To Paul,

To one of the ___ human beings on the planet,

with much Love,

Ziana de Bethune

(Ziana)

The Baron's Daughter.

by

Ziana de Bethune

Flat Hat Publishing

A division of Veritas Ventures Int. Inc.

Excerpt....

She spun around to find Gabriel behind her, which was a shock since she always heard those big boots long before he got there.

"Your Lordship," Denise interrupted with a bow, "may I be relieved to attend Mass with my kin?"

"Of course. Get one of the sentries to give you a ride to your father's home. Tell the sentry that he can attend the next Mass with his family, on my order."

"Much obliged, Your Lordship."

"I trust you will return by tomorrow night?"

"Yes, Your Lordship. May I go?"

"Yes, go. Don't let me keep you." He scooped Xavier from Viola's arms and transferred him into Denise's. "Drop him off with Chantalle on your way out. Tell her he needs his hair tidied."

"I already..." Denise began to speak but nodded instead. "Yes, Your Lordship." She turned and marched brusquely down the corridor.

Gabriel turned toward Viola. "You're wearing black again."

"It's indigo, not black."

"Must be the lighting." He said.

"It is the Lenten Season. It would be irreverent to do otherwise."

"You would know. You're the Nun." He pressed both hands to the wall above her shoulders and took a step closer, which brought him into her personal space. "You're getting under my skin, Sister Viola de Medici. Let's break a few Commandments."

"I am no longer a Nun...what are you doing?"

"Did you find him yesterday?"

"What are you talking about?"

"Your long-lost lover. You went searching for him, I assume. How did that go?"

"I'm feeling overpowered. I don't like that." She picked up the scent of soap on his skin and mint leaf on his breath, and could not make peace with the fact that her body and heart were beginning to want what her common sense did not.

He informed her, "I hardly slept a wink last night."

"I didn't mean to worry you."

"I wasn't worried. Look at me."

She stared at his mouth, watching every movement in case he planned to use it on her.

"I have to assume that your little tumble with him happened before you were tossed into a convent, and was perhaps even the reason for that sort of discipline. My eyes are up here."

Viola forced herself to meet his penetrating stare.

He went on, "If he discarded you then, what makes you think he'll want you now?"

"Why do you insist on badgering me with this?"

"Do you ever wonder about it?"

"About what?"

"Us." He answered.

"In what way?"

"In bed."

"I try not to."

"I want you, Viola."

"Please stop this."

He lowered his head to whisper into her ear, "Think about this."

Every fine hair along her arms stood on end as he kissed the side of her neck, her cheek, her temple, and then her forehead. Each kiss was slow and soft, accompanied by his warm breath brushing over her skin, which in some way caused her brain to start tilting out of its axes. She began to feel dizzy, and literally slumped back into the wall as he released her...

Prologue

1445. Somewhere in France.

The Aristocrat perspired heavily from exertion, his raspy breath cutting through the darkness after she left. His brain reeling from the experience, he thought that if he were to die now, he would die a happy man.

Who was she? In truth, he didn't want to know. It was better that way. The room had been blacked out with heavy drapery at his insistence, and the woman had been brought to him on this pitch dark, moonless night. For as long as he lived – which would not be that long, according to the leech – he would remember the insanely erotic sensations of discovery by touch alone. The thrill of intimacy with a total stranger, the curiosity of wondering what she might look like would be a delicious mystery for the remainder of his days.

He left that thought behind momentarily, knowing he would pick it up again later. This smouldering hot night would become a source of preoccupation while he waited to die. Instead, he thought about his deepest wish—to create a child before he left this world. He decided he would never tell his wife how deeply he relished this experience because he loved her too much to hurt her that way. She wanted a child as much as he, but she was barren. He hoped that in this most intimate encounter he had been able to plant a seed that took root, for he did not know if he would ever have the strength to try that again.

*   *   *

Stepping out into the dark corridor, Viola de Medici quietly closed the door behind herself. Immediately, a black velvet bag came down over her head, as if the man waiting in the hall had been holding it open all this time, to be at the ready. It was the same bag that she had worn to be brought to this unknown location.

Gaston Ste. Louis said, "That took longer than expected."

"He was...considerate," Viola explained. "He also wanted me to stay put for a spell so that his seed would have a chance to take root."

"I see." Gaston led her out of the building gently by her elbow—presumably the same way as he had led her into it. "As agreed upon, I will now bring you to another location where you will remain until the babe is born, after which time you will be generously compensated for your service."

"Assuming I am with child."

"Let us pray for the best. He did not hurt you, then?"

"Of course he did." She mumbled. "I told you that I had not been with a man before, and you had me examined by a leech to ensure that I was telling the truth, which was most humiliating. Did you expect that encounter not to hurt, *Monsieur*?"

"Of course, you are right," The elderly man said. "I apologise for having had you examined. The Aristocrat wanted to ensure that you carried no disease that could be passed down to the child."

She nodded her understanding beneath the bag. This anticipated compensation would give her the freedom of a new life, anywhere in the world she chose to live, except in France. What choice did she have? She had no money and no place to call home. She was alone, terrified, and so very tired of living in the streets of France, so she had traded the use of her body for less than one year, for a life of comfort. Once she fulfilled her end of the accord, she would never glance back.

"Be careful," Gaston said, as he opened the carriage door and assisted her in getting up into it.

"Is it necessary to have this bag over my head?"

"It is imperative that you do not know where you are, or where you are going. You did not see the Aristocrat's face at all, I assume?"

"No, it was pitch black in that room." She answered, as she settled her bottom onto the hard seat. There was a cushion, but it was anything but soft. A small heavy bag landed in her lap. The sound of metal clinked as she fingered the contents. "What is this?"

"Part of your compensation. You will get the remainder after the babe is born." Settling in beside her, he added, "I would advise you not to try to escape, now that you have the means to support yourself."

"Where would I go?" She mumbled. "I have no friends in this country, and none in my own, either."

"I can assure you, *Mademoiselle*, that you will be treated like royalty for the duration."

"Thank you."

The carriage began to rock as the horses pulled it over what felt like cobblestone streets.

"What if it did not take?" She asked. "Then what happens to me?"

"I assume that we will know in approximately two months. If the Aristocrat is still alive at that time, then we shall have to try again."

"And if he is not?"

"If he is not—God forbid—then you will still be compensated as if you had given birth to his child, and you will be set free to do as you please. The offer to own a home anywhere in this world will still apply, as you will have satisfactorily lived up to your end of the accord."

"Fair enough. Please tell me he was not an ugly wretch."

Gaston issued a chuckle. "He is strikingly handsome in his unique way, but I will let your imagination fill in the rest."

She sat quietly in the carriage for hours while rain pattered on its roof. Gaston Ste. Louis said very little, and she was not in the mood to speak anymore. Instead, she reflected on the intimate experience she had gone through in total darkness, with a stranger whose identity she would never know. If magic existed, she decided that her unknown lover possessed all of it in his hands. Once the first bit of pain subsided, it had been quite extraordinary.

The carriage came to a slow, bumpy stop. Assisted by the aging gentleman who was always ever so courteous, she stepped down onto what felt like pebbles. She did not see the sun as yet but felt its warmth caressing her shoulders as he led her up a gentle slope.

The bag was not removed from her head until she entered a building, and the door closed firmly behind her. The loud, resounding impact of wood on wood indicated that the door was much too high and wide for this to be the home of a commoner. After he removed the bag, she still could not see much as the entryway was dark, but not musty. It smelled like lye soap.

He said, "You will have a housekeeper and a houseman. They will see to your needs while you are here. There will be a midwife brought in when you go into labour. I will also bring you a personal handmaiden to keep you company. Her name is Louise. She is about your age. However, she will be under the same restrictions as you, during the duration of your stay."

"Thank you."

"Come with me."

She followed him up the stairs, immediately to her left. Judging by the circular shape of the well within which they were built, she assumed that this was a turret of sorts.

"You will not be allowed to leave your chambers at all, and neither will your handmaiden, but the suite of rooms is more than large enough for the two of you. Everything will be brought to you there. However, please do not think of it as a prison. Consider yourself a valued guest on the premises."

"I know what I agreed to, and I am fine with that."

At the top of the stairs, he unlocked a door and ushered her inside. The space was subtly lit by a dancing golden glow emanating from a marble hearth and beautifully furnished with an ornate, four-poster bed. Lovely tapestries hung over the walls, which she assumed had been recently added to provide insulation during the winter.

"*Monsieur* Ste. Louis, what is the date please?"

"Today is the fifteenth of November, *Mademoiselle*."

"Thank you. Does it get cold in here? It feels chilly."

" Your handmaiden will ensure that the hearth is constantly lit for your comfort."

"I suppose I will need some clothing."

"I will handle that."

She ventured further into the room. There were two fair-sized windows covered in red velvet drapery. She flung them open to let the sun blast into the room. Upon turning she noted that there was another open door that seemed to lead into a sitting area, which also boasted of a blazing hearth. All in all, it was lovely.

"All that you need is in this suite of rooms. Simply explore, and you will find. If you require something that is not here, ask your housekeeper, and she will ensure that you get it." He ducked out into the hall. "I must go. Your housekeeper will be up shortly with a good meal. She will also prepare a warm bath after the seed has had a chance to take."

"Thank you."

As the door clicked shut, she thought, *it would be better if I am not with child, but I will honour my part of the agreement, according to the whims of destiny.*

The Lady

&

The Count

Segment 1.

Chapter One

Five years later. France.

Valmont Ste. Germaine stole a furtive glance toward the young woman sitting in the indigo carriage across from him. Lady Viola de Medici rarely spoke, but when she did, she generally burrowed straight to the core of the matter without too much ado. Presently, she fondled a Rosary, her long, slender fingers drifting from bead to bead at intervals so equal, he knew she was praying. A closer look at those hands revealed a great deal of wear and tear around the knuckles—an indication of a lifetime of hard work. That was very odd, he thought, for a Baron's daughter.

They had been *en route* from Florence for two weeks and what a miserably sodden journey it had been. Rain the whole cursed time. Ordinarily, there would be an abundance of places of interest at which to stop along the way, to stretch the legs and grab a bite, but in this weather, it had been more considerate of him to just find accommodations at whichever inn was convenient and make do.

Occasionally, his companion raised her eyes to gaze out her window, and in them, there was always the pining of a tethered falcon — and the tenacity to keep pecking at the chain. She was thin as a pole, which was odd, considering her sisters were quite corpulent and bore no resemblance to her whatsoever. Neither did Lady Viola resemble her parents. He had to wonder if the Baron's wife had jumped the fence some twenty or so years ago. If she had, Valmont wouldn't pass judgment, for the man to whom she was married was a gluttonous pig.

Discreetly scanning her frame, he decided that Lady Viola's gown resembled monk's frock for it was loosely fitted and black with no bandeau around the waist. The color and shape of the horrid rag concealed any curves that she might have. In fact, she seemed to be so bony that the frock looked as if it was still on the hanger. Loosely draped about her was a shawl with fringed edges. Also black. Her Rosary, black. Her headdress, black – and it didn't nearly match the style of the frock. It was more of an afterthought. Her hair, what he could see of it, *almost* black. But what an unforgettable face. It was not that she was particularly beautiful. It was that she was so different.

Her Roman nose was a tad too small, her mouth substantially too thick, and her whiskey-coloured eyes too distant to give one the impression that she gave a flying bat's fart what they were saying. It was a real curiosity to him how these features merged into the image of drowsy sensuality. Correction. Behind those complacent, drowsy eyes was a volcano waiting to explode—and God help the man standing in the heat of that eruption.

Despite her diminutive stature, she would undoubtedly be too much woman for his own acquiescent manner, but perhaps a good match for his hot-headed brother. Valmont's gaze shifted to the lady at her side, her servant. Louise had been continuously touching her *Mademoiselle's* hand for the duration of the journey, apparently making an effort to comfort Lady Viola, but it seemed to him that the servant was the one needing reassurance. Viola herself seemed confident enough.

As they rode through the busiest section of *Orléans* on the first day of Aprilis, he couldn't help but note that it was another morbid curse of a day. The skies were grey and heavy, the rain pelting down in sheets. The usual beggars were wandering about, and the pitiful, hungry eyes of stray animals peered out from below staircases, but there was neither hide nor hair of an Aristocrat to be seen.

Every pigeon in the city seemed to be perched upon the dripping eaves of Ste. Michel's Cathedral set back a ways from the street, their beady little eyes fixed covetously on vendor's carts placed strategically in rows beneath the awnings. Everything was grey. Gray skies, grey streets, grey buildings, grey, grey, grey. Would the sun ever shine?

He glanced toward Lady Viola, thinking, *and there she sits, poor woman, all smothered in black as if she's going to her own wake.* He said, "We are nearly there, Lady Viola."

She offered no comment.

"There's something you ought to know."

"What might that be?"

"Your father allows you sixty days within which to entice the Count into marrying you. Or else."

"Or else he will beat me to a pulp, throw me back into the convent, or both. That is where I spent the last five years, up until a week before we met. Can you not tell by my lovely gown?"

"I regret your misfortune."

"It could be worse. If I had remained there another week, I would have been forced to take my final vows and been stuck in that prison for life."

"Many embrace that life."

"I am not one." She informed him, bluntly.

"I am participating in this plan, but I don't foster hopes for success. Many women are competing for Count Gabriel's attention."

Those heavy-lidded eyes came 'round to meet his. "Well then," she said, "I wouldn't want to burden the poor bastard with choices. They can have him."

"Then you won't be too disappointed when he rejects the whole notion of marriage?"

"No." One dark eyebrow quirking, she said, "If he won't have me, I don't suppose you would be looking for a wife?"

"I am flattered, but your father would have nothing to gain by an association with me. I've not one thimble full of noble blood in my veins."

"Hm. Well, fair-haired men never stoked my fire, anyway. No offence intended."

"None taken."

"You're a very kind, sweet man from what I've seen, but I believe I would need someone with bigger...what's a delicate way to put this...*balls.*"

Valmont nearly chocked on his own breath. Things were bound to get very interesting, very soon.

As the carriage careened down the long path between two large fields, Valmont noted that several serfs were out with teems of oxen, ploughing the soil in preparation for seed distribution. This in the pouring rain, the poor wretches.

This stretch of land nestled into the Loire valley was lush and fertile, the curves of yonder hills resembling a voluptuous woman's form if she were lying on her side. Down in the valley behind her was the primary region of Bellefleur, a village inhabited by peasants whose lives had been devastated by the war and the Black Death. Valmont's gaze shifted upward, where an ominous cloud glided in over her hip, which was not a good thing. When lightning struck around here, it felt as if the earth was trying to purge its guts. But presently, it wasn't thundering yet.

The wholesome scent of wet black earth and grass wafted on the pervasive breeze, taming the stench of cow dung from the endless pasture on the opposite side of the road. So many cows, with rivulets of rain drizzling off their lashes, lifted their cumbersome heads to watch the indigo carriage go by.

He said, "Yonder is our destination."

His companion shifted her gaze to his home in the distance – a monstrosity of an ancient, stone-block castle capped with a rampart around the top, and three eminent turrets occupied by pacing sentries. Though gloomy in appearance, she was a true fortress surrounded by a thirty-foot-high curtain wall.

Four hundred years ago the castle had been suitable for royalty, as it had been in the Valois family for many generations, but the heart of her carried the secrets of betrayal, murder, and war, and all of this sadness seemed to ooze from the clay between every stone. At one time it had been converted into a monastery which housed monks. After that, it was a penitentiary where men were sent to wither and die...or die and wither, whichever came first. Following that, the place had been under British occupation during this never-ending war. During that period, a British Queen had been sent here by her King, to be locked away in one of the turrets, where she was held prisoner until she died as a very old woman. Jean D'arc led the French to victory in 1429, and that same year Count Gabriel received his title, the territory of Bellefleur, and this long-neglected monstrosity as an inheritance. During the siege, the castle herself suffered no damage, but the front curtain wall had been knocked down by French canons – destroying part of their own pride to drive out the foreigners who had taken root in the heart of their motherland.

Two armoured sentries lowered the drawbridge to admit them. The wheels clattered noisily as the driver rode past the gatehouse and then straight along the path to the carriage house – a relatively recent addition. To the left of the carriage house was an outbuilding that served as housing for the outdoor servants and sentries and to the right a stable. All three buildings would appear substantial by themselves, but sitting well behind the enormous castle on the bottom of the rocky incline, they comparatively became a non-event.

As the driver stopped the carriage, a serf hurried from the outbuilding to come open the doors and let them out. Stretching his legs, Valmont addressed the man at his side. "Is the Count at home?"

"No, *Monsieur.* He has gone away."

"Where?"

"To do battle, *Monsieur.*"

Valmont assisted the ladies in stepping out of the carriage and gestured for them to walk with him. Leading them back down the path, and then up the winding incline toward the rear entry, he said, "You'll be quite comfortable here, Lady Viola."

"If you say so." Shielding her face against the drifting rain, she scanned the property, dubiously.

Chantalle, Gabriel's head servant, stepped outside to greet them as they strode across the covered portico. Chantalle was built like a very sturdy box—square torso, square head, and square hands—all features clearly representing the uncompromising nature of the bearer. Having been Gabriel's servant since he was ten, the Count had to occasionally remind her that he was her master and that she was not his mother. Understandably, it was difficult for her not to try to parent Gabriel and Valmont, since she had been their guardian, assigned by the King since Gabriel had received his title.

She wore her usual dark frock and a matching cap tied under her second chin. "*Monsieur* Ste. Germaine, welcome back."

"Thank you, Chantalle. As you see, we have company. Lady Viola, meet Count Gabriel's Head Servant. Chantalle, it's my pleasure to present Lady Viola de Medici, of Florence."

Chantalle performed a shallow but insincere curtsy. "Honored to make your acquaintance, My Lady, I'm sure."

"My name is Viola. Please use it."

"That would be improper." Chantalle's locked her russet gaze solidly upon Lady Viola with clear intent to stare her down, knowing she would win. She always won. Lady Viola's reaction was to nail her own eyes sharply open and to glare without blinking. The battle of wills was on...until Chantalle's eyes began to water...and it was she who looked away first.

Valmont cleared his throat. "Chantalle, this young woman accompanying Lady Viola is her personal handmaiden, Louise. Louise, Chantalle will show you about."

The women exchanged nods.

With introductions out of the way, he inquired, "Where is Gabriel?"

"His Lordship received word that the English forces advance toward Valognes. He said he was going to investigate, but since he was dressed in full armour, methinks he experienced a sudden yen to do battle."

"He's a seasoned warrior foremost and a Noble, second. He'll return feeling refreshed, the beast in him pacified for a time." He slanted Viola a smile.

"I can barely wait."

It was impossible to ascertain if she was sincere or serving up a shot of sarcasm. "Chantalle, if you would be so kind as to instruct the servants to prepare a bath for the lady, and a good warm meal. It has been cold and wet for the duration. Send a serf to the *Vacherie* for milk to soothe her skin."

"As you will. You ought to know that His Majesty ordered a raise in taxes to support the battle, but his Lordship disapproves of the whole notion."

"His *Royal Grouchiness* will have to comply, won't he? His Majesty may be his father, but he is our King and what he says goes. I'll see to the tax raise on the morrow." Valmont continued with instructions. "There is a small valise in our carriage, under the seat.

Have one of the serfs move it up to Lady Viola's quarters immediately. Also, a second carriage transporting the Lady's personal belongings should be arriving anon. They were immediately behind us, but we seem to have lost them. Upon their arrival, have the serfs move the Lady's valises up to her quarters as well. "

"As you will, *Monsieur.*"

"If you will show Lady Viola to her quarters that she may rest before eating? Louise may join you in the servant's quarters."

"I have no desire to eat," Lady Viola said, "but I will accept the bath and then go straight to bed."

"You will eat something." Chantalle once again attempted to get the upper hand. "You're but a sack of flesh and bones."

"Er…" Valmont opted to bail out while the getting was good. "I must go speak to the sentries for a few moments. Chantalle will see to your comfort. Chantalle, give the ladies a tour if you will, so that they don't find themselves lost."

"I don't do tours." Chantalle informed him.

"Try."

"I am concerned."

"About?"

"His Lordship left twenty-one days ago. He should have returned by now."

"You've received no word from him at all?"

"Not one."

"If we don't hear anything by morn's first light, I will go out there myself. Was there anything else?"

"No. Go!" She waved impatiently. "You may escape now."

Viola and Louise followed the servant into the dim, musty foyer, though it didn't exactly qualify as that. There was barely enough room for the three of them. The only source of light was one torch mounted to the stone wall, the flickering amber glow accentuating how badly the muddy wood floors needed cleaning. If the condition of her possible future home mattered to her, she would be crushed, but she had more pressing issues to occupy her mind.

Chantalle grabbed the wall torch and began climbing the stairs, each big square foot landing with great impression within the enclosure of the echoing stone tower. "Under these stairs is a door providing access to the kitchen, the *guarde robe*, the bathing room, and indoor servants' quarters. Follow me."

At the first landing, Chantalle led them down a dim corridor, which eventually opened up to a second-floor balcony overlooking a foyer. Situated back against the wall was a hideous gargoyle with a demonic face and pointed bat wings, parenthesised by two sets of stairs leading to the third level. She said, "His Lordship refuses to part with that hideous thing. He claims it is his stone likeness and I am not so sure I would disagree. How long are you visiting?"

"I don't know, yet."

"Don't get too comfortable."

Viola's jaw dropped. *"I beg your pardon."*

"What I meant was, it is not a very comfortable place. Always cold."

What was Chantalle's issue? It was as if she were trying her best to discourage her from staying at all. Viola crept to the edge of the balcony to glance down. From her vantage point, with several wall torches softly illuminating the vast area, it was not that bad. At each end of the balcony was a set of stairs curving down to the main level. The walls of the foyer were cream-coloured, with several white patches and protruding hangers where adornments had been removed. Though it was a massive space whose ceiling height was two stories, it was bare. There was not one single piece of furniture in it.

As if reading her mind, Chantalle said, "After she died, His Lordship commanded that we remove the hangings and furniture she had chosen and burn them."

"Who died?"

"Murielle. His wife."

"He's a widower?"

"Yes."

"What happened to her?"

"I'm not sure what *Monsieur* meant by giving you a tour. I don't have all day. We were not expecting visitors." *And I frankly do not like the imposition,* her tone supplied. "It is a massive place, and most of it is never used. The Count's private quarters are on the third level at the very easterly end. Not that you would need to know that. Let's go."

"One moment," Viola said, "it appears that this place is built backwards."

"It is not built backwards. We *use* it backwards."

"But the entrance – "

"The front entrance faces the river as it was meant to since boats deliver goods that way. You entered through the rear. I'll show you to your quarters now." She pivoted and squeezed between Viola and Louise to lead them back down the corridor from whence they came. At the turret stairs, Chantalle turned right, opened an old wooden door, and led them down another passage that was dark, mouldy-smelling and terribly narrow. There were no wall torches at all in this section, only a faint grey hue slanting across the floor from an open door halfway down. As they proceeded forward, the light from the servant's torch briefly illuminated a door every so often. Most were closed, and some were slightly ajar.

Viola ducked as a bat whizzed over her head, and puzzled over why this woman would see fit to put up a guest in the worst possible section of this place. However, she didn't want to seem ungracious, so she kept her mouth shut.

"In here," Chantalle grunted and gestured toward the open door.

The tiny cell contained a narrow bed and a bureau, both of which were covered in dust. Viola entered the room. "Thank you," she said, but she intended to speak to *Monsieur* to see if she could be moved to another room. That was, if she was going to remain for any length of time.

Beyond the brawny servant, Louise awaited in the hall, seeming none too confident with the notion of impending separation. Viola added, "Just so you're aware, Louise has permission to enter my quarters anytime."

"As you wish. Your bath should be ready within the hour, as well as your meal."

"I decline the meal, but I'll gladly accept the bath, thank you."

Scowling, Chantalle firmly closed the door, leaving her alone with her thoughts in this dingy, gloomy pit. There was no source of light, save for a dirty little window, which was now the home of a nesting spider. She shuddered to think about how many prisoners had died in this room over time. She wandered over to peer out but had to use her sleeve to rub a small circle in the grime to see anything. In doing so, she was careful not to disturb the spider. If that thing so much as looked at her, she would run screaming for her life.

Outside was a big dead tree that resembled a gnarly hand jutting up out of the ground, with long twisted fingers extending toward the dark overhead clouds. There was not a leaf on this tree, not a bird's nest. No sign of life.

Viola shuddered involuntarily, as her memories brought her back to the five years she had lived in a place too much like this one, where she had spent all of that time honestly believing it was her destiny to grow old and die in a convent. The place had not been this dirty, but it had been as dark and gloomy as this old monstrosity.

After giving birth to her daughter five years ago, she had once again found herself with no home and no finances. However, since she had agreed to depart from France and never return *Monsieur* Ste. Louis had put her on a boat to *Italia.* That had been her own choice since she hadn't known anywhere else to go. No sooner had the Baron laid eyes upon her than he stuffed her and Louise into a carriage, to be delivered to a convent in Rome, with the promise that she and her partner-in-crime would be there until the day they died. Others who were perfectly obedient ended up there as well because their parents believed that offering their daughters up in this manner would earn them a place in Heaven. It seemed to Viola that to offer up the life of a child to save their own souls had to be the gravest of transgressions, but nobody had ever cared about her opinions.

A week before she would have taken her final vows as a Nun, the Baron had decided to pull her out of the convent to use her as a bartering tool and send her here to marry the illegitimate bastard of the French King. But this was one move she wanted. This opportunity was like a smile from the Almighty because she was finally in France, and would at last be able to to track down her daughter. She *had* to make this Count want to marry her. Doing so would give her a sound, plausible reason for being here and living here. On that hope, she lay down on the lumpy little bed and fell right to sleep.

About an hour later, a dark-haired servant came to fetch her for her bath. She enjoyed that, and then went straight back to bed for another round of sleep.

Late that night Louise awakened her with a jolt, whispering frantically, *"Mademoiselle!"*

"What is the matter?"

"We must flee—now!" Louise stood over the bed, holding a candle whose upwardly slanting glow delineated the fear on her face.

Viola swung her legs over the side of the bed and sat up, repeating, "What is the matter?"

"Monsieur Ste. Germaine and Chantalle were speaking in the study. He told her not to repeat anything, but that you were brought to France as a possible wife for the Count."

"What's so frightening about that? It's the truth."

"Another servant entrusted to me that the Count had murdered his first wife and that he would likely do the same to you."

A cold shiver sluiced up her spine. "Murdered? How?"

"He threw her over the third-floor balcony." Louise hissed, her big green eyes stretching wide. So harried had she been to awaken Viola that she had not bothered to mind her hair, for the soft flaxen strands spilt out of her black cap like curling threads of gold.

"Oh, for goodness' sake. I don't want to hear this nonsense. You know what kind of gossip circulates in servants' quarters."

"We must get out of here!" Louise grabbed her hand and tried to yank her to her feet. "Let's go!"

"No."

"What do you mean, no?"

"I'm here for a reason, and I'm staying."

*   *   *

Gabriel frowned at the muckle of black clouds swallowing the turrets peaks as he rode through the gatehouse. He nodded at the sentries. "Anyone who thinks that France is romantic in the spring is full of shit."

One of the sentries bowed his agreement "Yes, Your Lordship. Have you sustained injuries?"

"Don't I always?" The metal of his helm rattled against his body armour as he tucked it under his arm, wincing visibly from pain.

The sentry didn't voice his concern. Perched atop his massive Belgian warhorse, whose muscles twitched restlessly beneath a sleek black pelt, the Count was a formidable sight. Fully armoured, his shoulders were so broad he would probably have to turn sideways to pass through a door. Nevertheless, he was human, and arrows killed humans. The sentry inquired, "Are we winning in Valognes?"

"Unless we recruit more warriors the English will win. At least, until the next round." Gabriel nudged his horse forward. A serf who was refilling the grounds' many torches with oil noted his arrival and trotted toward him.

He dismounted near the rear portico and handed over the reins. "Take him to be fed, watered, and brushed. The poor beast has been hoofing it in the rain for weeks. And it's still raining."

"Yes, Your Lordship."

"Would you look at that cursed sky? Do you suppose the Almighty hates me?"

"No, of course not."

"Go tend to the horse." Gabriel strode toward the door, his muddy black boots hammering into the stone portico floor. Pausing to look up, he decided he was glad he added this shelter. It made sense.

The door swung open, and Chantalle hauled him in by the elbow. "Well, it's about time! Have you been injured? Let me look."

"Don't mother me."

"It is my duty. I raised you." Grabbing his chin, she stood on her toes to examine his face. "What happened to you? Did you fall into a mud puddle?"

"Head first. Stop handling me."

"Given your caustic temperament, I would say you are fine. *Monsieur* has a matter to discuss with you in regards to the Baron in Italy."

"Cosimo is not a Baron. He's more of a King."

"Not him. Another one. A Baron."

"I don't know any Baron in Italy." Gabriel dumped his shield, sword, and helmet into her beefy arms. "Where is Valmont?"

"In the study, Your Lordship."

Unbuckling his double-belted dagger, he piled it atop the rest. "I'll go speak with him. In the meantime, prepare me a bath, will you?"

"I ordered the girls to start boiling water the instant I saw you riding through the gates."

"As usual, you're one step ahead of me."

"As usual."

He glanced around. "Why is it so dark in here?"

"Preserving the oil."

"Who's paying for it?"

"You."

"Then quit ragging and burn some." He hammered his boot soles onto the floor to knock off some mud, and then marched down the hall, pausing to glance back. "Chantalle, you have made some man out there very, very happy."

"Which one?"

"Whichever one you didn't marry."

*   *   *

Valmont's words only penetrated Gabriel's skull after he removed his gauntlets. The metal guards struck the corner of the writing table with a clatter, creating a dent in the dark, glossy surface. "You brought me a *what?*"

"A wife." Valmont, who sat at the table cleaning his nails with the point of a stag-horned dagger, dropped the knife to hand Gabriel a letter. "It's all detailed in this accord."

A big, dirty hand waved him off. "Hang that notion. Take her back."

"Read the offer before you decide."

"I have decided. Help me out of this contraption, will you? I'm hot, sticky, and sore. And I stink."

Valmont strode around the desk to assist Gabriel in shedding the heavy metal armour. The brothers clearly had different fathers, different looks, and completely different temperaments. Gabriel, the elder, resembled their mother. He had skin the colour of dark caramel, since their mother a Moor from Africa North, and his father a pasty-fleshed, red-haired King. His hair was a long mess of tight, dark curls streaked with red at the temples, an odd combination that lent him the appearance of a lion. Valmont resembled his absentee father, with fair skin, flaxen hair, and ocean-blue eyes. The former had a gut full of blazing fire while the younger tended to keep a cool head. But they were as close as the two middle fingers of the same hand. Reaching for him, Valmont said, "Since you refuse to look at it—Holy Mother of – phew!"

"I warned you."

Valmont continued to assist, but gingerly and at full arm's length. "Since you refuse to look at it I will tell you what the Baron told me. He is an absolute imbecile, by the way. I've never encountered a more offensive creature, him with his rotting teeth and stinking breath."

"And this you say to a man who smells like a goat?"

"Right. Well, Baron Mario de Medici sent his daughter in hopes that you'll take her as a wife. With her comes a dowry that the Baron says will make your head spin."

"I will shove the dowry so far up his arse that it will make *his* head spin."

"She's a lovely woman, Gabriel. She needs to be fattened up a bit, but she could be a real – "

"So was my late wife. We both know what a bitch she turned out to be."

"Point taken."

"If the Baron is offering his daughter, what does he want from me in return?"

"He seeks an introduction to His Majesty, that they may form an alliance. He wants you to put in a good word for him."

"Cosimo is already among my father's alliances. I introduced them myself, so His Majesty already does a great deal of trade with Italy." With the last buckle unfastened, the breastplate and back guards clattered heavily to the floor.

"The Baron wishes to form his own alliance with His Majesty."

Tenderly fondling the wound on his side, Gabriel concluded, "He's planning to undermine his cousin."

"That would be my guess."

"I happen to like Cosimo." More metal resounded as he removed his cuisses from his thighs and his greaves from his lower legs, and booted them aside. "So you can stuff that woman back into a carriage and return her to her father."

"I refuse to go anywhere until I've rested a bit—and that is not negotiable." Valmont returned to drop into the chair behind the desk. Finally noticing the dark, dried blood stains on Gabriel's once-white chemise, he said, "What happened?"

"It's nothing. I'll get over it."

"It doesn't look like nothing."

"I'm fine. Why is it so hot in here?"

"It's not hot. It's chilly. You may have a fever. Let me see the wound."

"Forget it." Gabriel squared his shoulders and stalked out, leaving his discarded armour where it lay.

Valmont sprang up from his chair to follow him out to the front foyer, "Gabriel, should I send for the leech?"

"No." He tossed over his shoulder. "I'll go find one on the morrow."

"Where are you going?"

"To dispatch a messenger to Florence."

"Why?"

"To inform Cosimo of the Baron's scheme. I'll have no part in this loathsome gambit. I'll not sharpen the blade that goes into my friend's back."

"I'll do that for you. Go have a drink. Relax."

"Fine." Gabriel spun around and headed for the stairs. "In that case, I am going to see my son."

"He's gone."

"Where?"

"He's being entertained at the King's Court until the morrow."

"Well, then. Go get this woman and tell her to meet me on the back portico in five minutes. I want to hear her side of the story."

"It's raining out there."

"It's a covered portico."

"It's cold."

"It's too hot in here."

"It's not hot. It's you."

A set of "II" lines drew Gabriel's eyebrows closer together. *"Valmont."*

On a heavy sigh, Valmont said, "Gabriel, I'm trying in every conceivable way to avoid restating that you smell like a pig and are not fit to meet anyone. You need a bath! Plus, it's been a horrible journey, and she's tired. At least allow her to rest till morning, and then you can be more presentable – "

"I'm not planning to woo her, Valmont. I'm planning to question her tactics."

"Question her what? Gabriel, she's not a war prisoner, for goodness' sake. She's a victim in this whole mess."

"She's a bloody Medici! The apple never falls far from the tree. Five minutes." He held up a big, dirty hand, all digits spread.

*   *   *

The distinctive scents of wet grass, mud, and burning whale oil swept into Viola's face as she opened the door and peered out. It was pouring outside. Distant rumblings of thunder announced that the worst of the storm was on its way.

Beneath the dancing glow of a wall torch, a muscled hulk of a man sat on the portico floor with his broad back to her. Two bottles of wine sat beside a dirty white chemise, which lay in a crumpled heap. A bushy, unruly mess of tight curls, caked in dried mud, extended down between his shoulder blades, lending him the appearance of a primitive beast that had crawled out of a cave. She didn't have to see his face to know that this creature was not going to be easy to palaver into anything.

Having second thoughts, she reasoned that if she quietly closed the door and went back to her room, she could apologise tomorrow with the explanation that she had fallen back to sleep. Maybe he wouldn't be so intimidating in daylight.

"I hear you." He spoke in a deep, quiet voice that was no less authoritative in its repose. If anything, his manner denoted that he was accustomed to not having to raise his voice to get results. "Come over here where I can see you."

Viola reluctantly padded to the end of the portico and waited for him to turn, but before he could, she covered her face with the black lace of her headdress. This small measure of concealment afforded her the slight advantage of being able to see him while he could not read her expression.

As he twisted around to investigate, his dark gaze crawled up the front of her frock. But those eyes were all that she could see, for he bore a thick beard that was also caked in dried mud. She resisted the sudden inclination to bolt as he stood and turned to face her—or more to the point, glare down at her.

The man stank. There was no nice way to put it.

Even in this poor lighting, she couldn't miss the many battle scars on his torso, or the muscles stretched over it. She suppressed a gasp when she spotted a big, festering wound at the side of his abdomen that was about the size of her palm and terribly swollen, with puss and blood oozing out of it. That was where the odour was coming from. Rotting flesh. She pretended not to notice but offered a hand to be kissed, the way any well-bred lady would. "Viola de Medici."

"Gabriel." He grumbled but didn't touch her hand.

"You're not what I expected."

"What were you expecting?" He reached down to snag a bottle of wine in his big fist, took a long swallow, and waited for an answer.

"Someone more —"

"Refined?"

"Yes." She admitted.

"Well, you gambled and lost. What you've got here is a Warlord." When he spoke, she could tell there was a mouth buried within his beard somewhere. "So, what's in this for you?"

She blinked at his unexpectedly blunt question. "Beg your pardon?"

"Your father wants a cosy little *tête-à-tête* with the King. What do you get out of it?"

"A husband."

"Anyone who would agree to marry a crusty bastard like me has to have an ulterior motive because let me tell you, I am no gem. Try again. And be honest this time."

"I am honest, Your Lordship. What else can a woman hope to gain?"

"My name is Gabriel. Use it. Money, wealth, and status are what you might hope to gain. Among other things."

"I don't care about those things. I simply want a home and a man who will treat me kindly."

"Where have I heard that before? Oh, wait. Yes, my late wife. She bought out half of *Orléans* in the first week of our marriage."

Viola began losing patience, and very quickly. "Your stupid mistakes have nothing to do with me."

"Right."

"Look," she said, "without having seen you before I had no way of knowing if you were a complete lunatic, a decrepit old dog, or a saint. It was a given that you would be wealthy since that's the only kind with whom my father will do business, but your financial assets wouldn't automatically make you someone I would want as a friend."

"No, but they would certainly make your life easier."

"I would think that having a derriere to grab any old time you want to is compensation enough. Did you expect to get everything for nothing?"

Muddy eyebrows lifted. "So, now that you have seen me, which category do I fit into? Lunatic, old dog, or saint?"

"I haven't decided."

"That bad, eh? Well, let's even this out, shall we?" He set his bottle down onto the stone floor and then plucked off her headdress and veil to expose her face. Pins went flying in all directions. "I feel as if I'm talking to a bloody coat rack."

Determined not to allow him to intimidate her further, Viola squared her shoulders under his close scrutiny. If he was expecting a long, flowing mane of gorgeous Italian hair, he was going to be disappointed. The Nuns at the convent had chopped it all off to within two inches of her scalp.

From somewhere within his facial hair came a barely audible, "Holy shit." His gaze slid down to her mouth and lingered there. He stepped back suddenly, grumbling, "Well, this doesn't change a damn thing."

"You ought to get that wound treated."

"It's been treated."

"It reeks. Do you have a fever?"

"Woman, I've had a fever for weeks. And I do not require a

mother. Let's talk about something else."

"I, uh...I'm sorry you lost your wife. Even if you did hate her."

"You mean, you heard I killed her. But draw your own conclusions. Everyone else does."

"I am not known to listen to other people all that well. That is why I ended up spending five years in a convent."

"And this you think is an asset?"

"I was just saying...well, I don't listen to gossip, either. It bores me."

"You're in good company." He picked up his bottle, leaned his back against the stone wall and drank till it was nearly empty. Silence stretched between them, punctuated by the heavy rain cascading over the eaves of the portico roof. Neither the extended silence nor the pelting rain seemed to bother him as they did her. In fact, he seemed to be a thousand miles away, staring reminiscently at that old dead tree in the yard. It was almost as if he were silently communicating with it. As if he and it shared a deep, dark secret.

This was not working out as she had hoped at all. She said, "Let us dispense with the nonsense, shall we? I'm not in a hurry to get married, and you clearly don't like me. If you want me to leave, I will."

Turning those dark, unreadable eyes toward her, he studied her but remained silent.

She continued, while she had the nerve, "All that I ask is that you allow *Monsieur* Ste. Germaine to assist me in finding alternative accommodations, because I refuse to return to Italy. I want to remain in France even if it means working as a domestic servant to earn my keep. I have no personal finances. Women seldom do, as I'm sure you're aware."

"Not so anxious to marry me now that I did not proclaim my innocence?"

"It's not that." She strode down the portico to collect her headdress off the muddy floor. "You clearly don't want me around here, and you don't trust me. Fair enough. Why should you? You don't know me. I don't trust you for the same reason. I will impose myself upon no-one." Snapping her headdress against her thigh to shake off the mud, she took a stance before him and waited.

"I know you want something, Lady Viola. You have an ulterior motive. I can *feel* it."

"What I want is something that you do not and never will have."

"Perhaps. But the real question is, will marrying me help you to acquire it more expediently?"

"It might." She admitted.

"Why?"

"As I said, I want to remain in France. Marriage to you would facilitate that."

"Why?"

"To avoid returning to Italy."

"Why?"

"Because I want to remain in France."

"This could go on all night." He frowned.

Viola squared her jaw. "Then stop asking the same questions."

"So you're not making any pretences toward any attraction to me whatever, hm? It's all just another business accord?"

"Attraction? Are you daft? I just met you, and I can hardly see your face for that—that *bush* growing out of it! You do not strike me as being stupid, so if I feigned attraction, you would catch me in a lie. Wouldn't you?"

"In a heartbeat." He agreed.

"And if I admit to this being just another business accord, I look like what I am—someone who is being traded like a bloody horse. Either way, I don't look too appetising, now do I?"

"I didn't say that."

She frowned. "Then what *did* you say?"

"Call me foolish, but I always thought that people ought to marry for...wait, what's that word?" He scratched his head as if rooting through his memory. "Oh, yes. *Love.*"

"Hearing that word come from the mouth of a banged up, battle-scarred, mud-encrusted savage would be as believable as Mother Maria Margarita telling me that she gave birth to a set of horn-bearing triplets." Jamming her muddy headdress onto the top of her head, she crossed her arms and defiantly glared at him.

He glared back.

"Do you want to know what I *really* think, Your Lordship?"

"I can't wait."

"Love has nothing to do with arranged marriages. I don't even think love exists. What men want is a woman to cook their meals and scrub their filthy clothes and their dirty floors and polish their boots – all without changing what they were before they married. After marriage, they're quick to take what they want in bed whether she likes it or not and then retake it from the next whore they meet at a tavern. After that, God only knows what variety of disease he will pass onto her. And then he will turn around and blame her for giving it to him, which provides him with just the perfect excuse to lock her up and throw away the key or have her beheaded for adultery. And this is supposed to be enticing? Where is the *love* in there? What damned reason on earth would be good enough to willingly lock myself into that wretched fate? All you need to do is say the word, and I will disappear at dawn's first light, just like the bad dream that you seem to think I am." As if nature were assisting her in punctuating her statement, a bolt of lightning flashed across the sky, followed by an earth-shattering explosion of thunder that shook the ground.

"Do you feel better now? Having gotten all that off your chest?"

"As a matter of fact, I do."

"At least we agree on something." He tilted the bottle up to empty it, and then let it hang loosely in his fist at his side. "Just so you know, I do not have the Whore's Revenge."

"Yet."

"I see you have sharp claws." Count Gabriel wound up and threw the empty bottle across the yard, causing it to crash into the dead tree and splinter into a hundred pieces. He hooked his thumbs into the waistband of his dirty black hose, the tips of his long fingers grazing against parts she didn't want to look at or think about. "Years ago I captured a young mountain cat and brought her home. I was going to try to domesticate her. Beautiful thing, but wild as hell. A lot like you."

"So?"

"For months she fought me. I had scratches up to my bloody shoulders." He pointed to various scars. "See this? And this? And this?"

"If you're stupid enough to play with mountain cats you deserve the scratches. Where are you headed with this fable?"

"It is not a fable." He argued.

"It is so." She stated. "There are no *mountain cats* around here."

"I captured her up in the French Alps, where there *are* mountain cats. In any case, *I won*. She comes and goes at will. At times I suspect she returns to her natural environment up in those mountains, but she always comes home."

"For God's sake, get to your point."

He did. "If I tamed her, I can tame you."

She made a double-take. "You just said, quite clearly, that you don't want me."

"I did not. I agreed that this business of arranged marriages is horse shit. *That's* what I said."

"Oh. So you *do* want me."

"I didn't say that either."

She marched toward the door. "I can't believe I left my lumpy bed for this."

Gabriel erased the distance between them in one long stride and grabbed her elbow. "I didn't dismiss you."

 *Chapter Two.*

"Kiss my bony arse!" She jerked her arm free, swung the door open, stepped in, and slammed it good and shut. Grabbing two handfuls of her frock, she lifted the hem and hammered her way up the stairs, knowing even as she went that she had gone and done it again. She had allowed her big fat mouth and her temper to over-ride her common sense. Maybe she did belong in a convent for life. But if they wanted her back, they would have to catch her first.

After the door slammed, Gabriel staggered toward the wall to grab a second bottle of wine. He popped the cork with two thumbs and then tilted the bottle to take a few more long drinks, thinking, *why would I want to saddle myself with another wife when the first one damn near killed me?*

None too steady, he navigated across the wet lawn in the downpour until he arrived at his tree, where he leaned his back against it, flinching from the pain in his side. Anchoring one boot heel into the sod, he lifted the other to secure it against the bark, and spoke to his tree. "After I inherited this place, I grew up swinging from your arms. I climbed up into your leafy shelter, and from there, I observed my whole world beyond the wall, my head full of dreams of one day becoming the world's strongest warrior. But lightning killed you the night I met that bitch. We watched the wrath of heaven and hell collide, striking you to your death. That should have been an omen. But what did I do? I fell in love, anyway. Stupid damn fool that I am."

As he got the last word out, another bolt of lightning flashed across the blackened sky, its long white tentacle needling into the hills on yonder horizon. The impact was fierce, causing his heart to quicken.

But rather than duck or hide, he planted both feet into the ground, spread his arms, and shouted, "Go ahead! Take your best shot!"

Hearing Gabriel challenging someone to shoot, Valmont grabbed his cloak and headed toward the back door to peer out. Swearing under his breath, he stepped out onto the portico and shouted, "What the hell are you doing? You will get yourself killed!"

"That's the point!"

"Get out from under that tree, you fool!" Quickly slipping on his cloak, Valmont raced across the yard to grab his brother and haul him toward the shelter of the portico. Once out of the downpour, he said, "Have you a death wish?"

"Did you ever get sick of running? Did you ever get tired of cheating death when it pursues you like a bloody Hell Hound? I'm fed up with all of it." The mud formerly crusted into his bushy mane was by now wet and sliding down the landscape of his face, to become an embankment in his beard.

"I thought you were interrogating Lady Viola? What happened?"

"I effectively scared her away. She'll be out of my hair tomorrow. Watch and see."

"Why did you do that? She's a good woman—and your son needs a mother."

"Right."

"Heed! If you died out there on the battlefield, who do you suppose will raise him? Chantalle? That useless wretch that you've chosen as his Nanny? The servants? Who, Gabriel? *Me?* I'll be too busy running your estate to have time."

"I do not wish to remarry. You know that, and yet you brought me a wife from Italia. A Medici at that. The Black Widows of *Maccaruni's Attic.*" He said, with exaggerated emphasis on the rolling r's.

"Not every woman is out to kill you, you know."

"Only the ones who marry me." Gabriel slurred and raised the bottle for another drink.

Valmont snatched it from his fist. "Why are you doing this? This is not like you."

"Pain control. See this?" He pointed toward his wound.

"It looks like it's rotting. What happened?"

"Jean-Paul Simone, Mark's younger brother, took an arrow on the battlefield. I tried to pick him up and carry him to safety, but I couldn't do it with my armour restricting me."

"So you took it off. That was not very bright."

"He was only fifteen, damn it. A child."

"Right."

"I got him to safety, but as soon as I put him down, I took an arrow myself. A poison arrow. I managed to stay alert only long enough to watch him die, and then I passed out. I didn't wake up for fifteen days. Fifteen days of my life – gone forever. I could have died without knowing it."

"I am sorry about Jean-Paul, but you made it fine, Gabriel. You will recover, as you always do."

"I have a bigger problem than that."

"What?"

"I don't think I can go back out there again. God as my witness, I lost my gall. I am sick to death of the blood, the useless loss of lives, the suffering, the filth, the fear of dying. I've had it, Valmont."

"Then, don't go. Your responsibility is to oversee your territory, which you do well."

"I won't send my warriors where I dare not go myself. I am a Warlord. I need to be fearless, and I need to be hard, or else people will walk over me."

Valmont yanked open the door with an exasperated sigh. "Right now you need a bath. Let's go."

*   *   *

Viola stood at the window, peering through the spot she had cleared earlier, and watched that maniac screaming at the sky while drinking himself to oblivion. If he chose to marry her, this is what she would be stuck with. A horrible, filthy creature with bad manners.

Discouraged, she reached into the pocket of her frock to slip out a small ring box. She knew what it contained without needing to open it, but she did anyway, as she turned and padded quietly toward the small bed to sit.

How often had she done just this in her cell at the convent? How often had she taken out this ring in the dark, put it on to go to sleep, and then took it off again in the predawn before anyone saw it? It was the only tangible thing that she had, which had once belonged to the Aristocrat. Gaston Ste. Louis had delivered it to her seven days after her babe had been born and taken away...

*   *   *

Five years prior. Somewhere in France...

"Her water has broken! Go fetch the midwife! Quickly!"

The groundskeeper dropped his lathe and ran toward his horse, which he kept saddled up these days, just in case. In a swift, practised motion, he mounted, snapped the reins and shouted, *"Dépêchez-vous, allons-y!"* Hurry! Let's go!

The spotted white mare let go a shrill whinny and then launched into action, spewing pebbles and dust in her back trail.

"She had to wait for the hottest day in the summer," he grumbled inwardly, as he rode out of the cleared land upon which the chateau was built, and through a narrow path cut into the wood. Crouching low, he nearly pressed his face to the horse's main to avoid low-hanging branches. It would be a long, hot ride. The chateau was out in the middle of nowhere, entirely surrounded by trees on all sides. The Aristocrat had it built as a wedding present for his new bride a few years ago. He had intended it to be their "summer home," but the place had never been used. Not by him, and certainly not by her. A terrible waste of money, in these times when so many were starving.

These things the groundskeeper knew, because he had been living there alone all of this time, assigned to keep watch over it. It was no skin off his nose. He was being paid well to do nothing but keep the place tidy. And now, since that young woman's arrival, paid even more to keep his mouth shut and to ensure that she did not try to escape.

Viola got up and padded toward the open windows to suck in a breath of fresh air, but there was none. She peered out at the lush trees, wondering once more, where she was. It was a sweltering August day, with not one single breeze to rustle the leaves.

Dragging the sleeve of her white nightdress across her brow, she concluded, "Maybe it's just me."

"It is not just you. I feel as if I am cooking." Her companion, Louise, stated. She too resembled a wilted flower. "You ought to lie down. The woman said you should stay on the bed."

The woman. That was what they always called the housekeeper, for none of them was allowed to exchange names, except Viola and Louise. The housekeeper and groundskeeper were faces without names – though very kind ones who had been seeing to her every need since her arrival so many months ago.

Nine months? Had it been that long already? It had to be, or she would not be having her baby today. As another labour pain sawed through her lower pelvis, she ground her jaw and held onto the bedpost. When it began to subside, she said, "It's a fallacy that women should lie down during labour."

"All the midwives say so."

"They're wrong," Viola said, as she paced and rubbed the small of her back. "It is better for both mother and child to keep moving."

"How do you know this?"

"Gravity, Louise. Gravity keeps the baby lower in the womb, closer to the exit door, if you will."

"You are a Medici. Your family practices cures and such. Is that not correct?"

"Yes. However, I will now lie down because my back is killing me."

She stretched out on the red coverlet, rolled onto her side, and stared at the bureau across the room. Louise sat behind her, rubbing the small of her back.

"Has she sent for the midwife?"

"Yes, *Mademoiselle.* Relax."

Silence filled the stifling heat as her thoughts carried her back to the intimate encounter that brought her to where she was now. A few moments into her memories, she said, "Have you ever felt the wings of a butterfly on your skin, Louise?"

"No, I have not. Have you?"

"Yes. That night with the Aristocrat. His fingertips were like the wings of a butterfly. My whole skin came alive."

"It must have been nice."

"There are some who say that the conception of a child is just a duty and that no pleasure ought to be expected from it, but the merging of bodies...no, the merging of souls in this way can be sublime and even sacred. That is my opinion on the whole matter. And that is also why I will never wed. I doubt that I will ever find a man worth marrying. All the men I've ever known were liars, cheaters, and snakes."

"I don't mean to be insensitive, *Mademoiselle*, but why do you cling to the memories of a man who is dead, and whose face you do not even know?"

"I don't cling to those memories, Louise. They cling to me – ooooh." She curled up into a tight ball as another contraction began, stronger than the last. As it subsided, she added, "Besides, it is safer to cling to harmless memories than chance being used and abused by someone in the flesh."

The housekeeper opened the door to peer in. "Are we all right in here?"

"Yes," Viola responded. "It's not time yet."

As the door closed, she spoke quietly, "It's going to be a tough birth, Louise. The baby has decided to turn head up."

Nine hours later the right time had long since passed. The midwife had arrived hours ago, and upon inspection, had decided that the baby was indeed turned the wrong way. Very slowly, and with a great deal of external massage and manipulation, the baby was now side-wise.

"This is not good," the midwife said. "You have been having pains for hours, and the water broke long before that. It will be a complicated delivery."

Writhing in the worst kind of agony, Viola tried to raise her knees, but the servant held them down while the midwife continued to massage and probe at her rock-hard, bulging abdomen.

"Take deep, steady breaths." The midwife said. "The babe has almost turned around."

"I need to push!" She ground through her teeth. Her body wanted to do what it wanted to do. What was natural for it to do.

"No. Do not push yet. Hold back from doing that."

"I can't take this much longer!"

Louise came to her side and pressed a cold, wet cloth to her forehead. "It will happen soon."

In tears, she pulled Louise's head down to whisper into her ear, "I cannot go through all of this just to give up my child."

"Shhh. Breathe deeply, *Mademoiselle.* Don't think about that now."

"You may begin pushing." The midwife informed her. She handed the lantern to the servant and sat on the stool at the end of the bed.

"Do you see the crown?" Viola inquired.

"Not yet."

The pushing seemed to go on forever, and the pain was beyond words. Louise was by then sitting on the floor at the head of the bed, with one hand atop Viola's head and the other rubbing her stomach.

"One more hard push!" The midwife commanded.

Viola pushed with all of her might, fighting against the pain and sweat and heat of that hot August night, until she felt herself tearing, and then, the flesh of her flesh gliding out of her body. She immediately tried to spring up to look, but the housekeeper pushed her back down with a firm hand to her chest.

"Please, just let me see! Is it a boy or a girl?"

"A girl." The midwife informed her. She turned her back to Viola and flipped the babe upside down. "I must clear the lungs." She said, and then there was a slapping sound, and a loud, shrill wail.

"Please, I need to see her!" She tried again to sit up, but the housekeeper held her down.

"That is forbidden."

"I want to hold her!" She fought against restraint, and all that she had been able to see in that dim light was a brief glimpse of the backside her daughter, covered in blood, hanging by her feet from the midwife's hand. Tiny arms shivered and flailed as the midwife wrapped the infant in a cloth, but in her right armpit, Viola spotted a birthmark like her own, in the very same place. "Give me my babe! I changed my mind!"

The midwife hurried from the room with her newborn. Viola got up from the bed and scrambled toward the door, mindless of the afterbirth hanging from her body, and the trail of blood she was leaving behind. The housekeeper pulled her back. "She is gone. And you will go back to bed now. We must clean you up."

Sobbing, Viola raced to the door again and flung it open. The housekeeper made it out before she did, and was able to pull the door shut and bolt it from the outside before she could get out.

"I want my daughter! I changed my mind! Tell them I don't want the money!" She banged on the door. "I changed my mind!"

*   *   *

"If the Aristocrat were alive," Gaston Ste. Louis said, "he would weep for joy while holding that precious little girl you created with him. She is glorious."

"Is she? I weep because I could not see her, *Monsieur* St. Louis."

"I know how you feel, *Mademoiselle.*"

"Oh, do you now?" Viola turned to face him, her eyelids stinging and her throat aching from withholding tears. "I felt her growing within my womb for nine months. I spoke to her, sang to her, I even gave her a name. Bella. My..." her voice cracking, she inhaled deeply to maintain her composure, and continued, "my breasts are full of milk that is meant for her. I ache for the need to feed her and hold her and to – for the love of God – just look at her. I am still bleeding from giving birth to my own flesh and blood. At night, I wake up sobbing because her first cry haunts me. I never got to hold her before they took her away. I never even got to see her. You tell me that you know how this feels?"

The old man lowered his head in shame. "That was a foolish thing to say. Please accept my apologies."

She returned to the bed to sit alongside him. "I should not have agreed to do anything so immoral."

"You were very kind to do so. You granted a dying man his last wish. You gave him an heir, and he will be eternally grateful, for I believe that souls live forever."

"An *heir?* Women do not inherit a damn thing, *Monsieur*. Their husbands get it all."

"This one will do fine. Things are different for those who have wealth." *Monsieur* Ste. Louis opened a small leather valise that he had brought with him, to show her its contents. It was filled with gold coins and jewellery encrusted with precious gems. "There is enough here to keep you in comfort for the rest of your life, *Mademoiselle*. I will also purchase or have built, a lovely home for you anywhere of your choosing, except France, as we agreed upon. As you know, you must leave here forever. That is part of the accord."

Viola dipped her hand into the valise, lifted a fist full of gold coins and then watched them flowing through her fingers, the sound of gold tinkling against gold making her stomach turn. "Do you know that Judas betrayed our Lord for forty coins?"

"Yes."

"I put a much higher price on my child, but does that make it right?"

"*Mademoiselle* – "

"I don't want that. Take it out of my sight."

"But we agreed –"

"You have my little girl! I have no idea where she has gone, but it is too late for me to get her back! Bad enough that I chose to do this wicked deed, I cannot accept that dirty money! Take it away!"

He quickly closed the valise and sat it on the floor next to his feet. Drawing her into a hug, he whispered, "I am so sorry, but it is done."

"In the bureau, top drawer, you will find the first amount you gave me. It is all there. Take that, too."

He slid a small ring box from his pocket, opened it, and handed it to her, in an attempt to make her feel better. Dragging her sleeve across her face, she glanced at a ruby ring, the stone square cut, the setting very simple. He said, "It once belonged to the Aristocrat's mother. He wanted you to have it after the babe was born."

"Why?"

"Read the note in the box."

She pried open the small square of parchment.

"Anonymous lover,

Please accept this ring as a token of my appreciation. Thanks to you, I will live on through my child, and my reason for having been born has been realised. I wanted a child so badly that my heart ached. Thank you, thank you, thank you.

Angel, you need to know that your touch reminded me of what it felt to be alive, even as the cold claws of death pulled me toward my grave. Because of that, I will carry the memory of your touch into eternity with me. Though my eyes did not behold you, into my hands has been imprinted the image of your glorious, slender form. I wish you the most beautiful life on earth.

The Aristocrat."

"When did he give you this? Is he still alive?" Her brain reeled with questions.

Choosing his words carefully, he explained, "The Aristocrat gave it to me two days after the babe was born and delivered to him. He passed the following day, with her in his arms."

Her heart sank. Her fingers trembling, she placed the note and ring into the box and slipped it into her pocket. "This I will accept. Thank you."

Monsieur Ste. Louis said, "I will return in thirty days. In the meanwhile, I want you to consider where you would like to go. I will have you delivered there. Once again, I reiterate that you must leave France for good."

She nodded.

"Do you wish to keep Louise?"

"She is not property, she is a human being. Besides, she belongs in the Aristocrat's domain."

"She belongs to no-one. She was selected by me to keep you company. If she wishes to go with you as a good friend, she may. I know that you two have become like sisters."

"I'll ask her. It must be her choice."

"Very well." He picked up his valise and stood. "I must be on my way now."

"Don't forget the rest of your money in the bureau. I don't want to touch it." She stood and marched into the adjoining room. She could not stomach the idea of listening to more gold clashing against gold as he reclaimed the first half that he had given her.

Thirty days later she and Louise were blindfolded until they arrived at the shores of Marseille, where they were put on a boat that was bound for *Italia*. Gaston Ste. Louis paid for their passage. As they sailed out, she glanced back at the shores of France and said, "I am going back there one day soon to find my child. I just need some time to regain my strength."

"But you promised never to go back."

"I also signed an accord which stipulated that I would receive a considerable remuneration for my services, but I did not take any of that money."

"But what of the Aristocrat, *Mademoiselle*?" Louise asked. "You would be letting him down."

"The Aristocrat is dead, Louise." She whispered. "He has his offspring, and that will never change. The only difference will be the arms that hold my daughter before she goes to sleep each night."

The Baron, Mario de Medici, had been enraged that she had

publicly humiliated him by running away and leaving her husband-to-be when she was sixteen. She had fled the country by stowing away on a boat, eventually winding up in *Tours*, France, where she had lived on the streets until Gaston Ste. Louis had found her and offered her that accord. She had been gone for nearly two years. Ergo, upon her unexpected return to *Firenze*, the Baron had her *and* Louise shipped off to Rome, where they spent the next five years in a convent. After their first botched attempt to escape, they were watched like hawks and unable to converse or spend any time together, but they saw each other from near distances and had to be content with that.

*   *   *

Viola caressed the ring in the dark. Oh, what measures she had gone to, to keep the Sisters from knowing that she possessed an item of sentimental value. Before her father could stuff her and Louise into the carriage destine for the convent in Rome, she had hidden the box and note behind a beam in the wine cellar of the Baron's home. She had stuffed the ring up inside of her womanhood, because she knew that they would search her and strip her of all that she wore, including her long beautiful hair, which they had chopped off.

She thought, *I should despise the Aristocrat for taking my child. I want to. I can't because it was all done honestly.* In the passing of five years, she had come to accept the fact that he had not gone back on his end of the deal one bit. It was she who had changed her mind when she had given birth. The fault had been her own for getting into that situation in the first place. Also, she had come to realise he had to have wanted that baby as much as she did, only his longing for a child must have been eating at him for a great deal longer than hers, for him to resort to buying a womb. All things being equal, there was no room for resentment in all of this, and as far as blame went, all of it should fall upon her own shoulders. This she knew.

Viola placed the ring into its box, returned it to her pocket and pulled out her Rosary. In the dark, she knelt at the side of the bed to pray for Divine Intervention, while at the same time knowing that this sort of help was only available to people far holier than she. Tonight, she would try again.

Her eyes stinging with new tears, she began whispering, unsteadily, "Father in Heaven, I don't know if You can hear me or if you have disowned me. I have no right to come to you begging for favours, considering the unforgivable transgressions that I have committed, but I'm afraid, and You are the only one who can help me. I don't know what to do. I have finally made it back to France. I need to find my daughter so as to make amends to her, and to You, and yes, even to my tortured soul. I made a terrible mistake entering into that accord, but You know that in the end, I took no money. I couldn't. I made a mistake! Have not even the best of your children made mistakes?"

Her tears flowing like small rivers now, Viola went on, "When summoned before the Pharaoh, did not Sarah blatantly lie and claim that she was Abraham's sister? An untruth is a transgression. Did she not send Abraham into the bed of her servant, Hagar, so that he could have a son? Did those two, who were among Your favoured, not sin against You when they did this? Yet, you still forgave them, and You blessed Abraham and Sarah with a child of their own flesh, a blessing so great that she gave birth in her senior years. Since then, the descendants of Abraham continue to multiply, by Your Grace. Can I not be forgiven, too? I plead with You to please help me find my child. I know she's in France somewhere. She is all that I have in this world. I have no family here, God. I have no family anywhere, and no home anywhere, and no friends anywhere, except Louise. Please, will you help me..."

*   *   *

As the quiet, blue light of predawn chased away the dark, a lone white dove landed on the ledge of Viola's window sill. Silent in her surveillance, the dove scanned the moistened grass in hopes of spotting worms. Swiftly, she swooped down to peck one from between the blades, and lifting off, carried it up to the eaves of the castle. There, she perched on the ledge to enjoy her breakfast. Tucked away neatly under the eaves was her nest. As she ate, she continued her surveillance, finally spotting her mate as he flew toward her with the gift of a straw in his beak. A bit of material, for her to repair her nest. Joining her, they began to coo at each other.

This was the sound to which Viola awakened, with intense pain shooting down her legs and up her back. She had fallen asleep face-first on the bed, still in prayer position.

After shaking the kinks out of her legs, she padded to the window to see if it was still raining. The sky was blessedly clear, a mysterious twilight shade. As she turned to retrace her footsteps, she noted that her valise had been placed just inside her door while she slept, and also, that a basin, a pitcher full of clean water, a towel, and some soap sat on her bureau. *Thank you, Louise!*

She wished that she had clean clothes to put on, but she did not, since her personal property had not yet arrived. Her tiny suitcase contained only a nightdress, hairbrush, and a few personal grooming items. Still, she was at long last in France and more than ready to begin her search. She hurried to undress, wash up, and redress just in time to answer a rap on her door.

It was Chantalle, and she was still scowling. "His Lordship said you are to join him in the Grand Hall."

"Good morning to you, too."

"He hates to be kept waiting."

"Well, I hate to be rushed."

"Hmph!" Chantalle turned and marched officiously down the dark hall, which was barely wide enough to accommodate her girth.

Shutting the door, Viola stood before the dirty, wavy looking glass over the bureau, trying to tame her hair. The least the Sisters could have done was cut it all evenly, but no, she was stuck with spouts of various lengths that went every which way. Her hairbrush only made it worse, so she used her fingers.

Forget it. It's pointless. Viola lifted her headdress from the bureau and frowned. It was smeared with dried mud and dust. Everything around here was filthy. Tossing it across the room, she decided that since that beast had wrecked her headdress, he would have to look at her ugly hair.

She found her way down to the foyer, viewing it from a different perspective than on the balcony. The floors in this section were dark wood and highly polished, reflecting the glow of the wall torches. Her light footfalls echoed in the massive empty space as she proceeded, all the while gazing upward and about to take it all in.

"In there!" Someone barked behind her.

Viola leapt within her skin and turned sharply to spot Chantalle marching across the foyer with a silver tray swinging from one hand.

"In where?"

"To your right. That's the Grand Hall. He will join you shortly."

"Thank you."

"Are you waiting for me to take your hand and walk you in?"

"Oh, *would you*?" She offered the woman a sticky-sweet smile. *Bitch.*

"Go!" The head servant marched past her and straight-armed the door which led to the back end of the castle. It banged shut in her wake.

Viola wandered toward the designated room, peered in, and was somewhat surprised that it boasted of all the pomposity found in such places. Based on what she had been told, that the Count had torched all of the furniture that his late wife had chosen, the things in this room had probably been selected by himself before he had married.

As it was with most Great Halls, at the far end was a raised platform for the High Table, where the Lord and other nobles would sit "above the salt." That table was presently dressed in white linen with a row of candles down the centre. The tables below the Dias were arranged in long rows, uncovered, and would be occupied by serfs, servants, and everyone else on his property who had to be fed.

She stepped inside the massive hall to explore since it was empty. It was lit by wall torches placed at equal distances apart, which allowed for good viewing. Three of the white walls were decorated with colourful murals depicting the lives and times of the people of France, with particular attention given to the Church and the King. Each of these boasted of an abundance of gold paint interspersed throughout – a costly luxury that most couldn't afford. The fourth wall held tapestries, shields, and banners displaying the Valois Coat of Arms. There was a large, field-stone hearth at both ends – one behind the head table and one at the opposite wall – and both were lit, filling the room with the aromatic scent of burning wood. Several narrow, highly-wrought tables lined the outer walls, displaying collections of busts and artistic objects from foreign countries. An obscene amount of money had gone into decorating this room.

Her footsteps echoed softly as she perused the space, her attention drifting from one painting to the other, from one object d'art to the other. She turned sharply at the sound of heels thudding decisively in the direction of the entry, which was by now, a good forty feet from where she stood.

A very imposing gentleman, whom she didn't recognise, entered and strode toward her. He was positively breathtaking. She began her quick perusal at his tall black boots and worked her way up along his white hose, a double-belted dagger slung around his hips, and white chemise, sharply contrasting his bronzed skin. He did not sport the supposedly-stylish bowl haircut but wore his dark hair pulled back, which implied that he bore a tail or braid. How strange, that he had a coppery streak at each temple.

"Good morrow." He said. "I trust you slept well."

Viola Crossed herself. "Oh, dear God. It's *you*."

Chapter Three

"I assure you that I am not God," the Count said, "though I *am* one of His most abominable creations."

Although clean-shaven, there was nothing soft about Count Gabriel. He was a robust masculine force. A leader. A conqueror. Yes, a Warlord. He placed his fingers under her chin to close her gaping mouth. "We get lots of flies around here."

"You look different."

"Not so much like a mud-encrusted savage?"

There was no point in worrying about things said, which could not be unsaid. "Not so much."

"Have you been crying?"

Not since last night. "No."

"Let's sit." He ushered her toward the head table up on the Dias, which was a long walk that felt like it would never end. There, he pulled out a chair. "After you."

She did as expected, but kept her eyes on him as he sat beside her.

He inquired, "Where did Chantalle put you up?"

"At the rear." She gestured with her thumb. "Facing that big dead tree."

"There she goes again. I'll have you moved."

"Thank you."

He stood abruptly to exit the room by a side door at the end of the platform, which she had not previously noticed, and swiftly returned with a pitcher of milk and two silver goblets. Reclaiming his chair, he filled both vessels and set the pitcher down at arm's length. "Valmont has received notification that all but one of the men delivering your personal property have been attacked and slain *en route* from Florence."

"Oh, no."

"All of your property has been damaged or stolen." The legs of his chair scraped the floor as he turned to face her more directly.

"Those poor men...their families...I am so sorry."

"I will see to their families' well-being, as I've always done."

"Good."

"Now, what about your personal losses?" He inquired.

"My property consisted of another ugly frock like this one, four hand-me-down gowns that are twice my size, and a few pathetic headdresses. No big loss, I promise you."

"You are to go into the city at first opportunity to replace your things. Hopefully, with items that appeal to you."

"I don't think – "

"Good idea. *Don't think.*" He further unfastened the front of his chemise to gingerly fondle his wound, which caused him to flinch in pain. "And don't leave without an escort. Valmont will assign you one."

"I don't have the finances to purchase new things. What I'm wearing will have to do."

"He will also provide you with a list of places to go. There's a growing trend of purchasing pre-made items. My late wife would have been able to send you to places where they sew with *gold thread*." He spat, as he pulled his hand out, sniffed it, and made a face. "Ugh...in any case, I suggest that you find a place that sells those since you need clothing immediately. If you don't see anything you like, they will create something according to your specifications. I will cover the expenses."

"I can't accept charity."

"That wasn't an offer. It was an order." He stood and marched around back of her chair to snag a letter off the mantle, dropping a sheet of well-worn parchment before her as he returned to his seat. "Now, let's get down to business."

"What's this?"

"The proposed business accord that your father has sent to me. He will trade you for an introduction to His Majesty, so that they may form an alliance."

"No, my father wanted to meet yours to show his approval of our union. A familial gesture."

The Count slanted her a doubtful glance. "He told you that?"

"It wouldn't make sense for him to form an alliance for trade or anything else." She explained. "Cosimo is already doing business with His Majesty. I assumed that he did have something more financially profitable in mind as an eventuality, but nothing that would undermine his cousin. It is on account of Cosimo's generosity that he has such a good life."

"Can you read?"

"Of course I can read."

"Read the accord. It's right in front of you."

"I shall forgo that dubious honour."

"You won't read it because you know as well as I do that your father is a pig." The Count gulped a drink and slammed the goblet down onto the table. "He would not only stab his cousin in the back, but he would use his own daughter as a bartering tool to line his pocket."

"Don't all fathers? That's how it's done. The sons inherit the land while the daughters get traded off for something better."

"Don't start on that again. I have a headache you could frame."

"Your headache – "

"And don't tell me that I wouldn't have this headache if I hadn't made a drunken sot of myself."

"I was going to say that your headache comes from the poisons in your own body. That wound of yours is rotting, and if you don't get it treated properly, it might kill you."

He gazed at her studiously. "What is your age?"

"Twenty-two."

"I can see why you're still unwed. You talk too much. Do you mind if I complete my thought, now?"

"Go ahead."

"I am doing quite well without this insulting dowry that he offers as part of the accord."

"The dowry is supposedly a gift to me as a wedding present – "

"That's horse shit, and we both know it. Our laws prohibit women from financial independence. Therefore, these dowries always end up in the hands of her husband."

"Now you're getting it." She smirked. "It's all designed to keep us under the control of men."

"Tell you what. You drink that milk. You could use some meat on your bones. I'll do the talking."

Viola frowned but drank.

"He's offering land on the periphery of *Firenze*." He scoffed, his white teeth flashing in the glow from the torches. "What in hell would I do with land in *Firenze*?"

"He must be referring to a vineyard that he owns."

"I can grow my own damn grapes. In fact, I *do*."

"I suppose it's settled then." She slid back her chair and prepared to stand. "I see no point in wasting your time. I'll go pack."

A large brown hand clamped around her wrist. "I am not through with you. I will take you as my wife, but your father gets nothing.

"Wh—what? You can't do that." She whispered. "I wouldn't mind escap—I mean—leaving promptly."

"Watch me."

"The Baron will retaliate. You will bring war upon your home, I promise you."

"Heed," he said, poking a long index finger onto the table, "once Cosimo gets wind of his underhanded machinations, the Baron will have war aplenty to fight in his own back yard."

"This could get very ugly."

"It already has. The Baron has tried to chisel the wrong man this time. I will keep you, but that manipulative whoreson gets nothing."

Long silent moments stretched between them, him staring at her, her staring at him. The stubborn line of his jaw cautioned her that this was not going to be a marriage made in Heaven. "What made you change your mind?"

"I've been re-thinking this situation. You have something I need, and I have something you need."

"Specifically?" She probed.

"You need a decent home, and my son needs a mother."

"You have a son?"

An eyebrow quirked. "Do you have a problem with a ready-made family?"

"No. It's just that I haven't seen any children here."

"His name is Xavier. He's visiting with my father," the Count informed her. "He should be returning today. Know this – if you ill-use him in any way you will have to answer to me."

"I would never harm a child. "

"The only reason I will marry you is so that he will have a mother if I am killed and trust me, that can happen. This last round on the battlefield was a real eye-opener."

"You're lucky to be alive."

"Your timing is perfect, but I will be watching you." With a deep breath, he leaned back into his chair, seeming to release his anger along with it. In the amber glow from the torches, the hardness in his eyes seemed to melt away. "That's one hell of a pair of lips you have there, *Sister* Viola de Medici."

"I am no longer a Nun."

"You're too damn gorgeous for my own good, and I suspect you already know that. So, don't try to soften me with temptation. You can wave the apple all you want. I won't bite."

"My name is Viola, not Eve. When do you want this marriage to take place, Your Lordship?"

"Gabriel. It will take time to have your personal items replaced and a new wardrobe created for you, as well as a gown for the occasion. Invitations must be sent out, and I suppose we'll have to get some furniture into this place. I'll leave that up to you. A couple or few months."

"Thank you."

"Don't sit at my table and thank me when you would rather slit my throat."

"That is something that my father would do, but not me."

"I see that fire in your eyes, and I don't for one moment mistake it for passion." Scraping back his chair, he stood abruptly and strode toward the end of the table. "Your meal will arrive shortly. I must go hunt down a leech. That damned arrowhead is still inside me."

"The poison on it is most likely hemlock. If the leech tries to use mandrake root, opiate, and hemlock to put you out before treating you, that concoction will kill you faster than the arrowhead."

He paused. "How would you know that?"

"Aside from absorbing the Medici's medical knowledge by osmosis, the Nunnery trained me to be one of the Sisters of Mercy, caring for the wounded who came from the battlefield. I may be able to help you."

He stepped down off the Dias and kept on walking, creating more distance between them. "The only Medici I trust is Cosimo."

"Why?"

"You Medici's are masters at concocting the very poisons that kill."

"True. But the Medici's are also masters at creating methods of healing that no-one else has heard of."

"For all I know the poison in my gut was brewed by your lovely little hands, so you won't mind if I decline your offer." He paused at the door to add, "When you replace your wardrobe, choose some colour."

"Do you have a preference?"

"Anything but black. I was married to the devil the first time. The last thing I need this time is to marry a bloody Nun!"

Viola dropped her pretend-to-be-nice face, and expelled a deep breath that she hadn't realized she had been withholding. The echo of his boot heels hammering down the corridor punctuated the silence that suddenly fell into that large hall, and the space that seemed too small to fit the both of them expanded to its normal size. She told herself she ought to be relieved that she would have a place to live while she conducted her search, and avoided wondering how she was going to get out of this arrangement *after* she found her daughter.

Her hopes were high but her spirit was low. She wasn't fooling herself. Realistically, that could take years. By all accounts this man seemed to be a real bastard to live with and God knew that she was no prize, for it seemed that even *He* had given up on her. Life itself had turned her into a hard-edged survivor with a nasty mouth. But she would pay *any* price to be reunited with her child. Even this.

Gabriel encountered his brother wandering through the foyer with his head down, preoccupied with his own thoughts. "Valmont."

He raised his head, "Yes?"

"Are you busy?"

"Not terribly, why?"

"Did you dispatch a messenger to Cosimo?"

"I sent Benoit."

"Good choice. Chantalle put Viola at the arse end of the castle."

Valmont rolled his blue eyes. "She hates visitors."

"She'll have to get used to her. I'm going to marry her."

Sandy-coloured eyebrows raised. "You've come to your senses."

"Or lost them completely." Gabriel frowned. "I have to go hunt down a leech, so would you mind getting Yolande to move Viola's things to the chamber adjoining mine?"

"I will."

"My cat's been sleeping in there, so she'll have to change the linen and give it a good cleaning."

"Noted." Valmont grinned.

"And when you're done would you have time to ride out to Mark's home to let him know about Jean-Paul's death?"

"Of course. Anything else?"

"What happened to her hair?" Gabriel drew a halo around his own head. "It looks like a scrubbing brush."

"Who?"

"Viola."

"Does it?"

"You haven't seen it?"

"Not yet." Valmont said. "She wears one of those ugly bird cages on her head. Those things...you know what I mean?"

"A headdress." Gabriel supplied.

"Right. But her hair can't be that bad."

"It is, but the damn mess suits her. Would you do up a letter authorising her to purchase anything she wants, from whomever she wishes?"

"All-inclusive, Gabriel?"

"Yes. Watch and see," Gabriel said, as he resumed his pace toward the front door, "she'll come back with enough useless shit to fill the Great Room. Make sure she has an escort!"

$*$ $*$ $*$

Before departing the grounds, Viola hurried up to her room to quickly clean off her headdress, since it was forbidden for women to show their hair in public. It was a crime punishable by prison time. As she was marching down the dark, narrow corridor, a servant exited her room with her suitcase and headdress piled into one arm.

"Excuse me, but where are you taking my things?"

"Oh," the servant replied, "I have orders to move them to the other side of the castle and up one level."

"Good. Please lead the way. I'm Viola. What's your name?"

"Yolande." She answered, as she firmly shut the door, effectively blocking nearly all sources of light. There were but a few slivers of sunlight peeking almost eerily through the few doors that were ajar, causing luminescent streaks across the filthy wood floors.

Being much shorter, Viola had to trot to keep up. "Yolande, how many servants live here?"

"Inside, there are three. Myself, Chantalle, and Denise. Denise is a caretaker for the boy—when she's here."

"She doesn't live here?"

"Yes, but she goes away too much."

"I see. And how long have you been here?"

"Six years." She gave the exit door a swift kick to open it, and marched through.

The door smacked against Viola, knocking her off balance. Shoving it open, she followed Yolande into the more appealing part of the castle. At least the wall torches were lit, and the hall was wider. She finally caught up to Yolande on the balcony overlooking the grand foyer, thinking that the help in this place certainly didn't go out of their way to make anyone feel welcome. In better lighting, she noticed that the servant was well-proportioned and quite lovely in a dark, smoky way, though one had to look past the homely cap to realise it.

"We'll use the service stairs. It's a shorter walk." She led Viola up the to the third level via the turret stairs on the opposite end of the balcony, and then down another wide, torch-lit corridor. Yolande went on, "There are many more serfs and servants who live in the outbuildings, but only few inside. He prefers fewer indoor servants than most."

"He prefers quiet?"

"I would not say that. His background is different than most royals. He's more comfortable with fewer servants."

"Does he have mistresses who live here?"

"No!" Yolande suddenly flared up. "He finds other ways to satisfy himself!"

That was clearly a topic to steer clear of. "Tell me, where are the birth records kept in this vicinity?"

"Ste. Michel Cathedral. Speak to *Monsieur* Ste. Germaine. He will provide you with a carriage and an escort."

"His Lordship mentioned the escort, but I don't need one. Louise will come with me."

"You will not be permitted to go into the city without one. None of us is."

"None of you?"

"Only the men can do that. His Lordship insists. We will put you in here." Yolande paused at the second door from the east end and shoved it open. Sunlight flooded into Viola's eyes, though she didn't step inside. Yolande paused just inside the door to advise her, "I would not enter just yet. I must change the linen and clean it properly. His cat has been sleeping in here."

"I'm not fussy. And I like cats."

"You won't like *this* cat. His Lordship's chamber adjoins this one."

What? Viola leaned back to glance at the door next to hers. "Does the door between the two chambers lock?"

"Only from his side. You might want to put something against it to prevent him from entering." Yolande marched into the room to deposit Viola's things onto the bed, but held onto the headdress.

"Is he likely to intrude that way?"

"It wouldn't be the first time I'd hear screams coming out of there, but suit yourself."

"Screams?"

"You might be safe, though. He seems to like them older." She skimmed a disapproving glance down Viola's front. "And meatier. Be thankful that you are not going to the chamber at the other end of the corridor, My Lady."

"Why is that?"

"That is where she slept. Never, never go there."

"Do you mean, his late wife?"

"Yes. I should not have said anything."

"But you *did*. Are you trying to tell me something?"

"Steer clear of the balcony." She thrust Viola's headdress into her abdomen and fired down the corridor. "I must go fetch some clean linen and towels!"

Ste. Michel's Cathedral. In a red carriage manned by an escort in the driver's box, Viola and Louise waited for the noon-hour Mass to end. With a brilliant sun drawing all creatures out of their holes, the streets were crowded and nearly festive, but that same sun cast a harsh light on the worst case of class distinction imaginable, what with the wealthy dressed in ostentatious garb and the homeless in rags. The former behaved as if the latter were invisible.

Viola observed a particular young woman – a "purse-cutter" – following close on the tail of an Aristocrat dressed in red. Anticipating what her next move would be, Viola was not surprised when the street urchin "accidentally" bumped into the man, excused herself and escaped between two buildings before her victim would notice his purse missing.

Viola admitted, "That is a hard life. Begging, stealing, fighting, feeling horrible about it, but having to do it all again the next day to survive. I lived that life when I ran away from *Firenze*. Until *Monsieur* Ste. Louis found me in *Tours*, and...well, you know what happened."

"Yes," Louise said. "The accord that was supposed to change your life but didn't."

"Correct." She shifted her gaze to the cathedral. On the grounds was a serf swinging a lathe, chopping the tall grass down to within a few inches of the ground. "And here I am pretending to be Lady Viola de Medici when I was nothing but a servant to my adoptive parents and siblings in *Italia*. I am an imposter."

"You are not. The Medici's adopted you so you are a Medici, and they named you Viola, so that is your name."

"That is true at a superficial level. The Baron did ensure that I was well-educated, but that was only to advance his plan to use me as a bargaining tool. But who am I, really? The answer is, I do not know. I know nothing of the fabric from which I was cut. Most likely that fabric was cheap rags, and yet here I have a letter which authorises me to purchase whatsoever I wish at the Count's expense. In this letter I am labelled as the future Countess of Bellefleur." She glanced at the all-inclusive letter in her hand and reread it aloud to assure herself that she understood it correctly.

"Dated this Fifth day of Aprilis, in the Year of Our Lord, Fourteen Hundred and Fifty.

To The Merchants of the City of Orléans:

This is to authorize that the purchase of any items chosen by the future Countess of Bellefleur, currently going by the Noblewoman's title, Lady Viola de Medici – at her sole discretion – are to be charged to His Lordship, Count Gabriel Xavier Valois, by order of the same; the order to be in effect from this day, until otherwise dictated by His Lordship, Count Gabriel Xavier Valois.

Monsieur Valmont Ste. Germaine,
Per/ Count Gabriel Xavier Valois."

Refolding the letter, she finalised, "It bears the official red wax seal of the House of Valois."

"You could walk into any shop in the city and buy everything? Count Gabriel would pay for it?" Louise inquired.

"Yes. Generous on the one hand, a killer on the other."

"Crimes of passion happen every day." Louise pointed out. "Perhaps she had a lover, or he thought she did, and he became jealous and killed her by accident in a fit of rage."

"His own description of himself, 'a crusty bastard,' is a perfect fit, but he's been through seven levels of hell. It shows in his eyes."

"I have not even seen him as yet. I have been busy helping to clean."

Viola admitted, "His eyes are terribly unsettling and he is most difficult to get along with, but Holy Mother of God, he is handsome.

His braid goes all the way down to the middle of his back. Most men wear that stupid hair style that looks as if someone put a bedpan on their heads and cut around it."

Louise relinquished a small grin. "A bedpan?"

"Yes. Do you not think so?"

"I never thought about it."

"I have." Viola said. "His hair must be lovely when it's loose, and clean as it was today. Not dunked in mud, as it was yesternight. Don't ask. It's a long story."

"I won't. Do you know, that letter could be a trick." Louise speculated.

They glanced at each other, the inaudible clicking sound going off simultaneously in each of their brains. Viola recalled his comments from the previous night. *Money, wealth, and status are what you might hope to gain.* "Yes! That's it, Louis! He's testing my motives. You're brilliant."

"Let's go. The priest is there." Louise turned and shoved open her door.

Viola slid out of the carriage, arranged her dusty headdress, and strode toward the building with Louise. They waited on the sidelines while the parish priest shook hands with the men and conversed with the women on their way out. Virtually every one of the parishioners glanced down their noses at her and Louise, as if they were street urchins begging for a hand-out. Viola said, "I must look as if I've stolen this clothing from the trash."

"And I as well, *Mademoiselle.*"

"I'll get us both something nice to wear, Louise. Don't worry. Things will get better." That's what they had been telling each other for five years. *Things will get better.* They never did, though, for Viola had managed to create problems everywhere they went.

When the last few parishioners left, she and Louise approached the priest. He was a rather short, stout little man with a shiny bald spot at the top of his head, and piercing blue eyes. She said, "Father, I am Viola de Medici. This is my friend, Louise."

"Pleased to make your acquaintance." He smiled. "A beautiful spring day, isn't it?"

"Yes, beautiful."

"I'm Father Jacques. How may I assist you?"

Viola cleared her throat. "I am searching for the birth record of a certain child born in August, five years ago."

"Male or female?"

"Female."

"Was she born in this vicinity or close?"

"I don't know."

The priest scratched his head. "Do you know which date in August."

"Near the beginning or middle. I don't know the exact date."

"I see. What was her name?"

"I don't know that either," Viola said.

"I see. Well, do you know the names of her parents?"

"Not exactly."

The priest maintained his smile, but it became one of pity. "We have thousands of birth records down in the lower level, but if you do not know the child's name, her date of birth, her parents' names, or anything else, how can we possibly know where to begin looking? The records we keep in this Cathedral go back for centuries."

"But the approximate time of the month is a start, five years ago." Viola pressed.

"Yes, but not a good one. Do you have any idea how many children are born each day? What is more, common folk and peasants often do not register their children at all."

"She was born to an Aristocrat." She piped up, feeling glad to know at least that much.

"Ah, yes. Many of them have mistresses as well as wives," he paused to perform a Sign of the Cross, "which is blatantly against Christian beliefs. However, when a child is born, he or she may be registered under the name of the father, but the mother's information may be incorrect or missing entirely in some cases..."

The good Father's voice fading into nonsense, she thought, *this is too much information, and it doesn't apply to my situation.*

Father Jacques went on, "Or in the case where the father does not want to acknowledge that the child is his, then the child may not be registered at all. The wealthy, God help them, seem to make their own rules. In other words, I regret that I am unable to assist you unless you have more information."

Expelling a sigh, she whispered, "I understand."

"I could bring you down to the vault where we keep the records. Even if you could read, you would view them as thousands of meaningless names, while one might actually be the child whom you seek."

"I'll see what I can do about obtaining more information. Thank you all the same for your time, Father Jacques."

"It was my pleasure. Will I see you at Mass this Sabbath?"

"Maybe. Good day, Father – oh, wait. I do have one more question. Are you familiar with a *Monsieur* Gaston Ste. Louis?"

"If we are speaking of the same man, I did know him when we were young. We were both born in *Tours*, you see, but he never sired any offspring." The priest leaned in close to whisper, "I heard that he was injured in a most unfortunate place if you know what I mean."

Viola's pulse sped up. "You say he was from *Tours?*"

"Yes. We lost touch years ago. We were never very close, but as far as I know, he maintained a residence there until he died – though he was known to travel about quite a bit, as he was quite educated and worldly. I, on the other hand, was offered a post here and was glad to take it."

"Do you know to whom he answered?" Louise piped up.

"To my knowledge, he was appointed by His Majesty to oversee the financial operations of many different ventures between here and who-knows-where. His Majesty owns many properties, and many people, for that matter."

"I see. And you're certain that Gaston Ste. Louis is dead now?" Viola asked.

"Positive. I saw him in the casket myself. Rumour has it that he took his own life." With a sad shake of his head, the priest Crossed himself. "God forgive him."

"Why did he do that?"

The priest shrugged. "He left no clues."

"Do you know where he died? Where he is buried? Anything?" Viola now grasped at straws.

"He was found dead in his home in *Tours*, and buried outside the Catholic cemetery, though I do not know the exact location."

Viola pondered the situation for a moment and then tried another approach, "Do you think His Majesty would give me a few moments of his time...oh, no. Forget that notion." Her shoulders sagged. "Thank you, Father. Good day."

"It's just as well," the priest said. "Gaining access to the King is nearly impossible unless you are of noble or Aristocratic descent. He has no time to converse with street people."

As they turned and strode away, she whispered, "I was so desperate that I had hoped to have success with no information at all to begin with."

"Why did you not want to speak with His Majesty? I thought that was a brilliant idea. He might know with whom *Monsieur* Ste. Louis was close."

"Louise, the noble and their hangers-on, the Aristocrats, move in very tight circles. Those in Germany, Belgium, Spain, France – all over the world, they all know what the others are up to, and all of their dirty little secrets. They have an abundance of time and money to go gallivanting about. Word spreads quickly."

"That works in your favour. They might know something."

"It works *against* me, Louise." She paused to pull her to the side as they left the cathedral grounds since the streets were very crowded. "His Majesty is the Count's father. Would the King not become overly curious as to why I was trying to find a birth record of my daughter when I'm about to marry his son? Aside from that, Count Gabriel may have known about the Aristocrat."

"Precisely, *Mademoiselle!*"

"Don't you see? If that is the case, then what are my chances that His Lordship will give me any information, even if he has it?"

Louise shrugged. "I wouldn't know. But if the Count was friends with the Aristocrat..."

"The fact that he would not do anything to undermine Cosimo tells me that he protects his friends. He would want to protect the privacy of the people who now raise my daughter. Aside from that, he's made it clear that he doesn't trust me so all the doors would be slammed shut in my face forever. Count Gabriel must never find out my real reason for coming to France."

"I understand." Louise nodded.

"Let's go purchase some clothing."

"Look at that driver." Louise gestured toward their carriage with her chin. "He keeps his eyes on us like a bloody hawk."

"One of the servants told me that none of the women are permitted to leave the grounds without an escort. We're fortunate that he didn't insist upon following us to the Cathedral."

"Count Gabriel sounds like a man who has to have his nose into everything everyone does. A controller."

"Huh! What man is not?" Viola threw up her arms. "All women have been doomed to a life of subjugation just because one woman took one bite of one apple fourteen hundred and fifty years ago—and they tell *me* not to hold a grudge!"

Upon returning from the city, Viola raced up to her quarters to change into a pink silk gown that was adorned with pearls, and a matching scarf to cover her hair. She fished through her purchases until she located a jar of Punic Apple preserves, left everything else on the bed and hurried down to meet the Count's son. She assumed that he had returned home and that he was very young, since Gabriel himself appeared to be in his early thirties.

She hoped that the child wasn't spoiled, because if she had to marry Gabriel in order to remain here long enough to find her daughter, she really wanted to like this child and get along well with him. It wasn't the child's fault that his father was impossible. Not only that but she had been a child once—a very unwanted child—and definitely had a soft spot for children.

Gathering the folds of her gown with one hand, she hurried downstairs, poking her head into each door on the main level until she located the boy in the kitchen. He sat on the end of the utility table – a large wooden cutting block – playing with a toy horse and carriage set, while Chantalle stood behind it, hacking up vegetables as if she was dismembering a cadaver. Viola was surprised that the acidic old hag would allow the child to sit where food was being prepared.

A thirty-ish woman with red curls sticking out from under her black cap, stood beside the boy. She said, "We have not met. My name is Denise."

"Viola de Medici. I'm pleased to make your acquaintance," she nodded.

"*Lady* Viola de Medici." Chantalle corrected. "And that's what we will call her. Lady Viola, or My Lady."

"I wish everyone would just call me by my name," Viola said.

Chantalle barked, "We don't want the servants to get too friendly! They get lazy when that happens!"

Rubbing the small of her back, Denise said, "It has been an eventful few days, and I am exhausted. I believe I will go lie down for a spell."

Chantalle slanted her a chilled glance. "We sleep at night. Not during the day. And that child must be attended to at all times."

"It is not as if he will be suffering neglect with so many others around here catering to his needs." She finalised, and then turned on her heel and marched out.

"I'll take care of him." Viola offered.

"No. You won't."

"Why not?"

"I know nothing about you," Chantalle said, banging her knife through some greens. "That looks like a new gown."

"It is. Count Gabriel bought it for me."

Chantalle's bushy grey eyebrows knotted together. "A nice parting gift."

"I'm not leaving. I am going to marry Gabriel."

The head servant planted the point of her knife firmly into the wood. "You have come all this way in hopes of sweet-talking that surly man into marriage, but you have wasted your time and mine, too."

"It's already been decided."

"By you, I'm sure. Many women have tried, and all have failed, except that greedy witch that he married—and she is the very reason that he will never marry again."

"If you don't believe me, ask him yourself."

"You are delusional. Where do you want to take this boy?"

"To play out on the grass, if that's all right with you?"

She grabbed her knife and resumed chopping while she considered it. Viola waited. And then she waited some more, while the child didn't seem to be aware of her presence or anything else, for that matter. He was lost in his world of pretending.

Chantalle finally said, "I suppose that would be fine. Not the back where it's full of mud. The front."

"Thank you." Viola leaned down to peer into the boy's face. He raised his long black lashes to gaze directly at her, and her heart missed a beat. It was like staring into the eyes of Count Gabriel himself, only a much smaller, younger version with skin the colour of honey. She smiled and whispered, "Hello, darling."

He returned her smile with a shy one. "Hello."

"I'm Viola. What is your name?"

"Z'abier. You're pretty."

"Oh, my goodness. What a charmer. Thank you."

"Oh, bother..." Chantalle rolled her eyes.

"Xavier, would you like to go outside with me?"

He held out both arms as if he had known her all of his life, causing Viola's case-hardened, suspicious heart to soften just a little bit more. Setting down her small jar of preserves, she caught him by his armpits and set him down, but rather than land on his feet, his legs collapsed under him, and he sank to the floor. She laughed, "Come, let's go, silly."

"The child is not able to walk!" Chantalle hissed. "You'll have to carry him."

The

Betrothal.

Segment 2.

♥ Chapter Four.

"Beg pardon?" Viola flashed Chantalle a surprised glance.

"His legs don't work."

Viola's heart twisted within her chest. She whispered, "Whatever happened?"

"We *try* not to discuss it around him." The head servant said, with a piercing glare.

"Of course." Viola collected him into her arms, reached for the jar of preserves and handed it to him, "Would you hold this, please?"

"Hang on." Chantalle gestured toward the jar with her blade. "Do you plan to give him any of that?"

"Yes. His Lordship told me that his son would be returning today. I bought him a treat. Is he not permitted to have any?"

Chantalle grabbed the jar in her manly hands and cranked it open. Dipping the tip of the knife into it, she transferred a gob onto her tongue and then stared up at the ceiling.

"What are you doing?"

"Testing it for poison." She tapped away the seconds with her nails.

"Pardon me?"

"Just wait." After several moments, the Head Servant handed him the jar. "He can have some."

"Did you actually think I would harm this boy?"

"You're a Medici. Better cautious than dead."

"Oh, Lord. I give up. Have you seen Louise?"

"Outside, helping to get the dust out of the tapestries. At least *somebody* around here is useful."

"Until I steal her back. Come, Xavier. Let's go."

"My horse."

Snagging the toys off the table, she piled them into his arms and left the kitchen. Outside, she found Louise in the tall grass unrolling a tapestry and beckoned her to follow. She was no longer wearing a servant's frock, but a nice, simple blue gown that Viola had purchased for her.

They strode to the farthest end, where Viola placed Xavier on the grass and stretched out on her stomach, beside him. Louise sat on his other side. In the nest of his safety, he went back to playing with his wooden horse and carriage as if they weren't there.

"You look lovely." Viola said. "That is a great color for you."

"And you as well, *Mademoiselle*. I feel awkward, though. I am not accustomed to wearing this kind of thing."

"Get used to it, Louise. Take the small blessings wherever they appear so you can reflect on them when life takes them back away."

"Yelk. This grass is soaked, and I am getting soaked, as well." Louise complained.

"I am, too," Viola said. "But I'm ignoring it. It feels great to sit in the sunlight."

"The things I endure because I love you," Louise grumbled, as she wriggled around.

"I love you more." Viola averted her attention to the boy. "What a lovely horse. Where did you get that?"

"Papa made it for me." He held up the wagon, "And this, too."

"Well, it's very nice. Is it your favourite toy?"

"Yes. Papa is good with his hands."

Viola's eyebrows lifted. "That remains to be seen."

"He is. He can make anything."

"May I ask you a question?"

He raised his head to look at her. In the low evening sun, they were the colour of amber, all the more pronounced by fringes of thick black lashes. "Yes?"

"You don't have to talk about it if you don't want to, but do your legs hurt you?"

"I don't feel them."

"I see."

"Why?" He asked.

"I don't want to hurt you by accident."

He lowered his head as if in thought and then smiled. "Thank you."

"Child, you are the sweetest little thing." She whispered as she passed a hand over his soft, dark curls.

"May I play now?"

"Yes, go ahead."

Louise remarked, "He speaks very clearly for one so young. How old is he?"

The child didn't raise his head but held up five pudgy fingers. "Z'abier is a big boy."

Viola scanned the castle from the front. It appeared to be a newer, three-story addition, built onto the ancient back side of the same height, for the light stone gleamed in the sunlight. There were six large windows in the middle, with two spacious balconies at the northerly and easterly ends. The balconies were recessed, with a partial wall between them to allow for privacy, which was a nice touch.

"When spring finally comes, it feels like I crawl out of a dark cave." She remarked, while scanning the property. The periphery of the front yard was surrounded by low hedges, the space between them containing a blanket of tall green grass rippling in the breeze.

Two serfs, one at each side of the paths between stable and outbuildings, swung their lathes, hewing the grass close to the ground and releasing a spiky scent into the breeze. Another couple of serfs followed behind them, collecting the cuttings for other uses. As they did, the servants from the outbuildings went in and out of the castle, carrying rolled-up tapestries which they would beat the dust out of on the lawn. The serfs cutting the grass worked around them until they moved, and then returned to clear that spot as well.

Bouncing to her feet, Viola said, "Louise, keep an eye on him for a moment. I want to go see what's down there." Grabbing her skirts, she darted down the incline, stopping at the tall, wrought-iron fence.

Two armed sentries guarded the gate, beyond which was a set of stairs carved into the rock. Some thirty feet below a small vessel was anchored at the shoreline while a group of serfs unloaded crates of wine. She made a double-take when she spotted a mountain cat lounging on a boulder in the sun, observing them. Would that be the beast that the Count had tried to domesticate? She made a mental note to always check before going anywhere around here, lest it hated visitors as much as everyone else did.

Across the river was a smattering of small humble homes built into the inclining rocky embankment, the land between them green and lush with new growth. Turning, she surveyed where her own balcony might be, up on the third level, and gathered that from there the view would be marvellous. Pleased with her findings, she returned to Louise and Xavier and dropped onto the grass.

She said, "I think I may like it here. It looks so much more inviting from this side. Don't you think?"

"Yes." Louise nodded. "Much."

Wanting to get the boy's attention again, Viola reached beside her thigh and opened the jar of Punic Apple preserves, and slowly waved it under his nose.

Forgetting his horse, he glanced up at her with twinkling eyes. "That smells good."

"It is good." She teased. She dipped her index finger into the jar and licked it off. "Mmm. I tell you, I would squeeze through a knot hole for this."

"May I have some?"

"I don't know. Do you have fingers?"

He held up both hands and giggled.

"I don't know if they're long enough."

He began to pull on them.

Louise grinned. "You're playing with his mind."

"I know. Isn't he wonderful?"

Louise answered. "Like most men, the way to his heart is through his stomach. He wouldn't talk to us a moment ago. We didn't exist."

"So, may I have some?" The boy repeated.

"If you can get your fingers into the jar you can."

In went three fingers, and out they came, completely covered in dark red sauce. "I did it."

"Now you have to lick it off. That's how we eat this."

Nearly the whole hand went into his mouth. Laughing, Viola handed him the jar. "Here. Enjoy."

She lost his attention again, for he became completely immersed in his treat. "What a beautiful child. He looks like a proper little man in his blue hose, white chemise, and blue tunic." Ruffling her fingers through his hair, she said, "Are you enjoying that?"

"Mmm! So good!" He grinned and thrust his little fingers into the jar for more. His cheeks were by now smeared with dark red sauce.

Louise drew her knees up close to her chest, locked her arms around them, and stared out at the river. "We may have to go to *Tours*."

"Yes. It may be the only way to find someone who knew *Monsieur* Ste. Louis."

Louise nodded. "And well enough to know with whom he might have associated regularly."

"Whomever the Aristocrat was," Viola speculated, as she flopped onto her back to gaze up at the few clouds drifting across the sky, "he would have been someone closer to him than just a business acquaintance, wouldn't you say?"

"I would say so since the Aristocrat would have had to put his total trust in him."

"It's impossible for anyone to cover his tracks completely. Everyone overlooks some tiny thing that he thinks won't matter – oof!" She blurted, as Xavier rolled onto her and thrust his fingers into her mouth.

"Eat!" He giggled as she gently nibbled his fingers.

"I will eat *you!*" Viola laughed for the first time in God-only-knew how long, as she pulled his face down to lick the red sauce off his cheeks. He shrieked like a wild cat. "I tell you, there is nothing tastier than the pudgy cheeks of a child. Nothing!"

Catching a swift motion in her peripheral vision, she glanced toward it and saw Gabriel flying over the hedges. He didn't pause on the landing but kept running until he swooped up Xavier and took a good close look at his face.

Sensing she was in trouble again, Viola scrambled to her feet.

"Papa!" Xavier yelped. "You're home!"

"Punic Apples?" He fired Viola a glance. "I thought it was blood, for God's sake! You scared the hell out of me!"

"I'm sorry."

"Where did you get this? They won't be harvested until October."

"There is a bakery in the city that sells jars of it. The storekeeper said his wife is the only woman in France who can preserve them this way. Chantalle tasted it herself before she allowed me to give him any."

"Swing me, Papa! Swing me!"

Gabriel planted five hard kisses on his son's cheeks before he created a sling under his son's backside with the fingers of both hands interlocked. "Hold on. Here we go."

Xavier wrapped both of his small arms around Gabriel's thick forearms. "I'm ready.Make it count, Papa!"

Gabriel swung him in a wide arc, for which he was rewarded with jubilant shrieks. Then, drawing his son into a big hug, he said, "Did you miss me, my little man?"

"Yes! You miss me?"

"I missed you like you would not believe."

"I caught a fish all by myself!" Xavier announced.

"Did you now? Who brought you fishing?"

"Benoit."

"And did you eat this fish?"

"All of it. Ch'tel cooked it for me."

"What else did you do while I was away?"

Louise beat a hasty retreat toward the front door. "Pardon me. I have work to do."

"I rode a horse all by myself."

"Not so." Gabriel teased. "You're too small."

"No!" The child laughed. "I rode a baby horse. Charles showed me how. He had a special saddle made for me."

"I am so impressed. But you must call him, His Majesty when you speak about him, and Your Majesty when you speak directly to him. Never call him Charles."

"He doesn't mind."

"I do."

"He let me keep it. It's in the stable."

"Good." Gabriel smiled – an expression that seemed foreign on his normally grumpy face. His teeth were slightly crooked but gleaming white, and that smile caused his eyes to crinkle with pleasure. The difference in the two expressions was as jolting as the depressing, ancient section of the castle was to the new. "I'm proud of your accomplishment."

"I was like you. A big, strong warrior."

"Show me your muscles."

The boy bent his arm, his pudgy little fist clenched so tightly that his face turned pink. Gently squeezing the tiny muscle between forefinger and thumb, Gabriel said, "No. You won't be like me. You'll be stronger."

"Nobody is stronger than you."

Gabriel crushed his boy close and stuffed his nose into the side of his neck, whispering, "Mmm. This is what I live for, little man."

The ache in Viola's chest deepened, for she would give anything to hold her own child as he was doing. What a privilege, she thought, that so many take for granted. She hugged one fist inside the other, both of them pressed into her chest as if she was trying to prevent her heart from breaking.

"Lisbeth!" Gabriel called out.

One of the outdoor servants dropped her tapestry and ran toward him. She stopped and bowed, "Yes, Your Lordship?"

"Take him inside. Get Denise to clean him up and put dry clothes on him. He's all wet from the grass." To Xavier, he said, "I trust you will still have an appetite at mealtime."

"My apologies," Viola said. "Perhaps I ought not to have put him on wet grass—or fed him treats before supper."

He observed the servant carrying his son across the grass, while rolling up his sleeves, and then turned to Viola. "A treat never harmed a child, and neither did play time. Thank you for that."

She was stunned into silence.

"You look nice – but you could do without the red sauce smeared across your face." Tugging a white handkerchief from the pocket of his surcoat, he reached out to wipe it off. Reacting on sheer reflex, she jerked backwards. He locked one big hand around the back of her head, wet the corner of the fabric with spittle and dabbed at the mess. "Why did you flinch? Did the Baron beat you?"

The Baron beat her whether she was obedient or not. He even beat her for the things her siblings had done because they were his offspring by blood, but she was not.

"Viola?" He bent his head to peer into her eyes, which cut into her memories. "Did he?"

She nodded. "I got used to it."

"That bastard." His movements slowed down while he studied her mouth, and then time itself seemed to stop altogether as he raised his dark eyes to hers. They whispered, *I would take you in an instant.*

Viola's heart missed a beat for she was not expecting this after the way he had snarled at her earlier. She sputtered, "Di-did you get it off yet?"

"Not quite. No point in wasting this." Dropping the handkerchief, he passed a fingertip along her lower lip, and then slipped his finger into her mouth. It seemed to be an action of good intent, such as a parent might do with a child, and one that he had probably done with his own son countless times.

Viola swallowed hard—a reflexive action caused by pressure on her tongue. In doing so she closed her mouth, as it was physiologically impossible to swallow with it open. It was even more impossible to do it without sucking on his finger. She hadn't intended on doing any of these suggestive things, but the body did what the body did.

It was clear even to her that he hadn't intended to initiate such an intimate moment, for he uttered an expletive under his breath that even her foul, street-urchin's mouth would not repeat. As they both simultaneously stepped back away from each other, she noticed that the fine dark hairs along his arms were standing straight on end. All a-fluster, she somehow caused her veil to come loose and flow down over her shoulders. Scrambling to cover her hair, she stammered, "'A-a leech! Did-did you find a leech?"

On a restricted exhale, he answered. "I did. I shall live."

"Be sure to change the bandage every day. Don't wash it for re-use. Throw it out and use a new one. Washing doesn't kill the germs."

"I will get you to do that for me."

"You're not afraid I'll poison you?"

"I'll be watching you the whole time."

"I have no drugs in my possession," she said, "so you can relax."

"Nothing except that mouth, which will sure as hell be my undoing."

Clearing her throat, she answered, "Well, it's good that you'll be fine."

"Good for you, yes, else you'd be a widow before a wife."

"Good for your son. He needs a father. All boys do."

"They need a mother just as much. Inelegance comes naturally to men, but the finer things need to be taught by a woman." He countered.

"I understand why you are so protective of your son."

"Good. But the last thing he needs is your pity."

"I wasn't pitying...well, yes," she allowed, "I was. I understand."

"Do you?"

"He must be stronger than most to get through this life with such a condition."

"Exactly, so you must not do everything for him. I want him to be taught strength and independence, not reliance. Understand?"

"Yes. I'll do my best."

"I'm creating a chair with wheels for him so that he can get around by himself. Once it's ready, he will be on his own to get from room to room." He informed her, his gruff tone returning with the placement of both hands upon his hips. "The wheels will be big enough so that he can manoeuvre them with his hands. I have seen one that came from the Land of the Chin."

"Will that not be hard on those little arms?"

"Those little arms are stronger than you think." He said. "Did you replace your losses?"

"I got five gowns, along with the headdresses and the underthings to match."

"Anything else?"

"I also purchased a few gowns for Louise. Simple outfits. I hope that is all right."

"That's *it?*" He said.

"Yes."

"You'll have to go back for more."

"I hate buying sprees."

"There are approximately thirty days in each month. No wife of mine will go 'round wearing the same things, day in, day out."

"Fine." She conceded. "Perhaps I can find someone to tidy up my hair a bit if that is alright. The Nuns hacked it off. It will grow back. Eventually. I hope."

"It suits you that way—all tossed about. I like it."

Oh, God, there he goes again. "You should go take a rest. Your side must be killing you."

Working his long fingers through her hair, as if to mess it up even more than it already was, he answered, "No matter what I do with that hair, it just looks better. You should keep it that way, Sister Viola de Medici."

Things were back to normal. "Oh, for the love of God. I already told you that I am no longer a Nun, and it was never my idea to become one."

"Is there anyone in your past that I ought to know about?"

"What do you mean?"

"Have you had any lovers?"

Her cheeks suddenly flaming, she said, "That's not the kind of question a man should ask a woman."

"A woman's virtue is always a deal-maker or a deal-breaker in any marriage arrangement. Since your father can't vouch for you, you'll have to speak on your own behalf. Have you had any lovers?"

She figured that she may as well be honest since he would find out sooner or later, anyway. "Yes. One time."

"Might he get jealous over our union?"

"No."

"Is he liable to haunt our marriage bed?"

She gave him an impatient stare. "This is a very crude line of questioning, Gabriel."

"I would have a fit if I were bedding you while you dreamed about someone else."

She continued staring at him.

"Who is he?"

Silence.

"Viola?"

"All of that is in the past, where it belongs."

"That is not reassuring." He turned and stalked toward the door, the grass beneath his feet not lessening the intent of hammering heels one bit.

"What does it matter?" She called out. "It's not as if you feel anything but distrust for me!"

"Distrust, and something else far more primal, Sister!"

Viola dropped to the grass, wondering what in God's name she had got herself into *this* time.

"Viola!"

She glanced up to find him in the doorway. "Yes?"

"We're invited to His Majesty's palace this eve. Did you purchase anything a bit more formal than what you have on?"

"Yes, but I don't like those kinds of events. "

"Wear it." He slammed the door before she could object.

Bossy bastard.

*   *   *

Shortly after the blue twilight gave way to night, so many windows on the hilly landscape across the Loire River lit up from within. At that distance, they seemed to be a vast collection of candles flickering in the dark. Although the temperature had cooled down substantially, made worse by the fact that her dress was damp, Viola had not moved since earlier that day.

She was still sitting on the grass, hugging her knees and devising schemes to find her little girl when Louise appeared at her side. "His Lordship awaits you in the carriage by the drawbridge."

"I don't want to do this."

"Do what?"

"He wants me to go meet his father."

Louise's eyebrows slid upward. "Oh-oh."

"Please tell him that I must change first and that I will be there shortly, and then come up to help me dress?" She hurried into the castle, darting straight up the foyer stairs, and then up another flight alongside the hideous gargoyle. Once in her chamber, she untied the gold and white ribbon holding together the fancy fabric within which one of her new gowns was neatly folded. Gently shaking it out, she placed it across the bed just as Louise entered.

In good speed, they got her out of the damp, pink gown and into a more formal red one with glittering black stones along the neckline, cuffs, and hem. Unlike any gown she had ever worn, this one was in the latest fashion with the neckline swooping down to reveal her neck, collarbone and a slight bit of cleavage. She was surprised that this sort of immodesty was allowed while a thing so non-sexual as the hair had to be covered.

Finally, she sat upon the chair at the vanity. "Would you look at this gown? I have never seen anything like it."

"The cost of it could feed a family for months." Louise pointed out.

"Yes, and I love it."

"It is beautiful, *Mademoiselle*. Red is becoming on you."

"Thank you. Time for the headdress."

Louise picked up a matching headdress from the bed and was about to set it upon her head. Viola held up a hand. "Look at the size of that thing. Would I even fit into the carriage? It must be two feet high."

"It is hideous." Louise frowned.

"Can you remove the long veil from the top?"

Louise turned the thing round and round, finally answering, "Yes, it is tacked on here." She picked at it for several moments until finally, the lace came off. "Now what?"

Viola took the red veil and draped it over her hair. "I shall wear it like this. We can only see the darkness of my hair but nothing more telling. What do you think?"

"It looks beautiful. Now, hurry! He's waiting."

*　　　*　　　*

Gabriel swept a glance down her front as she crawled into the carriage beside him. Straightening the folds of the fabric, she said, "I hate crowds. How many people will be at this event?"

"Not too many. Mostly family and friends. You ought to know in advance that it is sort of a known secret that the King is my father. I am his illegitimate bastard. He insists on keeping up appearances because of his status and to honour his wife, so he refers to me as his good friend when others are around. In private, he recognises me as his offspring. Once we are wed, you will become Countess of Bellefleur, by Royal Decree."

"Thank you for the information." She remained quiet as the carriage moved through the dark, knowing full well that she would somehow manage to make a fool of herself at this affair. She was no royal, and she *felt* it.

She allowed her thoughts to drift elsewhere, while the sound of horses hooves reverberated into the night. As the moments dragged by, she began to feel his masculinity infiltrating her awareness, rather like a thief quietly breaking into a sanctuary. The scents of soap and water and man drifted around her head while his sturdy thigh pressed against her skinny one. There was one heck of a lot of him in that small space and very little of her. She fanned herself with her hand.

"Are you nervous, Viola?"

"No."

He lifted her other hand to show it to her, and it was, in fact, balled up into a tight little fist. "No?"

"Do I look all right? You never said anything."

"Believe me, Sister, you don't want to know what I'm thinking."

*   *   *

They were greeted at the door of the King's castle by a gentleman wholly dressed in black, with the collar of a frilly white chemise puffing out around his neck. Head high and back ram-rod stiff, he led them through a massive foyer fit for a king, which of course, it was, and then through a set of twelve-feet-high, white doors.

Viola stood paralysed with her mouth hanging open as the wall of voices and laughter lambasted her—completely unaware that this event would change her life forever.

The vast hall was packed. Along three of the outer sides were long tables dressed in white linen, with elaborately gilded chairs surrounding them. There were only a few guests at the tables, as most of them had gathered in the central area where they stood in groups, chatting and sipping from sparkling silver goblets. From high above suspended several chandeliers with up to thirty candles in each.

It wasn't as if she had never seen this sort of ostentatious display. It was that she had never attended one as an invited guest. The walls of this place were adorned in portraits with gold frames, which brightly reflected light, but they were not nearly as blinding as the jewels worn by the women in their flamboyant gowns and headdresses. She was glad that she left her own ugly headdress behind. Lord, but she detested these things.

At the far end of the room was the Dias, a raised platform upon which was the table of His Majesty and his entourage. His wife, Queen

Marie of Anjou, sat on his right. Nearly every seat was occupied except two, which were to His Majesty's left side. In the back of that table was another space which was held by musicians, softly playing tunes that more or less became lost in all of this ado.

A gong sounded near the door, nearly frightening her out of her wits. An immediate hush drew all eyes toward her and her escort. "Presenting! His Lordship, Count Gabriel Xavier and Lady Viola de Medici, of Florence!"

She felt like turning tail and running. Gabriel produced an elbow. "Here we go."

The stroll to the Dias felt like a long walk to the guillotine. As they stepped up onto the platform, everyone at that table stood, except King Charles VII and his Queen.

Viola hissed, "We are *not* sitting up here, are we?"

"We are."

Pausing before His Majesty, King Charles VII, Count Gabriel bowed briefly and said, "Your Majesty, it's a pleasure to be here. Your Majesty, *Reine d'anjou*, it's always an honour to see you. I would like to present Lady Viola de Medici, my betrothed. Lady Viola, meet His Majesty, King Charles the Seventh, of France, and Her Majesty, Queen Marie *d'anjou*."

The King, a rather small man with reddish hair and ashen skin, wore a conical hat with a turned-up rim, embellished with gold chains and jewels. The frilly collar of a white chemise appeared above the fur of his mantle, and at the arms, very wide puffy sleeves lent a certain elegance to his demeanour. He seemed to be a man who was not entirely healthy and who was at the brink of exhaustion. Without standing, he extended his hand, backside up, and nodded briefly. "Enchanted."

As was expected of her, Viola curtsied and kissed his hand. "I am honoured, Your Majesty."

The Queen nodded but did not present her hand. She spoke with quiet authority and great dignity befitting the modest crown that sat upon her head. "Good evening, Gabriel. It is nice to see you again. Lady Viola, I am pleased to make your acquaintance—and I admire that you have the gumption to forgo a hideous headdress. You look lovely."

"Thank you, Your Majesty." Viola curtsied. "Most sincerely. I detest them."

"As do I." The Queen said.

"Please, be seated." His Majesty gestured to the empty chairs on his left. On his order, everyone at that table reclaimed their seats. "You and Lady Viola will be here, Gabriel."

"Thank you." Gabriel assisted her in getting all of her movable parts arranged – the placement of her long train – before seating himself.

Hence, he turned to his father. "How are you feeling?"

His Majesty shrugged. "The same. Yourself?"

"Like I took an arrow to the gut."

"We are both shipwrecks. I trust you will be taking the appropriate time to recover?"

"Yes. Thank you for entertaining my son. He's quite proud of his new horse."

The King waved a hand, dismissively. "My pleasure. As usual, he had all of the women swooning over him."

"He has that effect on females."

"Indeed. I love that boy." The King whispered, while stealing a cautious glance toward his wife.

"As do I," Gabriel said.

"So, this is the young lady about whom you spoke earlier." King Charles VII glanced toward Viola and offered her a tired smile. "You don't resemble the Medici's in the least."

"I hear that quite a lot, Your Majesty."

"You have beautiful eyes, my dear. They pull at the soul."

"Thank you, Your Majesty."

"She is lovely, Gabriel. Have you set a date set?"

Gabriel shook his head. "We have a few matters to settle first."

"I see. Well, let us formalise this betrothal before the meal, shall we?" The King lifted his arm and nodded toward the rear.

The gong sounded again. Twice. All of those who were milling about promptly returned to their seats and fixed their eyes on their royal host. The music behind the Dias drained into silence with a few trailing strains of a violin.

His Majesty stood. "Friends and family, if I may have your attention for a moment before the meal arrives. I would like to announce the betrothal of Lady Viola de Medici of Florence to my dear good friend, Count Gabriel Xavier. No date has yet been established. However, being as her father is not present, we will satisfy the law by declaring the seriousness of Count Gabriel's intent in my presence, as King of the Franks, and in your presence as witnesses, by his offering to her a gift in observance of the same. Let it be noted that I approve, and so on, and so forth. Go ahead, Gabriel."

Viola wanted to crawl under the table and remain there for the duration. But here she was, ergo, she had to play along with this pompous soiree whether she wanted to or not.

Gabriel stood and gazed down at her. She stared up at him. *What does he want? What am I supposed to do?*

He offered his hand, along with a subtle head gesture for her to rise.

"Oh." Tiny rivulets of sweat began to trickle down between her breasts, and her gown was laced up too tightly. Suddenly, she couldn't breathe but forced herself to stand anyway.

He pulled from the pocket of his black surcoat, a sizeable golden brooch encrusted with diamonds and sapphires, nestled within an elaborate silver box, which was lined with midnight blue velour. Turning toward her, he said, "I offer you this gift as a gesture of my intent to take you as my wife. Do you accept?"

She nervously whet her lips. "Yes. Thank you."

Removing the brooch from its box, Gabriel leaned over to pin it to her gown, above her left breast. Lifting his lashes, he smirked, "Wear it in good health, *beloved*."

His Majesty issued a few light claps of his hands. Everyone erupted into a round of applause. Gabriel waited for her to sit, and then did the same. She thought, *until I hear angels singing 'Hallelujah' this shall not be proper in the eyes of God*. Arranged marriages never were.

Gabriel whispered, "I get a mother for my son, and you get to stay here in France—and you get to sleep in my bed while pretending that I am your long-lost lover."

Chapter Five

After the meals arrived, Gabriel speared a chunk of vegetable with his knife and shoved it into his mouth, chewing it thoughtfully while he studied her. She was a far cry from refined, although she should be, given her supposed status. It was apparent to him that she had no clue how to conduct herself in this sort of situation, which meant that she was probably some guttersnipe hand-picked by Mario de Medici so that he could trade her off for an alliance with the King.

Lady Viola—if she was a lady in any sense of the word—now spoke only when spoken to by the Duke at her right. Mostly she picked at her food and seemed to be having a thoroughly miserable time. Who was this man in her past to whom she had given her virtue, only to leave her? Better than that, would any woman give herself to a man who has no serious intent to marry her?

Stupid question. They gave themselves to men like the one he used to be, before he had fallen in love and settled down, and the one he turned back into after the bitch died. Men who disappeared after they got what they wanted. Or perhaps she was merely another opportunist like Murielle had been, and he wanted to give her the benefit of the doubt because her very unusual sort of beauty was beginning to drunken him. *Don't go down that road again, fool.*

His father's guests began to wander back into the central area to chat and circulate after a hearty meal. The Queen congratulated them, excused herself and politely left the hall with two escorts. Gabriel leaned toward Viola, whispering, "This thing can go on for hours."

"I was afraid of that."

"The formalities are over. Feel free to circulate."

"I'd rather not."

"I suggest that you learn to mingle. I have a business matter to discuss with His Majesty." He stood to pull back her chair and let her out, observing her still as she strode down the Dias.

Reclaiming his seat, he turned to his father, whispering, "May I speak with you privately?"

Feeling ill-at-ease completely, Viola ambled down the outside of the tables, wondering what to do now. She supposed she should interact, but she didn't know any of these people and was never any good at bursting into a crowd. She had never learned how. Needing something to do with her hands, she swiped a nearly empty silver goblet from the end of a table in passing and then pasted on a smile as she ventured further into the group.

An elderly lady in a black gown and headdress approached her and spoke in a thick rolling accent. "Lady Viola. I am Duchess Christina Krzywousty of Bulgaria. Congratulations on your betrothal. He is a fine man."

"Thank you." She nodded. "You are a long ways from home, Duchess Christina."

"As are you, my dear."

"If I may ask, what brings you to France, Duchess?" Was that the right way to address a Duchess? She wondered. Or was it *Your Duchness*? *My* Duchess? Your Lesser Noblewoman? *God, no.* That would be insulting! *I am failing, miserably.*

"Oh," the Duchess made a flicking motion with a long, thin hand, "my husband and His Majesty are very distant cousins. I come perhaps once every ten years to France. But only in spring. It's too cold to travel in winter."

"Are you enjoying your visit?"

"*Meh*...it's a change of scenery."

"What was that fellow's name? The Aristocrat who died of Lung Fever right after his child was born? Do you remember? He had silvery eyes. He was so divine!" Viola heard the questions coming from directly behind her. It was all she could do to prevent spinning around to join that conversation instead.

"Of course, the wine is outstanding, as well." Duchess Christina went on.

"Uh, yes. Yes, it is."

"But it passes right through." The elderly lady leaned close to whisper, "I must go find a privy. At my age, everything passes right through me. That was where I was going when I ran into you."

"By all means, Duchess Christina." Viola answered, "It was a pleasure meeting you."

As the Duchess wandered off, Viola stood still with her back to the women speaking, listening intently to hear more about the Aristocrat who had died of Lung Fever. Had he been *her* Aristocrat?

"Oh, I don't know." Someone else said. "I don't know the names of every Aristocrat in *Orléans*, for goodness' sake! Do I look like the Records Keeper to you?"

"Well, dear Lily, you get your nose into everything."

"Nevertheless, Lung Fever has taken many lives, regardless of social standing, so he's just one more casualty of this dastardly disease, and that's to say nothing of the Black Death, from which we are yet to recover. Go ask the fellow who buries them. If he is still alive..."

Sipping from his goblet, Gabriel stood beside the King in the darkest corner of the room. From his shadowed spot beside a larger-than-life statue of the Madonna, he observed Viola while he spoke to his father. Yet, even as he spoke he was distracted.

This evening's events brought back ghostly images of Murielle on the night his father had made this same sort of announcement years ago. Murielle had not been the least bit shy or reserved. Ten years his senior, she had had ample practice rubbing elbows with Aristocrats, lesser nobles, and nobles. Whoever was most revered at any event was the one who inadvertently got her undivided attention. After the formalities were done with, it was she who had excused herself and floated down among them make good and sure that they honoured her sufficiently on the night of her betrothal to a Count.

His father nudged his elbow. "What do you ponder so deeply?"

"Murielle."

"It's always our mistakes that we dwell on more than our victories. They eat holes in our guts."

"Yes. She was a striking woman with her golden hair and twinkling blue eyes." Gabriel admitted.

"But the heart of her," His Majesty said, "was as black as the soles of Lucifer's boots. If only you had been able to see through her as clearly then, as you are able to in hindsight."

Gabriel admitted, "I wanted to believe the best."

"Love can blind us."

"And it can make us quarrel with those whose intentions are good. I still feel bad that we fought over her, Father."

The King patted his forearm. "It's all water under the bridge."

"And here I am, getting set to marry her complete opposite. Look at her. She's so small I could stick my tongue into her belly button and spin her around."

"She is quite petite, yes." The King agreed.

"Under that veil her hair isn't more than two inches long, a bloody horrid mess that is just as seductive as hell. She's bony as wild dog, and yet I want to bang her skinny arse into anything I can lay her down on. I don't even like her, but by God she excites me."

His Majesty laughed aloud. "You could do worse. I like her."

"Do you?"

"Indeed. She's more than a little awkward, though. I have been observing her. She has no idea how to interact with these people. Perhaps we ought to find someone to train her on how to conduct herself in these situations."

"Perhaps. I had to learn. I had no idea what I was doing." Gabriel allowed.

"Do you know, she reminds me of a certain young woman I was enamoured with in my youth, but whom I was forced to leave."

Gabriel concluded, "My mother."

"Indeed. I never got over her. You look so much like her, except that her skin was the colour of dark, rich molasses. She was a good hand's width taller than I. What a marvellous armful of woman."

"She was beautiful." Gabriel agreed.

"Yes, and I would have married her, except that my fate was sealed before my birth, and so was my destiny. I had to marry into nobility. If I had been able to marry her, you would have been in line for the throne for you are my firstborn son."

"Hm! I gladly pass on that. I have enough of my own headaches besides inheriting yours, which are by far much more intense. I'm quite grateful for what you have bestowed unto me, else my brother and I would have died of starvation."

"I never would have let that happen. Of course, I didn't know you existed until you were eight years old. In any event," His Majesty flicked his wrist, "my eldest son, Louis, who is in line for the throne, is not someone with whom I can get along. I can't say that I blame him. What with this damned war and all of my responsibilities, I wasn't at home very much. I wasn't much of a father. I was merely a dictator who appeared infrequently to dole out discipline. My own children hardly know me, and they certainly do not appreciate all of the power and wealth that is their birthright—*because* it is their birthright. Entitlement spoils children. You, on the other hand, I can talk to, because you listen and because you don't spend your time dreaming about the title you will inherit once I die. It's quite unnerving to wonder if your own son will kill you to get you out of the way."

Gabriel waved a hand. "Louis wouldn't do that."

"It has happened to other kings. History tells us that the Assyrian King, Tukulti-Ninurta, was killed by his son. So were Sennacherib, Bimbisara, Ajatashatru, and numerous others, over time. Power, or the promise of it, can corrupt the best among us." Charles VII pointed out.

"Well, yes, that is true."

"That aside, this Viola has the same wild heart inside of her as your mother had, I think." His Majesty speculated, as he glanced toward her.

"Don't get too fond of her just yet, Father. I suspect she may be part of Mario de Medici's plot. Someone he hand-picked to pose as his daughter."

"That would explain why she looks nothing like them." His Majesty allowed. "Any association that she and Mario have would end at the Altar, with him getting his alliance with me, and her, a better life than on the streets of Italy. Is that what you were thinking?"

Gabriel nodded. "You nailed it."

"Would you like me to look into this?"

Gabriel shook his head. "I'll handle him in my own way."

"And her?"

"I will get the truth out of her, one way or the other—and I believe

I'm going to head home. My side is killing me."

*   *   *

A distinct chill washed over Viola as she entered her chamber. Since it was pitch dark, she wandered back out into the hall to snag a wall-mounted torch and re-entered the room. Noticing that the French doors leading to the balcony were ajar, she quickly shut them and then noticed a candle on the bureau, which she lit. She returned the torch to its wall mount in the hall before finally settling into her chamber for the night. Now that the day's activities were done with, she finally examined where she would be laying down her head each night.

It was a very feminine room, decorated in pinks, creams, and greens – a monumental improvement over the tiny cell that Chantalle had put her in. A stone hearth sat directly across from a large, deeply stuffed, four-poster bed, which, after the rough few weeks she had endured, seemed to be begging her to jump in and sleep for a week. *After* she hung her new gowns, some of which were strewn across the bed.

As she was about to begin that task, she noticed that upon her vanity was an assortment of feminine grooming needs that had not been there earlier. Moving the candle to get a closer look, she cringed when she noted that there were long golden hairs in the brush. There was a vial of perfume, which was obviously used, as well as a small assortment of cosmetic items—also used. Who would put these things here? She wanted to believe that someone's intentions were good, but her intuition told her otherwise. The help had made it painfully obvious that nobody wanted her here. But why this? What was the intended message? Well, whatever it was, she decided that she wouldn't dwell on it tonight. She was exhausted.

Just in case, she locked the door and then approached the hearth with intentions of getting a good strong fire going. As she arranged the kindling, she said to the vacant space, "Whatever happens, happens."

"Meaning?"

She spun so quickly in her squatted position that she nearly toppled over. There stood Gabriel at the adjoining door, hands on hips. She said, "I thought you would be asleep by now. It was a long day."

He strode toward her with a quiet command, "Allow me."

"I am able to start a fire."

"Yes, you've proven that."

She backed up until the edge of the bed knocked against her legs, and then deliberated on whether to stand or sit. She did not want him to get the idea that she was comfortable with him being there. There were things that a woman just did not allow, and that was for a man to be in her private chambers before they were married. If she were in her homeland, they would not even be allowed to speak to each other without a chaperone.

She observed him as he snatched the candle off the bureau and carried it toward the hearth. She knew it would take a while to get that fire going, so she gathered the items off the bed and moved them into the dressing room, where she proceeded to hang them.

"You did well this evening."

She peeked around the doorjamb. "I botched it up."

"His Majesty enjoyed you."

"I hope I won't have to attend too many of those." She answered.

"You won't. I detest them, as well."

"Then, why did we go?"

"It was my father's idea." He explained, as he added logs to the burning kindling. "Since your father won't be here to officially approve of our union, the King of France has authority to do so. He wanted to leave no room for error." Shoving to his feet, he returned the candle to the bureau. "There you go. You'll warm up fairly soon. Is there anything else you require?"

"That was fast. I expected it to take longer to get a fire going."

He answered, "You'd be surprised at how fast I can ignite a flame."

"I suppose you've lit many," she said, trying to keep his mind on the more honourable path, "being out on the battlefield so much, I mean."

"I've been told that I have magic in my fingertips." He held up a hand to wriggle his long fingers.

Deliberately ignoring his double-entendres, she ventured further into her room. "If I didn't know better I might get the idea that a gentleman is hiding behind your – "

"Mud-encrusted savagery?"

"You won't let me forget that, will you?"

"No – and don't get any notions that I am a gentleman, either. You'd be setting yourself up for a fall."

"Well, you're quick to appear when I need a fire so thank you for that, at least."

"I care for what is mine." He strode toward her, his dark gaze intent on holding hers. "Are you that?"

"Am I what?"

"Mine."

"I am going to be your wife, so...so I..."

"Are you getting warmer now?"

"I'm getting nervous." She said. "You should not be in here."

"The fire was for my sake as well as yours. There's not much meat on your bones. We don't want them knocking together, keeping me up all night."

"You sleep on the other side of that wall. You ought to be fine," she said, deliberately ignoring the goose bumps on her arms.

"I'm a light sleeper."

"Then I will put pillows between my knees to keep them from knocking."

"If you need something between your knees I may be able to help with that as well."

"*No.* I mean, I think I will be fine. Perhaps you ought to leave now."

"I'm telling myself the same thing. Now that you've had a little time to think about our situation, I'll ask you the same question that I asked you the first time we spoke. What's in this marriage for you?"

"A husband and a home."

Gabriel eyed her studiously. "Money, power, a title...those things don't entice you?"

"I know you want them to entice me because that would give you a reason to resent me, but they do not."

"That's what my late wife said. But that attitude changed overnight."

"I am not her, so please do not make me pay for her nonsense."

"Do I?"

Viola blinked. "What? Do you what?"

"Entice you?" He spoke quietly. "Or repel you?"

She eyed him studiously, and began to realize that he was not simply egging her on, or trying to annoy her. The man was actually looking for answers to questions that tormented him. "Enticement is a thing that happens on its own terms, Gabriel. It cannot be forced, or bought, or sold. Sometimes it occurs instantly when there is a certain magical connection and sometimes it has to grow. It's not a commodity."

"Damn good answer."

"I need to ask you something."

"Ask."

She gestured toward the vanity. "From where do those items come? To whom do they belong?"

He crossed the room to pick up the brush, and his expression darkened. "My late wife. This was her chamber until she moved down to the other end of the corridor. But none of this—this shit! – was here yesterday." He made a sweeping motion over the vanity.

"I see."

"No, you don't." He began collecting them. "Your brain is reeling with questions that you dare not ask."

"That's because you wouldn't answer them."

As he strode past her, he paused to say, "That's right. I won't."

"Why not?"

"The more a man proclaims his innocence, the guiltier he looks. Know me first, Viola, and then make up your own mind." With a dismayed shake of his head, he strode toward the door.

"I am curious about something."

He cast her an impatient glance. "And that is?"

"This room appears to have been freshly redecorated. Why would you have this room redone if nobody was occupying it?"

"One. I detest her and want no reminders. Two. I have not slept alone every night since she died. I like to offer some semblance of comfort and privacy to female guests."

A hot line crawling up her neck, she answered, "Must you be so brutally honest?"

"You ought to try it sometimes." He left and slammed the door.

She decided she had enough excitement for one day, and was not going to dwell on this encounter. She manoeuvred her way out of her clothing and then changed into her nightgown—a homely gray thing that an old man would wear. Afterwards, she blew out the candle and knelt at the side of her bed to pray.

Clementine Dupond. The name rang in her head. Clementine Dupond was the name of the young woman with the red hair, who had been speaking of the Aristocrat. As she had circulated around them, she had overheard as this young woman introduced herself to a gent wandering by. It was a name worth remembering, for now, she had to find out where this young woman lived so that she would be able to track her down and find out more. Perhaps this was her first real lead to the whereabouts of her daughter.

Focus. She told herself. There was a time to plot and a time to pray. It was time to pray. She Crossed herself, then said an Our Father, ten Hail Mary's, one Glory Be, and then crawled into bed.

But she couldn't sleep. Her over-stimulated brain began wondering what it might be like to be in the Count's bed. He was right on the other side of that wall. Did he sleep in the flesh, as some men did? She knew what his upper half looked like, but what about the bottom?

Oh, stop.

Clementine Dupond.

"What was that fellow's name? The Aristocrat who died of Lung Fever right after his child was born? Do you remember?"

The hairbrush had belonged to his late wife, but someone with evil intent had placed it in this room for her to find, along with another assortment of used items. Was someone trying to frighten her away? Was it Chantalle? The Head Housekeeper clearly didn't want her here.

Stop! Go to sleep!

In her fits of tossing and turning, she eventually heard movements on the other side of the wall and knew that Gabriel was getting ready for bed. Oddly, it was comforting that he was near, as something was going on in this castle that unsettled her.

When she assumed the title of Countess of Bellefleur, Chantalle would no longer have the authority to run this place as she wished, but she would have to answer to Viola. That was just how things worked. Could that be it?

For God's sake, go to sleep!

She flipped over again, with her back to the French doors, punched the pillow, jammed her head into it, and stared into the darkness. This was the most comfortable bed she had ever lain upon, but she couldn't sleep, damn it! The fire in the hearth had died, and it was getting chilly again, but she was not getting up.

Hm. There were only so many choices. Yolande, Denise, *Monsieur* Ste. Germaine, or Chantalle. She doubted that it would be *Monsieur*. He didn't seem to be the sort to put the dead wife's things in the betrothed's chamber. So that left her with three possibilities.

Oh, Viola, shut the HELL up!

She forced herself to close her eyes and try harder to sleep. As she began to feel drowsy, she thought she heard the French doors opening behind her, followed by a predatory snarl. An animal sound. She told herself she imagined things...until she heard it again, and then felt a cold gust of air blowing across the room.

That mountain cat! She remembered.

She opened her eyes and turned, just as the creature leapt onto her bed. She stared into the dark, frozen in terror, unable to see anything but a pair of eyes glowing yellow. As the wind blew the drapery wildly about, she let go a screech, believing that this beast was going to kill her.

The adjoining door flew open as Gabriel sailed in with a black coverlet draped about his hips, which trailed across the floor. In his hand was a lantern. "What is it? Oh. Melanie, this isn't your private den anymore. Get off the woman's bed."

"Get it away from me!"

Setting the lantern down on her night table, he caught a handful of fawn-coloured fur at the back of the big cat's neck. As he coaxed it off of her bed, he explained, "She is quite adept at tapping those latches with her paw."

"How in God's name did she get all the way up here?"

"I installed a ladder of sorts on the east side of the building. It runs diagonally from the ground up to the side of my balcony. From there she can go along the ledge and – "

"Why?"

"So that she could find shelter in my chamber when the weather is cold and miserable. She had a litter of cubs in this very chamber a few years ago." He said, as he led the big cat through the adjoining door. "You have no idea what an honour that is, for they seldom trust humans this much...what's wrong?"

"I just about shat in my night-dress!"

"You'll have to tame that mouth of yours if you're to spend time around other human beings."

"Where's that cat?" She craned her neck to peer around him.

"She's on my bed. Did you hear what I said?"

"Yes." She responded.

"And?"

"Don't you worry about me." She assured him. "I know how to behave when I have to. Sometimes. Maybe."

"I got a glimpse of your finesse tonight. You had no idea what to do, did you?"

"Well, I never said I was any good at licking boots." She crossed her arms, defensively.

"The mouth." He pointed to his own.

"You are worse than I am."

"I'm a man."

"Evidently. And let's not forget that your lance is bigger than mine."

"A hell of a lot bigger," he warned, "so be careful."

Annoyed, she spat sarcastically, "*Wooooo.* Watch me shaking."

"You will be when I kiss that bony arse of yours. That was the invitation you put out. Wasn't it?"

Tugging the cream sheet up to her throat, she said, "That was not meant literally – and threats do not intimidate me."

"Oh, that wasn't a threat, Sister. That was a promise. By the time I'm done with you, you'll be screaming out the Litany of the Saints." Grabbing his lantern, he said, "Put a chair in front of your door, and she won't come back in."

*   *   *

"I seriously do not believe that he murdered his wife," Viola whispered, as Louise laced her into her gown, the same lovely pink creation that she had worn the day before.

"Why not?"

"I don't get that feeling about him. He's a grouchy bitch...is there a male word for bitch?"

"Bastard?" Louise said.

"How fitting, since he is one. Well, he's a cranky bastard, but I am not convinced that he's a cold-blooded murderer."

"Whom do you think did it?"

"Well, first of all, we're going on the assumption that she *was* murdered. She may have died giving birth. The poor child is crippled, Louise. It may have been a terrible birthing process."

"Why would they say he killed her, then?"

"You have lived in servants' quarters all of your life and so have I. We both know how they can take a little smouldering ash and build it into a volcano merely because they hate their lives. It gives them something to do." Viola expelled a huge breath to allow her stomach to expand within the tight confines of her corseted gown, which was, of course, impossible.

Turning to face Louise, she whispered, "All I know is that the servants do not want me here. Perhaps they do not want to have another Countess overseeing activities in this home because they like things as they are. Or perhaps they do not like the idea of someone new moving in. What do you think?"

"Methinks you ought to keep your door locked."

"Oh!" She turned suddenly to face Louise. "I have a name."

Louise smiled. "As do I."

"Silly you. Listen, at the betrothal, I overheard Clementine Dupond speaking about an Aristocrat who died of Lung Fever shortly after his child was born."

"Who?"

"I don't know anything about her but I must find her. She may know more."

"Are we going to find her first or proceed with our plan to go to *Tours*?"

"I must ask His Lordship if this it is permissible for us to go there, but before we do, we can search for this woman. I need to see how much room I have to manoeuvre."

*   *   *

"Where is his Lordship?" Viola stuck her head into the kitchen to ask Chantalle, who was busy at the counter pounding the daylights out of a massive mound of dough.

"In the stable."

"Thank you."

"Was your chamber suitable this time?" She inquired, with an acidic bite.

"It is fine, thank you."

"He told me of his plans to marry you – do not fire up that spit!" She snapped at Yolande, who was at the end of the room preparing to set fire to a pile of kindling in the large stone alcove. "I told you to prepare the outdoor spit! We suffocated in here yester's eve!"

Yolande stalked out of the kitchen, her shoulder banging against Viola's as she went. So much for pleasantries. "Where is Xavier?"

"Denise is dressing him. She must take him to the leech to be checked over. He goes once each month."

"All right." She left the kitchen and the castle.

She found Gabriel brushing his massive black warhorse in the stable, and he was alone – although the very weighty odour of horse manure almost qualified as a tangible entity in itself. The stable doors were wide open, allowing a beam of misty pink light to encapsulate millions of dust particles hovering over the hay-covered floor.

Running along the northern and southern walls were countless stalls, which appeared to be empty, except for scuffing sounds coming from the front-most stall. All of the serfs were already outside, performing an assortment of tasks, ranging from sharpening lances and swords to building a fire in the outdoor spit, to churning soiled laundry in a giant vat of water.

If he noted her approaching he did not acknowledge but continued brushing the glossy black beast in long strokes, from mane to tail. As she ventured further in, she said, "He is a beautiful creature. Has he a name?"

"Yes."

"And what is that?"

"Horse." Gabriel lifted his head to angle her a cautionary glance. "And if you're not careful you'll be scraping shit off your shoes all day."

"I have a request." She nervously moistened her lips. "Um...I would like to go away for a few days."

"A few days?"

"Yes."

"When?"

"I'm uncertain. I thought I would check how you feel about that before making any real plans."

"Why a few days?" He stopped brushing to approach her.

"I need to...well...it's private. May I go?"

"No. It's not safe. What can be so private that you can't tell me?" He inquired, as he dragged a sturdy forearm across his brow. "We are to be married."

"I can't say. I need to go, Gabriel."

"Did you intend to go beyond city boundaries?"

"Yes."

"Absolutely not."

"You're going to make me a prisoner?"

"If I must do that to ensure your well-being, yes. But I will compromise. I'll go with you."

"You can't follow me everywhere. I will return in three days. I promise." She said.

"I said no."

"I intend to go whether you approve or not." She spun on her heel to leave, "so you might as well – "

Gabriel caught her arm and pulled her back, causing her to slam against the cast-iron wall of his chest. "This country is at war. You may not see it in this area, and you may not have gotten a whiff of what this war is like *en route* to this place, but it has been going on for over one hundred damn years. A day's ride in the wrong direction could get you raped, killed, or both. You are not going without me." Releasing her, he finalised, with a scowl, "I have another task for you."

Her jaw set in a hard line, she answered, "What?"

"Come with me."

Grudgingly, she followed him out of the stable and into the carriage house, which housed four of them, two behind two. Leading her down the narrow space between them, he shoved open a door and entered a nearly dark room. "Stay put for a moment."

He shoved open the second set of double doors at the rear, and the room flooded with soft morning light. It was a small room upon whose rough wooden walls hung an assortment of tools with which to build things. A long workbench occupied the length of one side, and the floor was covered in very rough boards, marked by the heels of many over time. In the middle of this space sat a small chair, with large wheels attached to its sides.

Viola's resentment evaporated. She knew what it was.

He turned to face her, hands on hips. "Would you try that out for me?"

"I don't know if I would fit into it."

"I made it big enough to that he can grow into it."

Nodding, she ventured further into the room, turned and sat in the chair. It was a tight squeeze. "What do I do now?"

"Put your feet on the rest there, and see if you can work those wheels."

Clamping her hands over the front of the wheels, she raised her feet and pulled forward, and had to smile in spite of herself. "It works."

He stood back to watch and study. "See if you can go backward."

She did. "It's not bad at all. It would take some effort for him but he could do it."

"Good." He rubbed the back of his neck, deep in thought.

"But how would I help?"

He grabbed a stuffed cushion and a considerable length of folded leather off the workbench, and strode toward her. "I need to put this cushion onto the seat and another one like it onto the back, and then cover the whole works with this leather. I suppose I could try to find someone else to do this if you object. It is a rather menial chore for a noblewoman."

Viola heard herself jumping in with, "No! I want to do it!" before she even had time to think it through. She wanted to be part of anything that would help that wonderful little boy to have a more meaningful life, even if it meant postponing her search a bit.

"You do?"

"Yes. What I mean is, I have never done that sort of thing, precisely, but I could try. Do you have any sort of glue and something to attach the leather to the wood?"

"I have everything, but these hands are just too damn big and clumsy for upholstery." He stared down at the items, "I want it to be comfortable. I hate that he has to go through life this way..." he paused, turned suddenly, and dropped the items back onto the table. With his back to her, he planted both hands on the surface and then fired a glance toward the ceiling.

She saw it then – a crack in his shell. It showed in the tension across his broad back and in the silence closing in around him – a silence made more poignant by the dust particles floating in the morning sun. She stood and approached him with her hands clasped together at her waist. "What happened to him?"

 # Chapter Six.

"She dropped him." Gabriel spat.

"Who?"

"Murielle." He cleared his throat. "My late wife."

"One accident can change a life forever."

"He was six months old..who am I fooling? It was no damn accident. His back was broken. He almost died...listen, go find something else to do. I need to clear my head." He turned suddenly and stepped out into the sunlight.

So many questions filled her head, the least of which was, how could anyone purposely drop a child? And the worst of which was, how could a mother do this to her own son? Was this the reason that Gabriel's eyes were always so troubled? She wanted to go to him. Perhaps to console him? But she honestly didn't know what to say or even if he wanted that from her. So instead, she quietly rummaged around the well-organised space until she found the tools and adhesive she would need to work, and began the task on her own.

She managed to get the cushions glued and then pounded a few tacks around their edges to secure them further. Cutting the coarse brown leather to the appropriate sizes was no small feat, but she managed and was tacking the last bit into place when Gabriel finally returned about four hours later.

He stopped dead in his tracks upon entering, obviously surprised that she was still there, and even more so that she had got the job done on her own. "My God."

"What do you think?" She said, as she straightened up and placed the hammer onto the workbench.

"I am speechless."

"I must have done all right," she said, wiping her hands on her gown, "because you always have something nasty to say."

"Not this time." Gabriel crossed the floor to crush her into a hug, which caused her nose to press into his neck. He smelled of sweat and man, and was unnervingly intoxicating because she didn't want him to have that effect on her.

"What an amazing job you have done, my lady."

My lady? "Thank you. I ought to go have a bath. I smell rather ripe from sweating all this time." Her breath caught as two strong hands settled around her shoulders, for she knew what was coming before it arrived.

Her heart began to pound as he bent his head toward her, but instead, he dropped a quick peck on her cheek. "Thank you."

"You are welcome."

"Do you know how to ride?"

"A horse?" She blinked.

"Unless you want to ride me, which would be even better."

She decided to ignore that one. "I do not know how to ride a horse."

The Count anchored his fists on his hips. "You had better learn so that you can figure out how to hang on tight. In case you haven't noticed, I am not a small man—and you are a very small woman."

"Are we going to get into a pissing contest now?"

"There *is* no contest. You had better strengthen up those thigh muscles."

"Ugh." She rolled her eyes. "Men."

"I will teach you on the morrow, and you will ride like a man. I will also teach you to fire a musket." He stepped around her and walked out.

She couldn't imagine why she would want to learn how to ride like a man or shoot a musket. She stared at the open doorway until it struck her that she already had plans for the morrow. She wanted to go find Clementine. Chasing after him, she called out, "Gabriel!"

Already halfway up the incline to the castle, he glanced back, "Yes?"

"I'll be busy on the morrow."

"Cancel your plans. This is important." He continued on his way.

Nothing was more important than finding her daughter.

Damn, damn, damn! Well, perhaps she could sneak away tonight. Nobody would miss her.

"Sister Viola de Medici!"

It was him again, and he was nearly at the castle, so she had to raise her voice to be heard. "Stop calling me that!"

"Go get ready for dinner! We'll be formally announcing our betrothal to everyone in the Great Hall this evening!"

*   *   *

"Do you know how to saddle up a horse?" Gabriel spoke over his shoulder as he strode toward the nearest stall.

"No."

"Well, you're about to learn that, too."

Without too much ado he saddled a small, fawn-coloured horse, providing instructions every step of the way. She knew she had better pay attention for he would no doubt test her later.

Viola stood behind him, arms crossed, and on the verge of baulking. She did not want to learn how to ride. She had to locate Clementine Dupond, yet she knew intuitively that the best she could do for herself right now was go along with this to gain his trust. She needed that if she was going to get away for a few days.

With the horse saddled, he led it and her outside, where he said, "Put your foot into the stirrup, grab the horn, and I'll help you up."

"What's a stirrup?"

"Right there." He pointed.

"Where's the horn?"

"Mine—or hers?"

"Gabriel!"

"Right here."

"What if I fall off?"

He grabbed her by her waist and lifted her as if he were a child, plunking her firmly into the saddle. "There. Let's go."

After the sentries lowered the drawbridge, they rode – albeit very slowly for her sake – down the path between the cow pastures and the fields where the serfs were tilling the soil. Gabriel was observant and generous with advice, as required. He eventually led her through a wooded area, and then into an immense field of tall grass and wildflowers, whose colours were intense in the strong morning sun. The wood surrounded this place in a wide arc, and beyond the trees were the soft curves of a low mountain range.

"Go round a few times while I watch," he said, "and don't be so stiff. Let yourself relax enough to feel the subtle movements of the animal, and let her feel yours."

"I don't understand."

"Horses are very sensitive. They feel your tension and your moods. If you are tense, so will your horse be. After a time you and the animal will become part of each other, just as you and I will someday."

"I won't be riding *that* much." She said.

"Yes you will, and that horse is yours to keep. She's a kind, gentle spirit and very young, so you two can grow up together." He slanted her a half-grin and draped the reins of his enormous black warhorse loosely over its neck. "There's no need to yank and pull on the reins as some do. A minimal indication is all that she needs."

"All right, and um...thank you for the horse."

"You're welcome. Go ahead. I will observe."

Several times she rode slowly around this field with him still atop his horse watching, with crossed arms. As she began to feel more in control, her thoughts drifted. All of this nonsense – meeting the King, learning to ride, learning to shoot – was wasting her time.

Riding toward him, she said, "My legs are getting sore."

He dismounted and then used his strong side to reach up and slide her off, setting her feet down into the tall grass. "Let's walk them over to the edge where we can tether them to a tree and take a rest."

"What's on your mind?" He inquired.

"Nothing."

"That is a lie." He spoke quietly, as he stepped up to a tree to tie the reins of his horse and then hers. "You have been elsewhere in your thoughts for over an hour."

"People come with a certain amount of baggage, Gabriel. I am no different."

"If you would tell me what it is that marrying me would help you to attain, I might be able to help you get it faster. This damned wall of secrecy between us could drop."

Averting her gaze, she answered, "I can't say."

"You can but you won't." He gazed out over the field of grass, whose swaying blades now seemed to be dipped in silver. "But why should you trust me? Trust is not something that I have an abundance of either."

"We are both wounded."

Gabriel turned his head toward the sound of her voice more than the words she spoke. As she gazed out at the mountain range, her whiskey-coloured eyes told the story of a young woman who had loved and lost. The ache and the pain within her was nearly a tangible thing. It was funny how direct sunlight could draw the soul right out through one's eyes. She bore the look of a bird in a cage, pining to be set free so that it could fly away...perhaps fly home to its mate.

Perhaps she wasn't trying for a better life, after all. Perhaps this whole thing was all about locating a man she could not forget. This marriage to him would be her passage into this country, where this lout obviously resided. It was possible that she planned to ditch him when she found the other man. It was the only thing that made sense, because if she already knew where this man was, she would be with him instead, not here.

The whole thing irritated him to no end. He growled, "You pine over him but where is he? Is he here, teaching you to ride so that you will be empowered?"

"What?" She gazed at him in confusion.

"Is he teaching you to fire a musket so that you will have at least a fighting chance of surviving an attack? Is he prepared to marry you? Clearly not. So where is he, Viola?"

"I – "

"You don't know, do you? So you're here to find him, and you'll tread over anybody's back in the process. Some people are not worth it."

Viola suddenly realised that he was providing her with the perfect cover-up. So she remained silent while he went on. "There is nothing sadder than a woman chasing after a man who wants no part of her. If he did, he would take her and hold onto her for dear life. Where is he, then?"

"You're correct. I have no idea."

"Well, I *am* here." He growled. "But you are young. You will learn as I've learned, that nobody can force the love of another human being." He turned and pulled the musket from its sheath along his horse's saddle. On a softer note, he said, "You will love firing a weapon. It feels good."

"Gabriel, may I ask you a question?"

"As long as it is not about my past marriage or my late wife, go ahead."

"What do you expect from marriage? That is..." she scratched her head, searching for the right words, "we agreed that we do not embrace the concept of arranged marriages and yet we are about to enter into one. What do you want from this?"

"I already told you. A good mother for my son. Now that you've met him, you understand why that is so important."

"Yes. What else?"

"More children. He needs siblings."

"Yes, he does. I agree. Anything else?"

Anchoring the butt of the musket against his shoulder, he gazed down the barrel through one eye while collecting his thoughts. Finally, he turned his head toward her. "You."

"I thought you didn't trust me."

"Trust and want are two very different things."

"Right." She said. "Well, can we return to the castle now? I did have other plans for today. I can learn to fire a weapon another time."

"What plans?"

"It's personal. We spent time together. Can we go back now?"

Slanting her a frown, he thrust his musket back into its sheath and untied the horses. "If you insist."

"Can I at least go into the city for a bit without a watchdog?" Viola trotted alongside Gabriel as he entered the stable, leading both his horse and hers by their reins upon returning from her lesson.

He handed the reins of his warhorse to a nearby serf, "You know what to do."

The serf bowed, "Yes, Your Lordship."

"Well?" She prompted.

Gabriel turned to face her. "You simply will not quit, will you?"

"No. If you please? I'm asking nicely?"

"Go. But you will still need to have an escort. The serf who drives the carriage will do. Don't wander too far out of his sight or else you won't get to do this again. *Ever.*"

"Wooo-hooo!" She threw both small fists into the air while dancing around in a tight circle, and then took off on a full run, the soles of her petite shoes hammering into the straw-covered floorboards.

In spite of himself, a small grin tugged at the corners of his mouth while he led Viola's horse into the enclosure.

*   *   *

Back at Ste. Michel Cathedral, Viola and Louise entered the tall arched doors at the main entry. Since there was no Mass in session, the church was empty. They dipped their fingers into the vat of Holy Water just inside the door, Crossed themselves, and ventured in deeper. As it was with most cathedrals of this magnitude, there was a vast display of religious icons, stained glass windows that were three stories high, and balconies around three sides.

Hers and Louise's footsteps echoed as they strode around the periphery of the pews, passing a section where a few hundred candles had been lit by faithful individuals, to burn for the salvation of souls departed, or whatever their personal intentions were. "Louise, do you see another door which might lead us to where the priest may be keeping himself?"

"May I be of assistance?"

Viola wheeled around at the sound of Father Jacques' voice coming from the door where they had entered. Quickly retracing her footsteps, she said, "Good afternoon, Father. It's good to see you again."

"Good afternoon. I heard about your betrothal to His Lordship, Count Gabriel. Congratulations."

"Thank you."

"I take it you have a bit more information with which to conduct your search?" The priest wore a long robe with free-flowing sleeves, into which he tucked his hands.

"After a fashion. Do you know a young lady by the name of Clementine Dupond?"

"I do. Each spring she comes from somewhere up near *Normandie* to spend some time with her uncle, Leo Dupond. He is the second cousin of a Duke who lives near *Calais*. At least I think he's a Duke..." The priest paused to scratch the dome of his shiny head. "In any event, Leo has a row house here in the city, quite a lovely home tucked in between the seed merchant and the fabric store. I can't recall the name of the fabric store."

Viola's heart sped up. "Thank you, this information is most helpful."

"May I ask...this child you seek, what relation is she to you?"

She glanced about, for she felt the omniscient Eyes of God staring at her from all angles. There was no way to consciably lie with the Almighty peering straight into her brain. "I would prefer not to say, Father, if that is all right."

"Of course," He nodded.

"I'm afraid I can't linger. I must return to the castle before dark, and I have other things to do. His Lordship keeps a tight watch on us."

"He is wise to do so in these troubled times."

She and Louise hurried out of the church. Before climbing into the carriage, she instructed the driver, who held the door, to take them to the fabric shop.

Clementine opened the door after the first rap. In sharp contrast to her very fashionable outfit of the previous evening, she wore a rather dull brown frock with a simple veil to cover her hair. She looked younger now than yesternight. Perhaps sixteen or seventeen. Still, she was quite pretty in a fresh sort of way with her freckled skin and blue eyes. Her visage lit up with delight when she saw who her visitor was.

"Lady Viola! Oh, dear, I look such a mess...but I am so glad to see you. I'm so happy for you in your betrothal to Count Gabriel."

"Thank you, *Madamoiselle* Dupond."

"Christine, if you please. Were we properly introduced yesternight?I think I may have had a bit too much wine. I cannot recall."

"No," Viola smiled. "We were not. I heard someone calling you by name."

"Oh, whew! Would you like to come in?" She stepped back and gestured toward a long, immaculately clean corridor whose floor reflected the sheen from the sunlight slanting in around her visitors.

"I'm afraid I cannot stay long. But thank you."

"Well, then, how may I assist you?"

"I overheard you inquiring about a certain gentleman, an Aristocrat who died of Lung Fever shortly after his child was born."

"Ah, yes! He was, oh so handsome. Very tall." She glanced about to assure herself that nobody was listening, leaned in close and added, "He was so virile. Oh, dear. I get the vapours just thinking about it!"

Viola's pulse sped up. "I don't suppose you – "

"I was only twelve at the time. I only saw him once, and then I later heard that he had Lung Fever. What a shame." She rolled her big blue eyes. "The ugly ones live, the beautiful ones die."

"Yes, without question. I don't suppose you happen to remember his name?"

"You would think that I would remember but I don't think I ever learned it. I know that his nickname was Silver. Perhaps because of his eye colour..." She paused as if recollecting her image of the man. "I was with my parents that one time that I saw him, and they were busy hauling me about. By the time I heard about the Lung Fever I had already developed a bleeding heart for another fellow who, as you might guess, was thrice my age. It was such a long time ago."

"When?"

"Mmmm...about five years, I suppose. There was a terrible outbreak of Lung Fever at that time. Many died of it. I can ask around." Clementine generously offered. "And if I learn anything else I will send you a message."

"Would you?"

"Absolutely!" She chirped. "Where do you live?"

"I'm at the home of Count Gabriel."

"You moved in before the wedding?" The girl blushed. "Good for you!"

"It's not like that. But heed, is it possible for us to keep any conversations that we have confidential?"

"Cross my heart." She swore.

"You have been most helpful, Clementine. I must run now."

"Must you? I could get you a drink and perhaps a snack to nibble on? I'm sure my uncle would like to meet you."

"Regrettably, I must head back now. His Lordship keeps us on a tight reign."

After leaving the Dupond residence, Viola asked the carriage driver to take her to an alchemist. Instead, he brought her to a leech, whose shop turned out to be one room situated on the main level of his row house, on the main street in Orleans. Yvon LeBlanc, a frail old man with obvious vision problems, squinted at Viola upon opening his door.

"Yes, how may I be of assistance?" He asked.

"I require a mixture to treat pain and disinfect a poison arrow wound," Viola replied.

"The best remedy for that would be a mixture of opiate, hemlock, and – "

"No. That kills more than it cures." She said. "I'm looking for radish, bishopwort, garlic, wormwood, helenium – "

"You won't find that here." Monsieur Leblanc interrupted her. "You're better off going to that old witch on the edge of town. I think they call her Adalsinda."

"Thank you." Viola turned and left without much ado. There was no point in wasting his time or hers, so she climbed back into the carriage and instructed the driver to take her to Adalsinda's place. Luckily, he knew where she lived. Perhaps everyone did.

Adalsinda lived in a run-down shack that was set back quite a distance from the road, surrounded by trees on three sides. The old woman most certainly did fall into the typical "old witch" description, with her stringy white hair, black sunken eyes, and toothless mouth. She wore a grey wool blanket with a hole cut out, through which her head poked. The walls of her home were lined with shelves containing labelled vessels.

"What do you require?" She asked Viola.

Viola named her list of ingredients, hoping this woman would have what she needed.

"Wait here." She grumbled and shut the door.

Viola and Louise waited on her verandah for more than fifteen minutes. Feeling antsy about the whole thing, Louise said, "Are you sure you want to give him such a concoction? You could kill him."

"I will cure him, Louise. I know what I'm doing. I was raised by the Medici's, after all."

Finally, the door opened again, and Adalsinda handed her a well-worn leather sack. "It's all in there. Do you know how to mix this up?"

"I do, thank you. I do not have money with me, but if you tell me what you need, I will purchase it, and have it delivered to you promptly.

"I need a new coat and some meat. Can you get me that?"

"I will find a way, Adalsinda. Thank you."

Once again they were back in the carriage, this time to go to a shop where Viola could purchase a pre-made coat, and then to a farmer to buy some beef. At both places, she charged the items to Count Gabriel and told them to deliver the goods to Adalsinda.

With that done, she and Louise finally headed back to the castle.

"What's that you're putting in there? What does that do?"

"What's that you're putting in there? What does that do?"

"What's that you're putting in there? What does that do?"

"What's that you're putting in there? What does that do?"

That was all that Viola heard from Chantalle the whole time she mixed up her cure in the kitchen. "You needn't be concerned, Chantalle. I aim to cure him, not kill him."

"How do I know that?"

"I'm not feeding it to him. I'm only going to put it on his wound. It will alleviate pain and make him heal faster. Do you have any white fabric that I can use to wrap his wound?"

The Head Housekeeper hedged. "I don't trust you."

"If you have any white fabric, can you please cut into strips so that I can wrap his wound once I treat it. And also bring me a clean white chemise. After all, we want him nice and clean when we bury him."

"That is not humorous!" Chantalle grunted, as she stalked out of the kitchen.

Viola strained her mixture and then poured it into a brass pot, where it would sit for a few hours until it turned deep red, and then she left the kitchen and went to her chamber where she indulged in a nap.

A few hours, while Gabriel sat with his brother in the study, chatting about trivial matters for a change, Viola rapped on the door frame and said, "Pardon the interruption. Gabriel, take off that chemise and come with me."

Gabriel's eyebrows slid up. "Why am I not offended by her bossing me about?"

"Probably because removing your clothing is part of the command." Valmont grinned. "If you're very obedient she might ask you to drop your hose, as well."

Gabriel promptly removed his chemise while following her to the Great Room. Already upon the table were a few rolls of white fabric, a bunch of folded white cloths, a small bowl partially filled with an ointment, a larger container filled with water, a sharp knife, and his best bottle of German Brandy, already opened.

He said, "How did you get your hands on that brandy?"

"Chantalle gave it to me. Please lie down on the table so I can treat your wound."

Sitting on the edge of the table, he responded, "I was saving that for a special occasion. Do you have any idea how hard that was to obtain?"

"This *is* a special occasion. You have someone here who is actually qualified to heal you. Take a good long drink, and then relax. I promise you, I will not do you harm."

On that, she rolled up the sleeves of her gown and washed her hands in the bowl of water, while he savoured the taste of his brandy. Working around his arms, she used the knife to cut away his blood-stained bandage and examined it before tossing it aside.

"There's still puss coming out of there." She remarked. "And it's a nasty colour. Keep drinking."

The brandy was excellent, so he was fine with drinking more of it, straight from the bottle. It wasn't the first time he'd done that and wouldn't be the last. "Here, have a swallow."

"I don't drink brandy."

"I insist."

"Why? Do you think I've put something into it to poison you?"

"You may have, so if I'm going to die on this table I'm taking you with me, Sister Viola de Medici."

She paused to slant him a dull glance. "So, let me get this straight. You want me to become inebriated *before* I do medical treatments on you?"

"You're not touching me until you drink from this bottle." He said. "It was already open when I got here."

Expelling a heavy sigh, she grabbed the bottle and took a good long gulp, which caused her to sputter, for it was powerful. He gestured toward her small bowl of red paste. "What's in that dish?"

"About a dozen ingredients. It will help with pain and draw out the poison."

"Take another drink. If you think I'm going to put that shit into my mouth—"

"I'm not going to feed it to you. I'm going to put it on the wound."

"Then why are we drinking my best bottle of brandy?"

"Because it's going to hurt." She said. "*A lot.* To use your own vulgar language, I'm going to clean all that shit out of your wound."

She hadn't dropped dead yet, and neither had he, so he decided to take a few more deep gulps. He handed her the bottle and then reclined along the table, on his back, as a mild warmth began to spread in his knees and within his abdomen. "Why are you doing this for me?"

"Because it's the right thing to do, Gabriel." She said, as she took one of the clean white cloths, dipped it into the water, and then poured some of the brandy onto it. She set the bottle down and applied the warm cloth to his wound.

He swore under his breath, for it stung like holy hell.

"The alcohol in the brandy will disinfect the wound." She spoke quietly now while dabbing the cloth. She rinsed the material several times, applied more brandy, and repeated the swabbing actions, going deeper into his gaping wound each time. Clenching the edges of the table, he bore down into the agony with his jaw clenched, determined not to cry out. He tried his almighty best to prevent tears from stinging his eyes, but he lost that battle. The seeped out anyway.

Finally, she left the room with her bowl of dirty water and returned moments later with it refiled. Gabriel was drunk and sore by now, and yes—even grateful for any help she could give him because this wound was becoming the bane of his existence, and the leech he had seen hadn't done much to help him. All he had done was dig the arrow head out, wash it with ordinary water, and bandaged him up. Dipping another clean cloth into the container, she wrung it out and came to stand beside him.

Dabbing his sweaty brow with a cool cloth, she softly inquired, "How are you holding out, Gabriel?"

He nodded. "I'm good."

"Do you trust me, yet?"

"With this—yes. Do what you must."

"Here, you keep this cloth on your face. The worst is over."

He grabbed the rag and quickly dragged it over his eyes, cheeks, and neck, while she proceeded to apply her disgusting ointment to his wound. Afterwards, she took another folded piece of fabric, spread a good dollop of the balm on that too, and pressed it into his injury— gently this time.

"Sit up, please. I need to wrap you."

Good and drunk by now, he wobbled into a seated position, and just let her wrap his abdomen, without any sort of objection whatsoever. He said, "You didn't have to do this, you know."

"I know."

"And your only reason is that *it is the right thing to do*?"

She tied the bandage off and met his gaze. "Is that not a good enough reason?"

"So, you'd do this for anyone who needed it?"

"I *have* done it for anyone who needed it—good men, bad men, and those whose hearts I could not read. I told you that I was one of the Sisters of Mercy."

He couldn't think of a better reason to help another human being, other than just because they needed it. And that got to him. It seriously got to him. In this very pivotal moment, his view of her took a dramatic turn. It was funny how one single moment in time could change everything. "Sister Viola de Medici, do you have any idea—any idea at all—how beautiful you are?"

"You are completely drunk." She said.

"Yes, I am, but I am not blind."

"You should go to bed and sleep that off before you say something you don't mean. By morning, you will have forgotten all of this, and life will go on as it always has."

Gabriel slid off the table and staggered toward the door. "Perhaps you're right. In case I turn back into a beast at the stroke of midnight, I will thank you most graciously now for what you have done for me... my lady."

*　　　*　　　*

While everyone in the castle lay sleeping, Viola enlisted Louise's participation in sneaking into *Monsieur's* study. With only a small beeswax candle providing light, Louise stood watch at the door while Viola squinted to identify the objects on his writing table. At last, locating the small jar of India ink, parchment, and quill, she hurried around the table, whispering, "Let's go."

Carefully shutting the door, they darted across the foyer and exited that floor via the stairwell at the back. As they climbed the stairs, Louise whispered, "We will be in so much trouble if we get caught."

"If he will not allow me to go with his permission, then I will go without it."

"To forge *Monsieur's* name on a note could land you in prison, *Mademoiselle*. Someone will know the difference."

"Nobody will," Viola assured her, as they exited the stairwell on the second floor, and then hurried to the row of empty rooms down the back end of the castle. Any of these rooms would suffice. "Heed, most women cannot read or write."

"But your writing is different than his."

"Louise, I have the letter that he gave me, which authorises me to purchase anything in the city. I will imitate his writing and signature from that sample."

"I do not like this." Louise followed her into a dark, dingy cell, where they shut the door and then dropped to the floor to begin the task by candlelight.

"I don't like it either, but I am left with no option." Flopping onto her belly, she arranged the items in order, along with the letter *Monsieur* had given her, as a guide.

"Can we not do this in your chamber? I get the feeling that rats and bats and spiders live on this side."

"No. He sleeps very lightly."

"*Mademoiselle,* to whom do you intend to show this letter and what, exactly, are you going to write?"

"A letter we can show to the sentries which states we are permitted to leave anytime, by ourselves."

"That is a terrible plan."

"I thought you were on my side?" Viola raised her head to glance across at Louise, whose face shifted on the other side of the candle.

"I am, and that is why I must ask you why it is that you think these sentries can read. We commoners cannot read."

Damn. Viola dropped her forehead onto the parchment with a painful thump. She had not considered that. "Louise, maybe, just maybe, one of them can read. It is worth a try."

"If you say so, *Mademoiselle.*"

She lifted her head to glance at her best friend, who also lay on her belly with her fists supporting her chin. "Louise, if you are uncomfortable with this, perhaps you ought to not come with me."

"Don't be silly."

"You are quite right when you say that I could get jailed for this. I wouldn't want to get you into that same mess."

"I have come thus far with you. I will go the distance."

"I adore you, Louise."

"And I, you. But when will we do this?"

"We will have to make our escape when both his Lordship and his brother are off the property so that the sentries can't check with them. I don't plan to do this immediately," she added, as she began to write, "I want to follow any leads that Clementine gives us first, but I want to have this ready just in case we need it. Now, please allow me to focus, as I want to get this just right."

"It will never be right, as it is morally wrong." Louise reminded her.

On that basis, Viola performed a Sign of the Cross before beginning the next line of her lie. "I am going to have to pray the Rosary until the day I die for this."

"That may be sooner than you think."

Two hours later, Viola dropped off to sleep as soon as her head touched the pillow, for she was exhausted from trying to do such detailed work in near darkness. But she fell asleep proud of her accomplishment, knowing that her passage off of that property was safely tucked away in her vanity drawer.

She slept until ten on the following day, which was a Saturn's Day, to be awakened by the sound of someone banging impatiently on her door. Without getting up to open it, she called out, sleepily, "Yes, who is it?"

"It's me." Chantalle barked. "And we will be leaving for church in one hour. Meet us outside the stable."

"Oh, bother..."

"I can't hear you! Speak up!" Chantalle growled.

"Would you please send Louise up with some water and towels?"

"As you will! Hurry! Nobody waits for anyone around here!"

Ohhh! That does it! She marched to the door, heaved it open, and said, "The appropriate reply would be, 'yes, my lady, and we shall await your arrival.' "

"Yes, my lady, and we shall await your arrival – but the Mass begins before the noon's meal, and the entire congregation will *not* await your arrival. Put a move on!" Chantalle squared her shoulders, turned, and marched officiously down the corridor.

As Viola left her chamber, she spotted Denise exiting the middle-most bedchamber on that floor with little Xavier in her arms. Viola said to the boy, "Ah, so your chamber is down the hall from mine. How wonderful! You could come to visit me."

As he opened both arms and reached toward her, she gathered him close and planted a big kiss onto his cheek. "Good morrow, beautiful thing."

"G'morrow. Papa said you're going to be my *Maman* soon."

"Did he?"

He nodded.

"Well, it's true."

"Will you tell me stories?"

"I will. Did you sleep well?"

"Like a baby."

"*Like* a baby." She laughed. "And you are no longer a baby, are you?"

"Z'abier is a big boy."

"Yes, and you are going to break so many hearts when you are grown. So handsome you are."

"Unlike his father."

She spun around to find Gabriel behind her, which was a shock since she always heard those big boots long before he got there.

"Your Lordship," Denise interrupted with a bow, "may I be relieved so as to attend Mass with my kin?"

"Of course. Get one of the sentries to give you a ride to your father's home. Tell the sentry that he can attend the next Mass with his family, on my order."

"Much obliged, Your Lordship."

"I trust you will return by tomorrow night?"

"Yes, Your Lordship. May I go?"

"Yes, go. Don't let me keep you." He scooped Xavier from Viola's arms and transferred him into Denise's. "Drop him off with Chantalle on your way out. Tell her he needs his hair tidied."

"I already..." Denise began to speak but nodded instead. "Yes, Your Lordship." She turned and marched brusquely down the corridor.

Gabriel turned toward Viola. "You're wearing black again."

"It's indigo, not black."

"Must be the lighting." He said.

"It is the Lenten Season. It would be irreverent to do otherwise."

"You would know. You're the Nun." He pressed a hand to the wall above her shoulders and took a step closer, which brought him into her personal space. "You're getting under my skin, Sister Viola de Medici. Let's break a few Commandments."

"*Stop. Calling. Me. That.*" She ground through clenched teeth. "Wait—what are you doing?"

"Did you find him yesterday?" He asked, as he ran a fingertip along her lower lip.

"Who are you talking about?"

"Your long-lost lover. You went searching for him, I assume. How did that go?"

"I'm feeling overpowered. I don't like that." She picked up the scent of soap on his skin and mint leaf on his breath, and could not make peace with the fact that her body and heart were beginning to want what her common sense did not. She cleared her throat. "How did you sleep? How does your wound feel this morning?"

"I slept better than I have in months and my wound feels much better already. Look at me."

She stared at his mouth, watching every movement in case he planned to use it on her.

"I have to assume that your little tumble with him happened before you were tossed into a convent, and was perhaps even the reason for that sort of discipline. My eyes are up here."

Viola forced herself to meet his penetrating stare.

He went on, "If he discarded you then, what makes you think he'll want you now?"

"Why do you insist on badgering me with this?"

"Do you ever wonder about it?"

"About what?"

"Us." He answered.

"In what way?"

"In bed."

"I try not to."

"If you have to try not to, it means you're fighting against it."

"Please stop this."

He lowered his head to whisper into her ear, "Think about this."

Every fine hair along her arms stood on end as he kissed the side of her neck, her cheek, her temple, and then her forehead. Each kiss was slow and soft, accompanied by his warm breath brushing over her skin, which in some way caused her brain to start tilting out of its axes. She began to feel dizzy, and literally slumped back into the wall as he released her.

Without another word, he left her shivering while he marched away.

* * *

"...Et in Jesum Christum, Filium ejus unicum, Dominum nostrum; qui conceptus est de Spiritu Sancto, natus ex Maria virgine; passus sub Pontio Pilato, crucifixus, mortuus, et sepultus; descendit ad iferna; teria die resurrexit a mortuis; ascendit ad coelos; sedt ad dexteram Dei Patris omnipotentis; inde venturus judicare vivos et mortuos..."

Kneeling in a pew at the very back of the cathedral were Viola, Louise, Chantalle, *Monsieur* Ste. Germaine, Yolande, and a long string of serfs who had decided to attend this noon-hour Mass. The arrangement, Chantalle had explained, was that half of the serfs would attend this one and the other half would make it to the later one so that the property was not left unattended.

Gabriel sat beside her with his son on his lap, trying to keep the boy occupied but quiet. This was no small feat for he seemed to have energy to burn this day. He had been keeping his father plenty busy since the moment Gabriel had arrived, which was shortly after they did, for he had ridden in on his horse.

Father Jacques and the whole assembly completed their recital of The Apostle's Creed in Latin, and all of the parishioners slid back and sat into their pews as the Mass continued. Gabriel leaned sideways to whisper into her ear, "I am going to take him outside. He's too wily."

She nodded her understanding. As Gabriel stood to leave, there were many eyes upon him...aaaand then they turned to rest upon her. The news was definitely out. She, who truly hated to be the focal point of anything, felt ill-at-ease. Soon, everyone began to file out into the aisles to receive the Eucharist at the front, and she fell into that lineup.

Eventually, she made it to the front and knelt along the Altar. Perhaps she had been preoccupied with other matters or maybe she was simply slow today, but the instant she glanced up at Father Jacques, she knew she had a problem.

Would he inquire as to how her search was going? Would he do this in front of Gabriel, after the Mass? Or in front of *Monsieur?* Or Chantalle? Would the priest assume that they were already aware of her search, and feel free to discuss it with them? Or would he instinctively know that this was a private matter? How was she going to prevent any of this from happening?

A violent wave of nausea washing over her, she pondered the notion of telling Gabriel the whole story as soon as possible, but that idea made her even sicker. Having received Communion, she went back to her pew, knelt to say a quick prayer, and then whispered to Louise, "I will wait in the carriage."

"But it is almost done," Louise whispered.

"I must go." She made a fast exit and then darted toward the carriage on the street to hide inside of it, and pray that her secret would remain a secret. Dear God, what am I going to do? Inhaling a steady stream of breaths, she tried to talk herself out of a panic attack. She sat up with a jolt as Gabriel's deep voice came through the open window.

"Viola."

The

Other Man.

Segment 3.

♥ *Chapter Seven.*

Her heart thundering, she whispered, "Yes?"

"What is the matter?"

"I am not feeling well. Perhaps it is because I have not been sleeping much. Where is Xavier?"

He gestured toward the door, where the parishioners began to flow out in groups. Chantalle chatted with the priest while holding Xavier in her beefy arms. "Over there. Would you like me to take you home?"

"Would that cause a disturbance?"

"Do I care?"

"Probably not." She whispered, stealing another worried glance toward Father Jacques. *Please don't reveal my secret.* "Let's go quickly."

He opened the door and helped her out. To avoid having to chat with anyone, he rapidly ushered her across the street, where he had left his horse tethered in front of the tavern. He wasted no time getting them up onto the beast and leaving undetected, which was not all that difficult on a very busy Sabbath.

As they left the whole thing behind, he said, "I'm just as glad to get out of there before we get coerced into an afternoon social."

"I agree."

"I can't see a damn thing." He quelled the beast along the side of the street and proceeded to remove her headdress since he sat behind her on the horse.

"I will get into trouble for thi – oh no – " She grimaced at the sound of ripping fabric. "Well, I don't like them anyway."

Tossing the headdress into the street, he draped the veil portion over her hair. "Use this."

"Thank you. I think."

"For?"

"Twice you have rescued me."

"When?"

"From the cat, and now from feeling overpowered by that crowd back there. I don't like crowds. I already told you that."

"Nor do I."

Preparing the way for the trouble that might come later, she thought she would try to get on his good side. In full-blown panic mode, she was so afraid of being found out that she may have tried just about anything. "You've made it clear that you don't like me and don't trust me, but I like you at times."

"Only at times, hm?"

"At times I like you quite a lot."

"You're laying it on too thick."

"Sorry."

"I want you to know something, Viola."

"I'm listening."

"I do not want a lukewarm bride. Lukewarm is just a few degrees above cold, and I have seen just how fast the temperature can drop."

"I've been taught that passion is not required of women."

"By whom? The Nuns? The Baron? A bunch of cackling old hens with dried up pudendum?"

Her jaw dropping, she sputtered, "Why, that-that is so vulgar!"

"Maybe so, but you take it from me—every man wants a hot, wet woman in his bed and I'm no different."

"That's why whorehouses exist."

"And that's why men go to them. I'll marry you alright—but not before I see what I'm getting this time."

"You will have to change your mind about that, as I won't be intimate with you before marriage."

"It isn't as if you're a virgin."

She nailed him with a backward jerk of her elbow. "One mistake does not make me a whore."

"*Was* it a mistake, or did you do it willingly?"

"Was every woman you ever bedded a mistake, or did you take them willingly?" Viola countered. Without waiting for a reply, she added, "Are you a whore, too, then?"

"Point taken."

"Thank you!"

A quiet moment later, he said, "With all the galavanting about that you do, I'm sure you've heard some nasty things about me. Be that as it may, I will treat you very well, Viola."

"God knows why, but I am inclined to believe you."

"It is because deep down, you know that I am a man of my word."

She was glad he was looking at the back of her head, because she found herself smiling in the intuitive knowledge that this rough-edged Warlord was telling the truth. What was more, she suspected that he knew no other way to be.

Shortly after they arrived at the stable and dismounted, Gabriel spotted a horseman riding swiftly toward the drawbridge, as if trying to arrive before the sentries closed it again. His gut warning that this was trouble, he commanded Viola, "Go wait under the portico."

As she was about to obey his command, he pulled her back by her elbow, kissed her cheek, and then let her go. He covered the distance to the drawbridge in long, purposeful strides, but by the time he arrived the sentries had already taken a letter and sent the messenger on his way. Jean handed it to Gabriel. "A message for Lady Viola, Your Lordship."

"Thank you." As he strode toward her, he flipped the letter over. There was no sender's name. Just a red wax seal with no image within the wax press to identify any house of nobility or Aristocracy. The wax appeared to have been depressed with fingers rather than a stamp. He supposed he could keep it and read it. He ought to do that, he told himself. Instead, he handed it to her.

"Excuse me." She stepped well aside to break the seal and turn it away from his line of vision before reading it. Then she rapidly folded the letter thrice and held it firmly to her heart.

He gut twisting, he inquired, "Is it anything that I ought to know about?"

"No." She said. "It's personal."

Gabriel turned on his heel and headed toward the outbuilding. "I have work to do." As he marched across the property, he decided that he was not going to ride this cursed wave again. This woman was getting to him and he had to put a stop to that immediately. Once in a lifetime was enough.

*   *   *

At the noon's meal the following day, a driver veered a red carriage up to the front of the Bras d'Or, an inn on Rue de la Vallee. There, he leapt down from the box to assist his passenger.

As she stepped out, he closed the door and bowed. "I shall be waiting out here for you, My Lady."

"Thank you." Viola waited for Louise to come round to her side, whispering, "Her message said we were to meet here. Listen carefully in case I miss anything."

Louise nodded. "She is nice but also very excitable and speaks too quickly."

"Precisely." As they approached the Bras d'Or Inn, a gentleman posted at the door swung it open and offered a bow as they entered. Immediately, a Steward approached.

"Good afternoon, ladies. We are not too busy, ergo, you may sit anywhere you please. Follow me, if you will."

"We are to meet *Mademoiselle* Clementine Dupond, Monsieur."

"Ah, yes. *Mademoiselle* Clementine awaits your arrival. This way, if you will."

Viola observed the Steward's rapid gait as he navigated between the small round tables, deciding that he reminded her of a thoroughbred horse, for some reason. Then, glancing about, she noted that the eatery at this inn was none too fancy. It was more utilitarian than anything, with plain wooden plank walls and floors, though the tables were dressed nicely in white linen. There were a few windows which faced the street, and a few wall torches to provide a pleasant ambience for that time of day. At a table near the window, she spotted Clementine.

Today she wore a yellow gown which was pretty and sweet in its simplicity, and a modest headdress. Waving a decorative white fan,

126

she briefly raised her hand to make her whereabouts known.

The Steward pulled out her chair, and with a bit of reservation, also did the same for Louise, for she was dressed as a servant.

"May I offer you a refreshment, *Mademoiselles?*"

"Just a glass of red wine for me, *Monsieur*." Viola said, "Nothing else. Louise?"

"The same, if you will. Thank you."

The Steward no sooner trotted away than Clementine jerked her seat closer to Viola. But before she could speak, Viola said, "I must first apologise to my good friend, Louise, for the last time we met you, Clementine, I had the manners of a boor. I was so self-involved that I neglected to introduce you. Quite informally, since we are all women, Clementine, meet my dear friend, Louise. Louise, Clementine."

Nods and brief smiles were exchanged.

"I apologise for cutting you off, Clementine. Please go ahead."

Clementine kept her voice low. "I must ask, Lady Viola, how well you know your betrothed?"

Surprised at her directness, she answered, "Not too well at all. It is, of course, an arranged marriage. You know how it is."

Clementine dove straight to the point. "His first wife was a bitch."

"Beg your *pardon?*"

"She married an old cadaver long before she met Count Gabriel. She was older than Count Gabriel by at least ten years, don't you know. At *least* that much! But that's not the issue. She married the first time for his money, and then poof! He died suddenly when he was perfectly healthy all of his Godforsaken life. But then, it turned out that he was terribly in debt, so any money she thought he had, she did not get, and neither did her greedy brother, who was all set to manage her inheritance since women are not permitted this privilege. So –"

"Wait." Viola interrupted. "How do you know all of this?"

"People talk." She pulled her seat closer still and continued in hushed tones. "After her first husband died, she married again, and that time, the man turned out to be a liar and a fraud, with not a pot to piss in or a window to throw it out of. So, who knows where he went? He simply vanished. Some speculate that she drove him insane and he ran away. I can believe that, but nobody knows for certain, and so that part could be all gossip. At least that is what my father tells me. Some years went by, and so the church declared the marriage annulled, thus, freeing her up to search for another husband. Or rather, another victim. She married Count Gabriel only to be introduced to His Majesty, so that she could connive her way into his circle, with intentions to eventually become His Majesty's formal mistress."

"Wait." Viola interrupted again. "I mean no disrespect, but this sort of gossip about a dead woman seems cruel and judgmental."

"Lady Viola," Clementine whispered, "where there is smoke, there is fire? *N'est pas?*"

"I suppose. Who told you that she married Gabriel so as to gain admittance to the King's Court?" Viola asked.

"One of the King's mistresses told the Duke of Belgium's mistresses, who happened to be visiting Orleans at the time. She told her handmaiden, who told my uncle's servant, who told me."

Viola shook her scrambled brain. "Good Lord, what tangled webs we weave."

"Indeed. Have you heard the rumour that he killed her?"

"Yes."

"She was found dead on the ground below his balcony, so they – whomever they are – came to the natural conclusion that he threw her over, because just the day before, they had got into a miserable quarrel in His Majesty's Court. Someone overheard her telling him that the babe was his idea, not hers, and that she wanted no part of raising it. *It!* Can you believe that?"

"I don't – "

"Personally, I don't think he did it," Clementine said. "But since he refused to speak on his own behalf at all, he ended up in jail. In my opinion, even if he had done it, the bitch deserved it."

Viola's heart went very still. "He was in jail?"

"Yes. Round and round it went," Clementine said, with exaggerated eye rolls, "and still he refused to talk. His brother stepped in to say that he had killed Murielle himself, and then Chantalle, his servant, said that *she* did it. It became such a farce. After eight months of this, His Majesty personally marched into the prison and ordered his release."

"Why did not His Majesty have him released as soon as the whole thing began? Why wait that long?" Viola asked.

"I heard that the Count had insisted on solving his own problems."

Her mind reeling with this new information, Viola whispered, "And all that you tell me now is the truth?"

"It is common knowledge, Lady Viola. Some still believe he did it, and some don't, but the truth remains a mystery. The only point nobody will argue is that Murielle got what she deserved." She said, pulling her elbows in as the Steward appeared with their wine.

He made a grand show of serving it up with impeccable manners and then trotted away again.

Clementine continued, "The only person who has not heard all of this is you, and that is because you're not from around here."

"I'm stunned."

"Small wonder." She snapped her fan open and flicked it rapidly a few times, adding, "I won't pretend to know Count Gabriel all that well. What goes on in his head, I mean. But my uncle says that you can know a man by his deeds. Do you believe that?"

"Yes, I do." Viola sipped her wine, for she knew there was more to come.

"Well, this is the thing. The area of Bellefleur that he inherited was like so much of France, full of peasants who suffered terribly from this war and famine and also the Black Death. It was a lost and forgotten civilisation. My uncle tells me that when Count Gabriel inherited that region, he had the land cleared and then from his own pocket, purchased massive amounts of seed for planting, and entire herds of cattle to fill those pastures—all of this when he was merely eleven or so years old. Hence, he created a source of local produce and meat with which to feed the people under his lordship. That does not sound like a bad person to me. Does it, to you?"

Viola shook her head. "Not at all."

"Now," Clementine continued, "I have another bit of information in regards to that Aristocrat about whom we spoke."

Her pulse accelerating, Viola leaned closer. "Yes?"

"I don't know these people at all, so what I tell you is what I have heard, and it may not necessarily be true. Lily is somewhat of a tonguester herself so..."

"Who is Lily?"

"Lily LeClerc. She knows everyone's business and what she doesn't know she makes up, so please take all of this with a grain of salt."

"I will. Go ahead."

"She said that Silver was married to a woman who was barren, until one day she showed up at Mass with a child which she claimed to be her own. It's rumoured that she did not give birth to this child herself, so perhaps he had a mistress who gave him a child. His wife stayed home all the time, except on the Sabbath. Some say she was mentally ill." Clementine touched her own temple. "Her home is on *Quai de Roi*, not far from the water. Her name is Lucianne Belleveau. I believe the Belleveau home is the one with a wrought iron balcony at the front."

*   *   *

Gabriel exited the tavern in time to see one of his own carriages careening by. The tavern was not a place he visited often, and he had only gone there to order another bottle of brandy from Germany.

The carriage wasn't all that distinctive, but the driver was one of his serfs. He spotted Viola within, and his temper instantly flared, even though it was only his own supposition that the letter she had received was about her long-lost lover or from him.

He quickly untethered his horse and mounted. Turning the beast around, he allowed the carriage to gain a bit of headway so that he wouldn't be spotted, and then followed. But for only a few minutes. Swearing under his breath, he jerked the reins and turned the horse around. He would not resort to spying on her, and that was that.

Trust was something he didn't have a whole lot of since his failed marriage, but he reasoned that he'd be sinking this marriage before it even got off the ground if he didn't allow her some breathing room. Then again, there might be no marriage at all if she got lucky enough to find the bastard. He turned his horse again and snapped the reins to catch up.

He turned his horse yet one more time and headed for home. *To hell with it! I don't need this shit!*

The Belleveau estate was a huge limestone chateau built upon a hill, surrounded by trees. It was set well back away from the road and rather poorly maintained. The path leading up to it was littered with twigs and small branches, and the black, wrought-iron fence on the front veranda leaned outward. Louise had opted to wait in the carriage while Viola approached. Her stomach tensing, she climbed the five sloping stairs and rapped on the door, hoping against hope that this was where she would find her daughter.

The door swung open and the frame filled with a huge, blubbery man who was terribly shoddy in all ways, from his overgrown beard to his lopsided, filthy clothing. "Yes, what do you want?"

"Perhaps I took a wrong turn somewhere. Is this the Belleveau residence?"

"Yes. What brings you to my door?"

"I'm searching for Lucianne Belleveau. I was told that she lived here with her child."

"You're two years late." Raising a colossal thigh of chicken in a filthy hand, he ripped off a chunk with rotting teeth.

"Why?"

"She's dead."

"Dead?" Viola blinked. "What happened?"

Jerome Belleveau dragged a dirty sleeve across his mouth. "Her and our parents were killed in an ambush *en route* to *Normandie* two years ago."

"I am so sorry. And the child?"

"Why do you want to know any of this?"

"I knew her when we were young...wh-when I visited from Italia," she sputtered.

"She never left the house to make friends."

"You are right. I lied." She admitted.

"No skin off my nose." He shrugged. "I never got on with any of them anyway, not even our parents. She came back home to live with them after her husband died. She didn't want to be in that house anymore. What else do you need to know?"

"What was her husband's name?"

"Arthur. Arthur Stephan Simone."

Arthur Stephen Simone. She whispered the name in her mind, finally able to put one to the Aristocrat, if this man had been him. "And the child?"

"After they got killed I sent the brat to live with Arthur's twin brother—as if one of him wasn't bad enough." The man tossed the molested chicken thigh out into the yard, over her shoulder. "The child was not my kin. Some other woman had his child, and he brought it home for Lucianne to raise. What else do you want? You interrupted my meal."

"I apologise." She whispered. "What is his brother's name?"

"Mark."

"Just one more question. Where would I find Mark Simone?"

"He lives in a big fieldstone chateau on the other side of the city. Follow the Loire River eastward until you come to a large horse farm. It's the home after that one." Jerome slammed the door in her face.

It was dark by the time she and Louise made it back to the castle, and supper was already underway in the Great Hall. She and Louise helped themselves to a bowl of stew in the kitchen and then entered the hall through the side door.

His Lordship sat at the head table up on the Dias, with an empty chair to his right, *Monsieur* after that, and then a long row of empty seats. To his right was Xavier and then his minder, Denise, and then another row of empty chairs to the end. Below the salt, all of the tables were surrounded by serfs, servants, sentries and everyone else that had to be fed. The din was deafening, as so many conversations went on simultaneously.

"I will go sit down there." Louise gestured toward the table at which the indoor servants dined.

Gabriel glanced at Viola, who stood motionless and awkward for her tardiness. Inhaling a deep breath, she crossed the Dias and felt ever more ill-at-ease as Gabriel and Valmont stood, which prompted everyone down below to rise as well, and wait for her to claim her seat. The whole incident might have slid by fairly unnoticed if not for this ridiculous protocol.

Thankfully, conversations resumed after she sat beside the Count.

She whispered, "I apologise for my tardiness."

"Where were you?"

"I met with a new friend in the city. Clementine Dupond."

"I see. And where did you meet?"

"At the Bras D'or."

He set down his knife in deliberate movements. "Did you take the scenic route home after that?"

"Pardon me?" She blinked.

"Anytime I go to the inn, I generally don't head out toward *Quai de Roi* on my way back."

"Well," she nervously responded, "we went shopping as well. I bought some more veils, and some Punic Apple preserves for Xavier, and – "

"Stop lying to me."

"I'm not lying. I could show you the things I bought."

"The stores closed two hours ago."

"Can we discuss this in private?" She whispered.

"We will discuss it right now and right here." He said, in a tone as cold and quiet as a cemetery in winter. "Where were you?"

"The carriage threw a wheel halfway home." She explained, and that was the truth. It had. "The driver had to wait until someone passed, and they give us a lift to the drawbridge. Go ask him."

"Even if what you say is true, that still doesn't explain why you were headed out toward *Quai de Roi.* There are no shops in which to buy one damned thing out there." His chair scraped as he shoved it back and stood. He turned on his heel and stormed out of the Great Hall by the side door, slamming it hard in his wake.

Viola hurried after him, finally catching him part ways up the curving stairs leading to the balcony. "Gabriel, I didn't do anything wrong."

He continued on, his big black boots banging into each step.

On the balcony, she said, "Why are you so angry? What is it that you think I have done against you?"

He wheeled around to face her with black fire spewing from his eyes, and the chill of that quiet, deep voice stating its position. "I'm going to give you one opportunity to tell me everything without omission. I'm listening."

What could she tell him to pacify him? What could she say that would make him hate her any less than he did right now? Her eyes stinging with tears that she refused to let fall, she stood her ground and maintained her silence, for the truth was far worse than even his wrath.

He exploded, "I'm waiting, damn you! Speak your piece!"

With his booming voice still echoing through the two-story foyer below, she fired back, "I have nothing to say! I'm sorry! "

"Don't." He held up a big palm that shook from his fury. "Don't say that you are sorry when you would go behind my back doing God knows what with God knows whom. Why in hell would I want to marry someone who lies every time she opens her mouth?"

Gabriel spun around and stalked toward the second set of steps that would lead him to the third level. Viola wanted to run after him but knew that he was too angry to reason with, so she turned and sat on the top step, gazing down into the foyer. Her heart in her throat, she studied the stark white patches where his late wife's wall hangings had been, and she wondered what Murielle had done to him to annihilate his trust.

"It was no accident." Gabriel's words rang inside her head, as she remembered him telling her about how Xavier had lost the use of his legs. *"She dropped him."*

What in the world had gone on in this home? Folding over to hug her knees, she thought, *I don't want to lose him*, and in that defining moment, she realised that she was beginning to develop real feelings for this very complex man. And why wouldn't she? Yes, he could be hard as flint, but he was also kind and generous. What was more, he had every right to be furious because she did lie to him at every turn, but for the life of her, she couldn't see any other way to find her child.

Viola shoved to her feet to descend as Louise approached the stairs. At the bottom step, she concluded, "He is so angry."

"We did nothing so terrible. We only spoke to a couple of people."

"It's deeper than that, Louise," she said, as they strode toward the door. "He's jealous."

"Of what?"

"He thinks I've come to France to try to find an old lover or some such thing."

"Where would he get such a silly notion?"

"I misdirected him," Viola whispered, in confidence, in case anyone was nearby. "When he asked if there was anyone who would haunt our bed, I refused to answer because I do think of the Aristocrat now and then. He's been carrying around this idea, so when I go out, I'm sure he thinks I'm searching for this other man who is actually dead. But he doesn't know that."

"Why didn't you tell him there was no other?"

"Because him thinking there is someone else keeps him distracted from the truth, which would be worse for him to find out. Louise, apart from not wanting him to know about my search for my daughter, I loathe to consider what he would think of me if he discovered my very unsavory past – that I sold my womb five years ago. That I behaved worse than a whore. That I had intimate relations with a man I had never seen before, and it was entirely in the dark, ergo, I have no clue who he was, but I enjoyed it immensely. That I agreed to accept a great deal of money for my daughter, but I changed my mind, and now I want her back. And then we have the reality that I do not have an ounce of noble blood in my veins. I was adopted. And he is the son of a king. Come on! That is a very long list of unforgivables to dole out to a man who has already been raked over the coals by a bitch who crippled her own son. "

As they stepped out into the darkness, Louise answered, "This is getting so terribly convoluted. *I* cannot even keep up anymore."

"You should see it from this side of my eyes, Louise. I have to remember these details when I'm trying to work around him."

"And you cannot simply tell him the truth?"

"No. If he knew the Aristocrat when he was alive –"

"Yes, I know. He might alert the people who raise your daughter now."

"Yes."

Louise expelled a long sigh. "How are you going to make this marriage work when you don't trust him, and he doesn't trust you?"

"Neither of us has a good handle on this thing called trust. Perhaps the best idea would be to try to keep it going as a business accord. An arranged marriage. Which, really, is what it is."

"That might work if you were not beginning to have feelings for him."

"I never said that."

"You didn't need to, *Mademoiselle.* I have seen how you look at him—and how he looks at you."

"I don't know what's happening to me, Louise. I don't fully understand it, but there is something about that man that draws me like a magnet. I love to be near him. I'm happy when he's within reach, even though I dare not reach out to touch him. As hard as he is at times, I just know in my heart that there is a very good man, deep inside. But I think he's done with me and is about ready to send me packing." Viola clamped a hand to her chest when she heard that big cat's low growl somewhere nearby. Grabbing Louise's hand, she inched backwards toward the door. "Don't make any sudden movements but let's go back inside."

"Why?"

"That damn cat is out here somewhere. I can hear it."

"What cat? There is no cat in this place."

"That lion I told you about...Louise?"

Louise bolted inside before she could finish. Viola wasted no time following. As they hurried toward the stairs in the foyer, Gabriel stomped down, passing between the two women and then stopping to glance back.

"Louise."

"Oh-oh." She turned slowly and bowed. "Your Lordship?"

"It's been brought to my attention that you've been doing more work around here than anybody else."

"I would not say that. "

"Straighten up before you get a knot in your back."

"My apologies."

"And don't apologise unless you have done something wrong. It makes you look suspicious—not that you don't already with the company you keep." He made a jerking motion toward Viola.

"Duly noted, Your Lordship."

"I hope you realise that you are under no obligation to lift one finger around here, so far as household duties go. You are Viola's private handmaiden. Now, where did Chantalle put you up?"

"In the servant's quarters, Your Lordship."

"Tell Valmont that I want you moved to a proper chamber on the second level." On that, he marched straight out the door and slammed it. The windows on either side of the door rattled.

Louise whispered, "I guess he's not going to send you packing."

A wave of relief washed over Viola. "I ought to take a break from my search for a while. Perhaps he needs time to cool his head."

"Perhaps you need to stop lying. It is a sin to lie."

Viola slanted her a moot glance. "It's too late for that now."

Chapter Eight.

Eight days before the Lenten Season would end, Viola hunted down Gabriel and found him in the workshop, sanding the wood on the wheeled chair that he had created. He had not spoken to her in more than a week, and wouldn't look at her, either. She had been waiting, moment by moment, with dread accumulating in her stomach, for him to evict her and be done with it. In the meanwhile, she had spent most of her time entertaining Xavier and feeling otherwise useless and restless.

There was nothing to do around the castle. After washing and dressing in the morning, Viola mostly wandered around feeling lost, for she had no idea how a future wife ought to conduct herself in her future husband's home. The lifestyle that everyone had already established was not in her purview to re-organise. Apart from that, she had no experience in running a home for she had always been more of a servant to the Medici clan. She needed to get out for a while, and was afraid to approach him now.

He was in a crouched position when she entered, focusing intently on his task. She didn't doubt for a moment that he was aware of her entering, but he pretended otherwise until she spoke.

"Gabriel."

"M-hm."

"I want to take Xavier into the city for a bit. I would like to get out before I go insane." She waited for a reply or reaction, but none came. She prodded gently, "Well, what do you think?"

He finally raised his eyes to glance up at her, "Make sure you – "

"Have an escort." She finished the sentence for him. "I know."

"Would you like some company?"

"Yes, I would."

Both dark eyebrows lifted, causing his brow to crease. "Yes?"

"Perhaps we could do something together."

"I ought to stay here and finish."

"But you were the one who suggested coming along...oh, wait. I know. You are testing me again."

He was quiet for a long, thoughtful moment, during which not one muscle in his body moved. "Not testing. Just trying to figure out where I stand, Viola."

She didn't know what in God's name came over her, but all at once she needed more than anything to know that he still wanted her. She had discovered that there was no place colder on this earth than the circle outside of his interest. She tilted his head up and awkwardly pressed her lips to his. Awkwardly, because she didn't know how to kiss. She had no experience with that, either. The Aristocrat had not once kissed her that night.

Losing his balance, Gabriel toppled over backwards and pulled her down atop himself, which resulted in the two of them rolling around on the dirty floor, locked into a gut-wrenchingly passionate first kiss.

He whispered, "Damn you, woman, you beguile me even as I know I'm walking into another trap."

"I am not trapping you," she breathed, "you know that I impose myself upon no-one."

"That's just the problem. I want that imposition."

"Gabriel – "

"Don't talk." He claimed her mouth again, and then locked them into the most intimate of embraces by wedging his thighs between hers and firmly grabbing two handfuls of her backside. The fire blazing within him spread into her, for she felt his erection grinding against her. The silence that enveloped them was interrupted only by gasps of wanton breath while but a few layers of fabric obstructed the merging of flesh.

One kiss led to another, each one more profound and more fervent than the previous, with him yanking at her gown to pull it up. Every bone in her body melted, and every muscle lost its power, while the core of her screamed like a wild animal that needed to be beaten down into submission. Never before had she felt this brand of insanity.

Without warning, he abruptly withdrew from her limbs and pointed toward the exit. "You had better get out of here before I close that door."

Viola grabbed the edge of the workbench and pulled herself up on trembling legs. Her breathing rapid, she said, "You're..uh...oh my God, I can't think...uh...are sure you don't want to come along?"

"I better get this job done."

Lingering, she admitted, "The depth of your fire frightens me, Gabriel. It seems to be all-consuming."

"Believe me," he breathed, "it gets worse."

She backed toward the door as if that was a threat.

"While you're in the city would you mind stopping off at the cobbler's? I've ordered a new pair of boots for Xavier. They're probably ready."

*   *   *

In Orléans, they didn't do much more than meander about, and for the duration, Viola's thoughts flitted between her urgency to find her daughter and her growing feelings for Gabriel. She did manage to stay focused long enough to purchase several beautiful arrangements from the florist for the Holy Day table, some treats from the bakery for the same, pick up Xavier's boots, and order a pretty, sky-blue gown for Louise. After that, she merely wanted to go home.

Admit it, she said to herself, as she assisted in loading the purchases into the carriage, she wanted to get near him again. He was a magnetic force. She was, quite honestly, losing her senses over this man and could not find one logical reason why this was so, for they were utterly incompatible. He did not trust her as far as he could throw her...no wait, with his strength that would be from her balcony right over to the Loire River. Scratch that one. The point was, they did not mesh.

As the carriage pulled out onto the street, Xavier said, "My boots."

Viola handed them to him and ruffled his hair. "They're very nice."

He made no reply but attempted to reach over and pull his foot up onto the seat.

"You want to wear them now?"

"Yes."

"We can do that. Let's get you turned around." She said, angling him so that his back faced Louise. "Put your head on Louise's lap."

As he reclined, she unlaced his black leather boots and pulled them off. As she was trying to get a new one onto his right foot, she froze when she spotted his toes moving. She said, "Did you do that on purpose?"

He raised his head to glance at her. "What?"

"Did you move your toes?"

"I don't know."

"Will you try to? Right now?"

He did, and again the toes moved.

"Good boy!" She smiled. Her pulse quickening, she hastily got the new boot onto one foot and switched to the other. It was the same. He could ever so slightly move the toes on the left foot as well. She thought, if this child could move his toes then there was still a part of his system working as it ought to be. If that were the case, then he was not completely paralysed. Hope fluttered in her stomach, but she remained silent, for she didn't want to mislead anyone. She held her thoughts within, got his new boots on, and then tapped his feet. "There you go."

"Thank you." He smiled and then yawned.

"Sleep, pretty boy," Louise spoke softly, stroking his hair. "We will awaken you when we get home."

They were silent until Viola was confident that he was asleep, and then she whispered, "He can move his toes, Louise."

"I saw that." She said, not seeming to understand the significance.

"If he can move his toes, there may be hope that this boy will walk again."

Louise frowned. "Not likely, *Mademoiselle.* As I understand it, he has never walked in his life."

"It's possible that for all of their good intentions, no-one has tried to get him to walk. Nobody believes that he ever will, but I have seen this before. I told you about Leonardo, my cousin?"

"No."

"He had a patient who could not walk. He had not walked in years, but then for whatever reason, he began to move his toes. Just one toe, actually. So my uncle encouraged him to try harder each day, and he did. Then with help, he tried day after day to strengthen the muscles. It took two years, but that man stood up by himself. Today he walks. Not perfectly, mind you. But he walks."

"Is that a fact?"

"Yes!" Viola whispered. "This child's muscles have completely gone soft, but if we were to try to strengthen them, there might be hope."

"How?"

"I know how. I watched Leonardo working with this man a few times. I will try this on Xavier."

*   *   *

"You cannot go in there," Yolande said, as she wiped her hands on the front of her brown frock.

"Why not? You just came out."

"Lady Viola, His Lordship is in the tub."

Viola's temper instantly flared. Jamming her fists on her hips, she demanded, "Then what were *you* doing in there?"

"Scrubbing his back. He hates when Chantalle does it. She's too rough."

"And I suppose you have a nice, gentle touch, hm?"

Yolande's dark olive complexion began to flush.

"Does he enjoy your method?"

"I wouldn't know."

"Better still, do *you* enjoy it?"

"My Lady – "

"I am going in there." Viola stepped around the servant and grabbed the latch. "I am bound to see his precious little pecker sooner or later – and I hope you have been relishing these moments enough to last you a lifetime because you won't scrubbing his back again! Go! Get out of here before *I SHRED YOU!*"

Yolande raced down the narrow service hall, disappearing into the dark end of it. Resolving not to look directly at Gabriel, Viola entered and shut the door. The room was quite small, and his presence seemed to fill it. She only realised then that her face burnt with jealous rage, and she felt this redness intensifying when she realised what she had so angrily marched right into.

Before she could open her mouth, Gabriel said, "Precious little pecker? Is that what I heard?"

"I...well, yes." She focused on a lantern, which was mounted to the wall above the tub.

"You are in for a delightful surprise."

"That's not what I came in here to discuss."

"Who is going to scrub my back now that you've banished her?"

"You can scrub your own bloody back. You are not a cripple."

"A little jealous, are we?"

She squared her jaw. "I need to ask you a favour."

"I like you jealous." He said.

"I do not."

"Your face is beet red. Do you know what that's called, my lady?"

Needing to do something with her hands, she straightened her neckliner. "Embarrassment."

"It's called passion—and I want to see more of it."

"Quit baiting me, Gabriel. I need to ask you a favour."

"Go ahead."

"Xavier said that you were good with your hands, and I have seen that this is so – "

"You haven't seen anything yet."

"I can feel you smirking. Stop that."

"What do you need, Viola?"

She cleared her throat. "I require a contraption of some sort, made of leather, that I can sit Xavier down into, and that he can't fall out of. And I need it to be strung up to that old dead tree in the back yard so that his toes cannot quite touch the ground. Would you be able to create that for me?"

"Yes. Is this meant to be some sort of toy? Like a swing?"

"I wasn't thinking of it that way, but that would also be a good use for it. How long would it take you to create this?"

"An hour, perhaps."

"Good. I am much obliged."

"I'll get at it right now." An explosion of water blasted upward with him as he suddenly stood.

Oh, shit! She whipped around and reached for the door handle, but was hauled back by two big wet hands around her waist.

Hugging her back against the heat of his drenched body, he whispered, "God help me, but I find it impossible to stay angry with you."

"I guess I will have to work harder at that."

"Is it your intention to drive me completely mad for the rest of our lives?"

"I don't do it purposely."

"But you do it so well."

She held her breath as he turned her around. "Wh-what are you doing?"

In a series of swift motions, he reached down to shove one arm under her knees while securing her back with the other. He jostled her into place, turned – and dumped her into the tub of water.

"Gabriel! Damn! Oh, damn!"

Reaching for a towel which was draped over a stool, he wrapped it around his hips and said, "Come find me in the workshop when you're done in here." The door clicked shut, and she was alone.

She fought her way out of the tub in a gown that was wringing wet and restricting her every move. Her foot slipping, she fell back into the tub, and grabbed the floating bar of soap to hurl it at the door. As her luck would have it, Chantalle opened it just in time to get soundly knocked on the forehead. If that were not bad enough, the Head Housekeeper slipped on the soap and ended up going arse over kettle in the pool of water that Gabriel had caused.

Grabbing the side of the tub, Viola was finally able to haul herself out. Stepping over Chantalle, she growled, "I am going to kill that man!" As she stomped out into the dark corridor, she heard a snorting sound – much like a pig – and turned back to see if the woman was all right.

Rolling her large square body into a seated position, Chantalle commenced to laugh and to laugh from deep in her gut.

"I do not see the humour in this at all," Viola grumbled. Still, the woman had the most ridiculous laugh she had ever heard.

Snort, snort, hahaha! "What was that man do-doing, running down, down, down..." *snort, snort, hahaha!* "down the hallway..." *snort,*

snort, "naked?" *Snort snort, snort, snort, hahaha!*

"I can see why you don't laugh much." Viola said, but despite herself, her mouth gave in to a small twitch, and then a bigger one, until she folded down to the floor and laughed along with the housekeeper.

*   *   *

By the time Viola tracked down Louise, went up to her room, undressed, dried herself off, and recruited her friend's assistance in getting into her cream-coloured gown, the hour had passed. She draped her black veil over her hair and went to find Gabriel in the workshop.

He was sanding the seat of the contraption she had requested. The sun was by now low and red on the horizon, filling the space with a soft, filmy glow.

He fired her a marginal grin, which, for this surly bastard, was a pleasant change. "I decided to make the seat of wood, but the containment around it, leather. Leather seats tend to buckle too much. Tell me what you intend to do with this thing?"

"Are you aware that he can move his toes?"

"No. I never dress the boy. Denise does. What is the significance?"

"The significance is that the message to move his toes is making it from his brain down to his feet."

"And?"

"There is still life in those legs. Listen, I am very reluctant to breed hope where there may not be any, but..."

"Shit." His expression went blank. "Don't tell me that."

She told him the story of her cousin Leonardo's patient, and finalised, "Is it not worth a try? What can we lose by trying?"

"Nothing," he said, "but don't get his hopes up, just in case."

"I won't. I will make it like a game. But I find it difficult to accept that the leech has not noticed this before."

Shrugging, Gabriel explained, "He's not a very good leech, Viola. He never was. His training was very rudimentary – a bit learned from this one and a bit from that one. Nothing formal. Our best leeches were killed during this damned war. They'd go out to help the wounded and not come back. We make do."

"That is unfortunate."

"I was so happy that he lived after...well, I was so glad to still have him that I never even thought to ask for more, or expect more, or even hope for it, for that matter. He is the air that I br—" His voice broke, and he could speak no more. He continued sanding, putting every ounce of his concentration into the task.

The intensity of the emotions that he fought so hard to contain was her undoing. She didn't have a clue how to deal with this crack of vulnerability so wide that she could walk through it. Yet, she fully understood how much it must have cost him to allow her to see this side of him because she had her own secret sorrows as reference points. She had no experience whatever in dealing with the dark fires that men held in their hearts. She only knew of the fury shown by the Baron who beat her but never told her why and expected her to learn how to take it without complaining. So silently she had suffered, and silently she had lived, until running away seemed to be the only way out.

Nervously wringing her hands, she said, "Send someone for me once that thing is ready."

Gathering the swing, Gabriel left the workshop, summoning one of his more agile serfs to follow him. Once the swing was hung from the dead tree, he sent the same serf inside to fetch Viola and his son and made the appropriate adjustments so that Xavier could sit in it, with his feet an inch or so above the ground.

Afterwards, he sat on the cold stone floor of the portico with his back against the wall, observing, while she tried to get him to reach down with his toes to touch the earth. His heart broke, for the amount that those little toes were able to move was so minuscule that it was not even worthy of mention. But she gently swung him to and fro while she did it, so the boy was at least getting some fresh air and enjoying her company.

And she was good company for his boy, he fully realised. She was excellent, with her youthful, spontaneous laughter and the animation in her voice, and her willingness to just be with him so much of the time. Clearly, she had fallen head over heels for his son, though she had not once said as much. He decided that love was not about saying the right words. It was about doing the right things.

Gabriel wished that she could love *him* that much because in spite of his resolution not to love again, he was falling for Viola and falling hard.

*   *   *

The Holy Day meal finally came 'round, and it was a good one. Afterwards, Gabriel grabbed his son and said, "Let's go out to the foyer."

Viola followed him out and was delighted to find the wheeled chair that Gabriel had made, sitting near the front door.

Setting his son into the contraption, Gabriel said, "There you go, little man. A present for you, from Viola and I."

Xavier glanced from her to his father, as if not understanding the importance of any of this. Gabriel placed the boy's small hands around the wheels and began to move them back and forth, and those eyes lit up like a pair of lanterns. As if to illustrate what kind of freedom this would bring, Gabriel pushed the chair around the foyer.

Viola sat on the bottom step to watch. Without realising it, she began gnawing on the knuckle of her index finger, for the look of amazement in the boy's eyes nearly broke her heart.

Xavier said, "Let me, by myself, Papa. Z'abier's a big boy."

Gabriel stood back, hands on hips, to watch, as his son slowly struggled with the big wheels to get around the room.

"I can do it!" Xavier cried. "Watch me!"

"Yes, you can," Gabriel said. Crouching down to be at his son's eye level, he added, "You can do anything. Do you hear me? Anything."

"I can do anything." The boy repeated. And then he unexpectedly collapsed into sobs in his father's burly arms.

Stroking his hair, Gabriel whispered, "What is wrong? Did I hurt you?"

"N-no." The boy hiccuped. "I'm just so hap-happy. I can go pla-places by my-myself now! All by myself!"

Gabriel's expression twisted with emotion. Holding his son closer, he fought against the tidal wave until he was able to speak again. "Now, when we go into the city, we can bring that chair, and you can get all over the place with your own strength. You can get all over the castle on the main floor, but not on the upper floors. You could fall down the stairs. Fair enough?"

"Thank you, Papa."

Gabriel said, "You must also thank Viola. She helped."

"I didn't do much." She whispered.

"Thank you, Viola."

"It was my pleasure. You know that I would move the world for you." Viola pondered the complexities of their relationship. Thus far, it had been a rambunctious ride. Gabriel was so quick to anger, always seeming to teeter on the edge of it. Anger, passion, love, hate...his emotions were unlike her own, which were buried deep within her soul, and which she didn't allow to show all that much. Gabriel's were just under the surface of his skin—and she decided in that moment, that she absolutely loved that about him.

But how quick was he to forgive? She wondered. She was going to need to rely on that grace existing deep within his soul when he found out the dark, disgraceful secrets of her past.

*　　*　　*

The following morning she encountered Gabriel in the corridor as they were both leaving their rooms. Draping an arm around her shoulders, he said, "Good morrow, my lady."

"Good morrow, Gabriel. Did you sleep well?"

"No." He said. "I felt you on the other side of that wall. I keep the adjoining door unlocked, you know."

"That's good to know. Listen...uh...I would like your permission to go into the city today."

"Would you like some company?"

She answered, "No, thank you."

He stopped in his tracks. "We're back to that, are we?"

"I won't be very long."

"History seems to be repeating itself. "

"Gabriel, you need to understand that I am not doing anything against you as much as doing something for myself."

Releasing her, he continued down the corridor, speaking over his shoulder, "You are obsessed, but go do what you must."

*　　*　　*

The residence of Mark Simone was exactly where Jerome Belleveau had directed. Louise decided to wait in the carriage, as she felt uncomfortable with the idea of being in the same room with Viola and a man who was a twin to her late lover. "I would feel in the say," she said.

Viola was greeted by a servant who ushered them to the sitting room, where Mark sat on a chaise, sharpening a sword with a stone and spittle. He glanced up from his task and then put his weapon aside to stand and greet her.

He was a stunning man – very tall and well-built, with dark hair and piercing, silver-grey eyes. "Good day. How may I help you?"

Viola extended a hand, while otherwise paralysed by his eyes. If he was the Aristocrat's twin brother, was he identical to the man with whom she had been intimate five years ago? "I am Lady Viola de Medici, of *Firenze*."

"I have in-laws in Florence." The gentleman said, as he kissed her hand and gestured toward a red and white chaise that matched the overall decor in the room. "Please, sit. May I offer you a refreshment?"

"Thank you, but I won't be that long, I don't think." As she seated, he reclaimed his own chaise.

He prompted, "What can I do for you?"

"I am seeking information about a certain child born to your deceased twin brother."

"Yes, and I lost my youngest brother, Jean-Paul, in battle recently. Perhaps it is true that the good die young."

"I am genuinely sorry to hear that, *Monsieur.*"

"Thank you. Go ahead. Ask your questions."

"My first one may seem odd, but are you identical to your twin?"

"Yes. Everyone got us confused. When he got married he relocated to *Lausanne*." He shrugged, adding, "He got this idea in his head that he wanted to try farming. He always did like the feel of soil between his fingers. As well, his wife didn't want to be in the city where there were so many others around. It made her feel trapped. Or something. I'm not sure. But I am rambling. One tends to do that when they lose a loved one. I apologise."

"Please, don't apologise. About the child, do you know the circumstances surrounding her...or his...how shall I put this...this child's conception?"

"A very indelicate topic to be sure." Mark nodded. "I will try to be diplomatic. Arthur wanted a child and his wife could not give him one. She was barren, you see."

"Yes."

"And she wasn't well. I don't know if she was stable enough to be anyone's wife. She was a charming woman, but she had some sort of mental sickness which made her terrified of leaving the house. So," he sighed resignedly, "Authur had an involvement, shall we say, with another woman, who agreed to carry his child. He and his wife agreed on this arrangement since she also wanted a child of her own. There was some speculation—by tonguesters, mind you—that her parents had done something to get her sterilised so that she would not be able to reproduce. She had been mentally ill since birth."

"That is most unfortunate," Viola said. "Tell me, were they living in *Lausanne* at the time of the child's conception?"

"Yes. Arthur was very ill. Lung Fever. He wanted more than anything to have a child of his own before he died. So time passed, and he was brought a child. Now, I don't know who the child's mother was or what arrangements were made for this conception to happen, and he never talked about it. I didn't pry."

"I see. Her brother, Jerome, said that she and their parents were killed *en route* to *Normandie*?"

"Yes. Shortly after the birth of his daughter, Arthur passed away. Lucianne, his wife, returned here to live with her parents, for she was afraid of living too far away without Arthur. She was well aware of her mental condition and was afraid of not being able to raise a child on her own. Her parents were more than happy to accommodate her. She began to try to go out on the Sabbath, for the child's sake. She wanted to get better, but for some strange reason, she could not bring herself to mix among other people. Ergo, her parents heard of a specialist in *Normandie* who might be able to treat her. So they stuffed her, kicking and screaming, into the carriage and headed out that way, but they never made it."

"That is very sad."

"That lout who inherited the Belleveau estate somehow managed to finagle the entirety of what the child should have inherited, but he was clever. He worked within the requirements of the law, you see. Any properties inherited by the wife would either go into the King's coffer, or to his eldest male offspring, or a male member of the wife's family. This evil bastard protested that the child was an illegitimate female, since Arthur's wife was not the child's birth mother, and in fact made a point to mention that there was no proof that Arthur was the child's father, for that matter. It went 'round and 'round for a bit, but he won, and the estate began to quickly fall apart after that. Some say he has squandered the entire fortune."

Viola said, "He pointed out quite succinctly that he didn't want the child as part of the package."

"Absolutely correct. Jerome called the child *Arthur's little bitch-bastard*. So I took her home with me. I've been raising her as my own ever since."

Viola's heart leapt against within her breast. "Is she here? May I see her?"

"I am afraid not." Mark smiled. "She's gone with my wife and our three other children to visit her parents. They ought to return in a few hours."

"I came back in a few hours, may I see her then?"

"Of course."

Viola stood and straightened the lines of her gown. "I will go now and return later. Thank you so much for indulging me, *Monsieur* Simone."

"No worries. I'll walk you to the door." As he ushered her down the hall, he added, "Now, I that have answered your questions quite openly, perhaps you will answer a few for me before departing."

"Certainly."

"Why do you seek this child? Is she related to you?"

For a change, Viola opted for truth. "She might be."

Those piercing silvery eyes met hers. "Might you be that woman who provided my brother with a child?"

"I might."

"And if it turns out that she is yours, would you want her back?"

"If she is mine, yes."

"Would you be able to give her a good home? She has everything she wants with us. We adore her as our own."

She considered that very deeply while he patiently waited for her answer. "Well, if it turns out that I could not provide adequately, I would not be so selfish as to remove her from this loving home for my own sake. I would just like to...to find her." She went one step further, "I didn't even get to see her when she was born, *Monsieur* Simone."

"Mark." He smiled. "Please call me Mark."

"Thank you. Mark, if I cannot provide her with a good home, I would at least like the freedom to visit her regularly, and I would not upset the arrangement that you have in place now. I wouldn't even have to tell her that I am her mother. Honestly, my heart just breaks that I can never even see her."

"That is fair enough."

"Mark," She said, grasping his arm. "I must plead with you to keep this between us no matter what happens?"

"Of course. I give you my word."

"The issue is that I am about to be married. I don't want to wreck it with him, and yet I cannot give up this quest to find my daughter. If this child that you are raising is mine, then it might take some time for me to break this news to my betrothed. You understand?"

"Completely, My Lady."

"Just as you wish to be called by your name, so do I. Considering the most delicate nature of our...um...situation, perhaps we may be friends if you are comfortable with that. It may turn out to be that there is a little girl whom we both adore."

He sighed. "Yes, Viola, I agree. The more compassionate we are toward each other's common interest, the better for the child."

"Thank you with all of my heart."

As Mark swung the door open, the intense morning sun slanted into her eyes. Standing in the halo of it was Gabriel. He stood beside her carriage, talking to her driver, who was one of his serfs.

He turned to face them.

Viola's knees all but gave out on her.

Gabriel left his horse next to the carriage and approached the door with his eyes fixed steadily on the man standing behind her. He said, "Mark. How are you?"

Chapter Nine

"I'm good, Gabriel."

"I am sorry about Jean-Paul. I tried to save him."

"And almost got yourself killed in the process." Mark said, "Valmont told me. Thank you for trying, Gabriel."

"You're welcome."

"How are you recovering from your wound?"

"Very well. I see you've met my wife-to-be."

Mark's dark eyebrows slid upward. "Viola is your betrothed?"

Gabriel smiled, though it did not reach his eyes. "What a small world. But then, you do travel to Italy quite often, don't you? Where does your wife's cousin live again? Florence, isn't it? Is that where you two met?"

"Yes." Mark lied with a straight face. "Viola and I met there some years ago."

"Small world," Gabriel repeated, as he produced an elbow for Viola to take. Her knees shaking, she accepted it and allowed him to lead her away.

He said, "I thought you didn't know anyone in France?"

"Um...I forgot about Mark. It's a long story."

"I bet it is and it must be a very involved one, for he calls you by your first name."

"Many people do that."

"Men of good breeding do not address women by their first names, and he most certainly is well bred." Opening the door to her carriage, he assisted her in climbing inside and then studied her knowingly through the open window. "Go home, Viola."

"Are you coming?"

"I will when I'm through here."

"I would that you come with us. We require time to talk. "

"Go home." Lowering his voice, he added, "From now on you will go nowhere without me."

Louise reached over to squeeze her hand reassuringly, but she was only vaguely aware of it. Her head reeling from shock and from the fear that Gabriel might just convince this man to tell him the whole story, she had no choice but to allow this carriage to take her helplessly away.

As they turned out onto the street, she said, "I think I'm going to be sick."

Louise answered, *"Mademoiselle,* when we begin to tell lies, we need to make up more lies to cover the first."

"I didn't know what else to do, Louise."

When they arrived back at the castle, she went upstairs and straight to her room, for she felt absolutely ill. Pressing a cold, wet hand towel to her face, she lay down across her bed and tried to imagine what was going on between Gabriel and Mark, in her absence.

Gabriel wasn't interested in obtaining any of the details of their past romance or what they were cooking up now. The whole thing made his stomach convulse, as he already knew what was going on. He felt the fire of rage searing through his brain and his gut. Small wonder her lover didn't want to marry her. He was already married with four children.

Somehow, over the years, he had mistaken Mark for a good man, he thought, as he turned and approached him. So this was the man she pined over. This was the one that she would travel so far to find. And this was the one she would be dreaming on when she came to his bed. A close friend of his. Someone he had known and trusted for twenty-two years.

He wanted to draw his blade and gut the bastard. But as he stood staring at him, he wondered if Mark wanted to rekindle the fire with her? Perhaps he had decided at some point to return his loyalty to those who depended upon him, namely, his wife and children. Was Viola pursuing someone who was no longer interested? Perhaps Mark was a man who had made a single mistake and regretted it? Many did. And they never cheated again. Deep down he wanted to believe that Mark was too good a man to carry on like this.

Was a deceptive woman worth throwing away twenty-two years of very close friendship? He had almost destroyed the relationship with his father over Murielle. He figured he would try, for once, to keep a cool head and watch how this thing played itself out.

"Would you care for a drink?" Mark asked, as he leaned against the door frame.

"No, I ought to get going."

"What's on your mind, Gabriel? Is something wrong?"

"I know it's short notice but why don't you and your family come over for a visit? I'm sure Xavier wouldn't mind some play time with Lise. It's been awhile."

"They're not here," Mark said. "They've gone out for a few hours."

Ahhhh... Gabriel thought, bitterly. *Of course, they are not here.* Of course. No man wanted his wife to meet his plaything. Well, then... "What about later today?"

"Certainly. My family will return soon. Put a bottle of white wine on to chill for me."

Gabriel smiled, ruefully. "White wine. You always did have a taste for the finer things in life, didn't you?"

"I always did."

"Yes. Well, I'll see you soon, then."

Gabriel strode toward his trusty warhorse, who hadn't budged an inch since he was left unattended. Now he knew why she wanted to remain in France. To be near Mark Simone. It was finally starting to make sense. *Well, we shall see how interesting this gets when the lover meets the wife.*

*   *   *

At five in the afternoon, Viola was awakened by a firm rap on her door. Peeling the hand towel off her eyes, she sat up and answered groggily, "Yes?"

"His Lordship wants you outside in the front." Chantalle barked.

"Why?"

"We have visitors."

"Who are they?"

"*Monsieur* and *Madame* Mark Simone and their children."

Scrambling off the bed, she raced over to the basin to rinse and dry her face, straighten her veil, which she had been lying on, and then she raced downstairs. Her heart banging like a drum, she paused at the door to peer out into the yard before exiting. A large wrought-iron table had been set out on the grass, and around it was Mark, a woman who was most likely his wife, and Gabriel. A bottle of wine sat upon a crisp white tablecloth whose edges fluttered in the breeze.

Over near the hedges were five children. One was Xavier and the other four, presumably Mark's, except for one. And she just might be Viola's daughter. Her knees began to tremble so fiercely, she wondered if she would be able to walk. She wondered why Gabriel had brought them back. Had Mark told him the whole story after all? And did he understand rather than condemn? She would have to play it by ear.

As she crossed the distance over the grass, she forced herself to smile and greet. "Mark. Good to see you again."

Both men stood. Mark kissed the back of her hand and said, "Viola, it's my great pleasure to introduce you to my wife, Elisabeth. Dear, this is Lady Viola de Medici, the lovely young woman about whom I spoke earlier."

"So pleased to meet you, *Madame* Simone," Viola answered, and fired a glance toward the girl and four boys playing near the back hedge.

Elisabeth stood to lower her head in a gesture of respect. "The pleasure is mine, Lady Viola."

Mark said, "Come, I will introduce you to our children."

In her peripheral vision, she noted Gabriel's eyes fixed upon her and they were judgmental. She followed Mark to the rear of the property, where he got his children's attention. "Children, I would like you to meet Lady Viola de Medici, of Florence. You know how to greet nobility. Please do so."

All four of them promptly stood at attention and issued awkward bows, while Xavier tilted sideways to grab her around her calves.

"Viola!" He yelped. "You're up!"

Smiling in spite of herself, she collected him into her arms and then glanced at the other children, each little face individually.

Mark went down the line, placing a palm upon each of their heads as he spoke their names. "This is Jean, who is eight, Lise, who is five, Durand, who is nine, Christian, who is five, and Stephan, who is four."

Bang! Viola's heart slammed against her ribs. A pair of silver-grey eyes, fringed by black lashes, gazed up at her, sparkling in the late afternoon sun. The other children may or may not have had silvery eyes, but she barely saw them. The little girl's hair was also very dark, producing a mesmerising effect. Forcing herself to remain composed, she bade them each a friendly hello, and then said, "Go back to your game, children. We grown-ups are boring."

She glanced toward Mark, who had questions in his eyes, which she could guess. *Do you think this is your daughter?*

Xavier grabbed her face and twisted it toward his own. His brown eyes shining, he said, "Did you get more Punic Apple goo?"

"Punic Apple goo?" She laughed, even as tears formed in her eyes. "Oh, Lord, I do love you! Yes, I did. Don't you know that I would have walked to the ends of the earth to get more of that goo for you, little man?"

"I know." He giggled and plastered a wet kiss on her cheek. "May I have some?"

"Yes." Glancing at Mark, she said, "I will be right back." She turned and hurried inside, to run into Chantalle in the foyer.

"Chantalle, would you be so kind as to prepare some of your bread with Punic Apple sauce on it, for the children?"

She stole Xavier from her arms. "Come with me, little warrior. You can tell me exactly how much you want on the bread."

Viola turned and hurried back outside, and Mark was where she had left him. Stepping very close to him, she whispered, "I'm not sure. She has dark hair but otherwise, does not look like me at all. She is absolutely beautiful, though."

"She looks like her father—and me, I suppose."

An image flashed in her mind. A brief image shifting in the glow of a lantern in the room where she had given birth. With her back to Viola, the midwife had held her crying babe upside down, and beneath her tiny right armpit was a birthmark that was like her own. But what was she supposed to do? Undress the poor child seconds after meeting her – if ever?

"Let's go back," Mark suggested. "Gabriel seems to be watching us very closely for some reason."

"Did you tell Gabriel anything?"

"No. It is for you to tell the secrets of your past to your betrothed, not I."

"Thank you. I am so indebted to you."

The afternoon was one hell of a long one. The Simone's were lovely, their children were well-behaved, and Gabriel was the perfect host in all ways. But when he glanced at Viola, there was something barely detectable in his eyes that was meant only for her, and it was not kindness.

The tension of it all was enough to give her a stomach ache from her upper ribs down into her navel. Even with that, she couldn't take her eyes off the child with the beautiful silvery eyes. And she hoped to God that she was her own blood. Even if it meant losing Gabriel, she hoped this child was hers, because her soul was weary and she wanted her daughter back.

Finally, as daylight succumbed to twilight, Mark stood and beckoned his children that it was time to go. As they raced toward him, Gabriel strode across the grass to collect Xavier into his arms, and then rejoined them around the table.

Madame Simone made a clicking sound with her tongue and said, "Oh dear, you are a mess, Lise. Look at your chemise. That will get all over the carriage seat that we have just had reupholstered."

"Punic apples stain for life," Viola said. "I am sorry. I didn't realise this would happen."

"Oh, it's not a great disaster, but perhaps she can borrow a chemise from Xavier? They are nearly the same size."

"I will go fetch one," Viola volunteered, and then turned and raced inside. It took but a moment to run up to the third level, find a clean chemise and run back down. By the time she returned the little girl was stripped to her waist. Madame Simone used her dirty chemise to wipe her face clean, and the faces of the other children as well. Viola handed her the clean chemise and then took a chair next to Gabriel as she waited for the woman to put the clean chemise on the child, hoping to get a glimpse under her right arm.

At last, she did get her wish. Her eyes fired to the spot in her little armpit, and her stomach nearly dropped into her shoes.

Lise was not her daughter. Birthmarks like these did not just go away as one grew. They only got bigger. Oh, no. Dear God, no. After all of these hopes...

She held onto her composure and held onto it some more, while they bade their long farewells on the walk to their carriage near the drawbridge. After Monsieur Simone got his wife comfortably seated and shut the door, she managed to catch his eye long enough to very discreetly shake her head, no. And that was when the tears began forming in her eyes.

In the act of pure compassion, Mark drew her close for an embrace and whispered into her ear, "Never give up hope. It will all work out. Come to me if you need anything."

Gabriel was close enough to hear it—and draw his own conclusions. As their carriage drove off, Viola turned abruptly and ran toward the rear entrance under the portico, for she hated for anyone to see her crying. He caught up to her quickly and grabbed her elbow to spin her around.

He saw her tears glistening in the soft evening sun and ground through his teeth, "It's a real bastard, isn't it? Hurting this way?" *I watched you two exchanging furtive glances all evening, and every one of them cut me through and through.*

"Not now, Gabriel."

"There's no good time for it, Viola."

She wrenched her elbow free, growling, "I said—not now."

"What the hell is it that you want?" He demanded, as he grasped her shoulders and pressed her firmly to the stone wall beneath the portico. "What can he give you that I cannot?"

"It's not like that!"

"Horse shit! I heard him whispering words of love when he thought that no-one else could hear!" Not knowing what in blazes he was thinking, he hauled her into his arms and forced a kiss upon her mouth, as if that would make a bit of difference. For it was he who had told her that one could not force the love of another. But here he was, trying.

Still trying. It was happening all over again. What was that saying that they quoted in her homeland, Italia? Ah yes. *One always kissed while the other turned the cheek.*

She shoved him back and ran inside.

Gabriel punched the stone wall so hard that his knuckles bled, and then stormed to the stable to saddle up his horse. He needed to ride hard and fast.

*   *   *

Resigned to his loss and determined not to allow her to weasel her way back into his heart, Gabriel did his utmost to avoid her in the upcoming days, but he wasn't all that successful. It was difficult when they lived under the same roof. At times he thought he should simply find her alternate accommodations so that she would not have to return to Italy. But the part of him that remembered the good moments simply did not want to give up, for even when they had fought, he felt more involved with her – more alive and entangled – than he had ever felt with any woman. Sometimes, in those weaker moments, he thought that he would rather take a slap in the face from her than all the kisses in the world from anyone else.

As well, she was right for Xavier. She began a practice of bringing him out to his swing every eve after supper, and playing games with him to get him to try to touch his toes to the ground, now less than half an inch away. To any other man with a healthy child that might mean nothing at all, but to him that half an inch of progress meant the world. Each time he saw that he loved her more, even as he hated her more for making him love her.

But what the hell was the point? What was the point, when all of the emotion that he was putting into her was one-sided? He despised himself for his inability to get her out of his blood, and for his failure to completely cut the strings and send her away. But mostly, he despised himself for weakening every couple of days and thinking that if he tried a different approach, they would be able to work it out.

On the second of May – a day he would remember forever – he returned from the city to hear a jubilant screech coming from under the dead tree. He shielded his eyes against the afternoon sun with his hand, to see what was going on. Viola was under the tree with Xavier, who was in his swing. Viola saw him riding in on his horse and for the moment, forgot their differences, for she excitedly waved him over.

Dismounting, he handed the reins of his horse to a serf and strode toward them. His expression dark, he said, "What is going on?"

"He did it!"

"What?"

"He touched the ground!" She exclaimed, excitedly.

"I did it, Papa! I grew some more!" Xavier joined in, clapping.

"You grew?" He glanced toward Viola, not understanding.

She whispered, "I told him that if he could touch the ground, it means he has grown. Incentive," she smiled from ear to ear. "Watch this! Do it again, sweetness!"

Gripping the ropes with all of his strength, the boy began to turn pink from exertion, but then, sure as hell, his little toes bent downward, ever-so-precisely, and touched the ground.

"Oh...my...God." Gabriel squatted, wanting to see a repeat. He was no leech, but he knew enough to realise that for a child who had no use in his bottom half at all since he was six months of age, this was miraculous. For him to be able to do that, he had to have been using at least his calf muscles. "Again, little man. Do it again."

He did, with a big beaming smile. "I grew some more!"

"Yes, you did. You grew some more. I am proud of you. Keep at it." He straightened to kiss the top of his son's head and then strode toward the portico to lean back against the wall.

Viola got the swing going to and fro on its own momentum, and then rushed toward him. "Isn't that wonderful?"

"I had no faith in this idea of yours at the start, but now...I'm hopeful."

"It's *all* about hope, Gabriel, and it's about faith. If we have those, we don't quit until we win. Wooo-hooo!" She let go a whoop and ran toward Xavier again, giving him another gentle push.

His son shrieked with glee. With his heart in his throat, Gabriel observed as she lifted him from his swing, and said, "Tomorrow, we will get your Papa to raise the swing another little bit, and then you can try to grow some more. All right? Do you want to do that?"

"Yes!"

She pressed a kiss into his cheek and carried him into the castle by the rear entrance.

Glancing toward the door, he thought, *how in the hell can I unlove you?* In that moment he realized that she was also hurting. She had to be, for one did not just get over the kind of pain she had to have been feeling that night the Simone's had come over. She had to see Mark there in front of her, with his wife and their children. That had to hurt. She had to have been feeling as miserable as he was feeling now, and yet, she could find within her heart, the time to do this for his son. From where did she get this goodness?

"It's about hope, Gabriel, and it's about faith. If we have those, we don't quit until we win."

Was it really that simple? Could he, with faith and hope, beat the odds working against them? Did they stand a chance of making it? Chewing his lip, he pondered this, and it seemed to him that she had not been trying to get off the property since their last quarrel. At least, not that he was aware of. While the fear inside him screamed not to be tested again, he beat it down and entered the castle, feeling sick to his stomach and yes, a little hopeful at the same time.

He strode through the narrow corridor at the rear, shoved the door open and entered the main foyer as she was handing Xavier over to Chantalle.

"He has earned a slice of bread with Punic Apple sauce," Viola said.

"And he shall get it." Chantalle marched forward, stepped around Gabriel and kicked the door open, letting it bang shut at his back.

"Viola." He spoke hoarsely.

"Gabriel." Coming toward him, she wrung her fingers at her waist. "I know I ought to leave this place. I know that you hate me for what you think I've done to you, but I just wanted to work with him for a bit. He deserves a chance."

"Come here." He folded her into the tight circle of his embrace, and the way she just fit right in there, with her arms around him and her head sliding in under his chin caused a surge of protectiveness so great in his Warlord's heart that he nearly broke down. But he had to remain strong. He was, after all, a man. He whispered, "Why can I not complete you, Viola? What is it that I lack?"

"Not one thing. I would not change you for the world."

"Then why can't we make this work?"

"Perhaps we are both too complicated."

"I can't accept that as an answer. Where do we stand? What are we?" He asked, stepping back from her to see her expression. "Are we only friends? Are we still going to be married? Are we over? What are we?"

"What do you want us to be?"

He growled, "Don't play that game. Talk to me! What do you *want?*"

"I want to marry you."

"Are you sure?"

"I am very sure." Tears shimmered along her lower lids when she raised them to study something above and beyond his shoulder, and for a very brief instant, it appeared that she would reveal something of utmost importance. Something that would seal them together forever, or tear them just as surely apart. But then she shrugged and said, "I am tired. It's been a very long week."

"All right. But we need to discuss this further."

"We will."

"I have your word on that, do I?" He pressed.

"Absolutely."

Heavy hearted, he released her. "Go get some rest, my lady."

She turned and walked away, her light footfalls echoing in the grand foyer. Gabriel watched her climb the steps and then disappear into the darkness at the rear of the balcony above. He wanted to believe. He so wanted to believe, but his gut cautioned him that this wasn't the end of his misery. She was still withholding information, and he knew it.

* * *

"We have a change of plan. I have taken some serfs clothing from the clothesline. We will disguise you as a male serf, and you will pretend to be my escort as we leave."

Louise issued a heavy sigh. "*Mademoiselle,* you are at it again, devising a different plot. Can we not rest for a bit?"

"I can't, Louise. I swear, I am possessed but I cannot. You have no idea how it felt like to be me when I thought that I had finally found my daughter. I need to feel that hope again."

"Fine, but I will never look like a man."

"You will when we are finished. We must get some cosmetics from somewhere, though."

"Why are we doing this? The letter you created states that we both have permission to go anytime, *Mademoiselle*."

"Yes, and I have reconsidered that because it might raise suspicions more quickly than if you were to be an escort."

Louise pondered this idea for a moment. "Yes, I agree, but how will we make me look like a man?"

"I have an idea. I don't know anyone on the premises who uses cosmetics, but there is one place where we may find some."

"Where?"

"In the late wife's quarters."

"Oh, no." Louise backed toward the door. "I will not steal from the dead."

Viola shrugged. "She doesn't need them anymore."

"It is the same thing. What if her ghosts still lives there?"

"If her ghost is still here, I suspect that it would be haunting my quarters, not her own. Look, I don't like the idea of touching her things any more than you do, but we must be creative, and we must get past our fears if we are to find my little girl."

"Supposing I go along with this. The letter says that we both are permitted to go. You would appear to be alone with the escort."

"I wrote another letter which states that I have permission to leave provided I have an escort. This letter is only about me. Can you lower your voice to sound male?"

"Not too well. I do not like this at all."

"Then you will remain silent, and I will do the talking." She grabbed Louise's hand and hauled her toward the door. Thankfully, there was nobody in sight, though the corridor was lit by the wall-mounted torches. Picking up her pace, Viola hastily tiptoed down the hall with Louise behind her. At the very end, she swallowed a mouthful of sawdust, and then let herself into Murielle's quarters. "Close the door after yourself, Louise."

The door shut.

Viola said, "Well, holy dow dung. It's pitch black in here. We need a torch."

"Mademoiselle –"

"I will go." She stuck her head out, darted across the hall and snagged a torch, and then ducked back inside.

"I feel her in here," Louise whispered, hugging herself.

Viola moved about very quickly and quietly, examining the items on the vanity, where a wide variety of cosmetics lay neatly arranged upon the dark, dusty surface.

Louise shook in her shoes. "Hurry!"

"I think I have found some things we can use. There are sticks of colour, rouge, hair pieces over here, some adhesive...for what would a woman use adhesive?"

"Those black dots that they wear on their cheeks, *Mademoiselle.*"

"We can use all of this. Do you have pockets in your frock?"

"Yes, but I am not touching her things."

"Hold your pocket open, and I will shove them in."

Tightly closing her eyes, Louise held open her side pocket while Viola filled them. A long hair piece she wadded up in her free hand and then turned to leave. "Let's get out of this mortuary. We have enough."

One hour later, Louise stood before Viola's vanity mirror, sporting the garb of a male serf, and a golden beard stuck on chunk by chunk. What survived of the hairpiece, she wore on her head, which was mostly covered by a hat. Pleased with her creation, Viola said, "It works. You are quite tall. Yes, it works."

"Good, now how do we get out of here without being spotted? If they see a male serf leaving your room or any of these upper floors, they will sound all of the alarms."

"I have that figured out. Come with me." Viola quickly darted toward the door adjoining hers and Gabriel's rooms and led Louise through the Count's chamber. Curious though she was about what items and details she may find in here, she did not stop to look, for time was of the essence. Leading her out onto the balcony, she said, "If you look around the corner here, you will see a ladder of sorts running diagonally from here down to the ground."

"Are you insane, *Mademoiselle*? I abhor heights!"

"Louise, you are somewhat of a monkey. Do you recall that time we escaped from the convent the day after you arrived? We scaled down the wall, four stories."

"*We got caught!* We were both throttled! You still bear the scars on your back, as do I! Hideous scars! And we were guarded like hawks for the remaining five years afterwards! Stuck there in that horrid prison! *Five years!*"

"This time we won't get caught. Now you go to the stable and I will meet you there. We will take two horses and go that way."

"I have a terrible feeling about this."

"Louise, we have come thus far. Now, you know that I would never force you into anything, so if you truly want to change your mind, you may stay, and I will find another way off the property by myself. But you know that I must do this. I must, Louise. I want to find my child. Nay, I *need* to find my child."

Stalling, Louise inquired, "What if *Monsieur* Ste. Germaine or His Lordship catch us?"

"*Monsieur* has gone for a ride, and His Lordship has gone to visit his father. And it is dark enough that they won't see who you really are. Let's go!"

Issuing a heavy sigh, Louise grabbed hold of the stone balcony, climbed up, and crawled to the edge...

Her heart pounding like a drum, Viola rode to the exit gate with Louise behind her. At the gate, two sentries stepped forth.

A tall one with dark, angular features bowed briefly and spoke up to her. "My lady, it is unwise to leave the premises after dark, as I am sure you are aware."

"I have an escort." She gestured back to Louise. "He is dumb, ergo, he cannot speak, but he hears and is quite able."

The sentry glanced toward Louise. "I don't recognise him."

"Here," she said, producing the forged letter from her pocket, "read this. It is written by *Monsieur* Ste. Germaine, authorising me to leave the property anytime, so long as I have an escort, which I do."

"I am unable to read." He skimmed the parchment and then glanced toward the other sentry. "Jean, do you read?"

"No. But His Lordship changed the order so that Lady Viola cannot leave without him. He didn't mention the brother's permission."

This is not going too well. Viola's knees began to feel weak. "I assure you, all is in order. *Monsieur* Ste. Germaine consulted with his brother before writing that letter. I was there."

"Neither is here for us to consult with." The first sentry said. "His Lordship has gone to meet with his father and *Monsieur* Ste. Germaine has gone for a ride."

"Heed, we will return shortly. I simply want to go out for a breath of air. I'm feeling a tad restless this eve."

"How long will you be gone, then?"

"Not more than ten minutes."

The sentries glanced toward each other, and then at her. Jean said, "If you have not returned in ten minutes, someone will come to find you. We could be seriously reprimanded for this if all is not as you claim it is."

"All is well." Viola forced a smile.

The sentries lowered the drawbridge, and they rode off into the night, down the road between the fields and the cow pastures.

The taller sentry spoke to his companion. "I don't like this feeling in my gut. The letter didn't have the red wax seal upon it. Go get your horse and follow them. Be discreet in case I am wrong. Tell Renauld to come out here and replace you until your return."

"Good idea."

"Here. Take this letter and bring someone with you in case you need him to relay a message to His Lordship. If you find that this is not as it ought to be, send the messenger to His Lordship to apprise him of the situation.

*   *   *

At the stroke of midnight, a knock fell upon the door of His Majesty's Palace. A serf delivered a verbal message and a letter to the servant who answered. The servant delivered both to one of His Majesty's mistresses, who crept quietly into the sitting room to whisper it into the King's ear and pass the letter onto him.

King Charles' expression did not shift, nor did he read the letter. After his mistress left and the door closed, he said, "Gabriel, it appears that your betrothed is on her way out of the city, on horseback, and er...she is with a man."

Gabriel's eyes went black. "Say that again?"

"You heard me."

"How do you know this?"

"One of your sentries followed her and sent this message to you." He held out the letter.

"Where is she now?" Gabriel said, as he pried open the parchment.

"I don't know, Gabriel. A messenger is waiting at the outer courtyard, beyond the gates. He will lead you back to your sentry, who will point you in the right direction."

Upon reading the forged letter of authorisation, Gabriel knew immediately that Viola had written it, for his brother never authorised anything without his approval, and he most certainly never forgot to attach the official Valois seal of validation.

As he marched purposefully toward the door, His Majesty spoke quietly behind him. "Gabriel, things are not always what they appear to be. You, of all people, know this."

He paused at the door with the knob in his tight fist. "I have been betrayed and lied to. Again."

"Heed." His Majesty said, as he stood to approach Gabriel. He placed a bony hand upon his chest and peered up into his eyes. "Do you remember what I told you when you were ten, the first time we met?"

"That we surrender our dignity by allowing people to disrespect us, or claim it by commanding respect."

"That is correct. What I'm telling you is this: Murielle robbed you of your dignity, and you allowed it. In doing so you earned her complete disrespect. She belittled you, and she shamed you. You could have ended her game swiftly, but you did not. You let your heart rule your head. Thus, you have paid a very hefty price."

His jaw set in a hard line, Gabriel admitted. "I acknowledge that fully. I live every day with that mistake when I look at my broken boy."

"Lady Viola seems to me to be a fine human being, but what I think of her is irrelevant. You are the one who lives with her. If in your heart you honestly believe that she is leading you down that same path, you do have the authority to put a stop to that nonsense once and for all. And you know what that means, I'm sure."

"*Nobody* will take me down that damned path again," Gabriel swore.

"You are my firstborn son, Gabriel. Had I been able to marry your mother, you would be next in line for the throne. I was not permitted to marry her because she was not of noble descent, however – "

"Father, you know that I don't give a damn about that. Louis can have it. I've told you that at least a dozen times and I mean it."

"I'm not finished, son. The blood that you have coursing through your veins is noble, and it is proud. Regardless who steps into my shoes, you and I both know who belongs there. You need to grow a backbone and assume your authority, knowing that whatsoever you choose to do in this matter, I will back you up. Now," His Majesty said, with a nod, "You go do what you feel is right according to your heart, your conscience, and your noble bloodline."

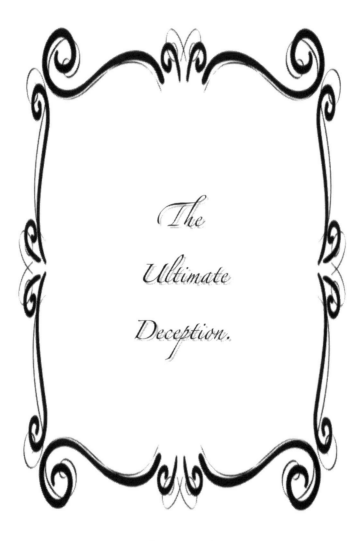

The

Ultimate

Deception.

Segment 4.

Chapter Ten.

4. am. Valmont's Study.

Valmont sat at his writing table with his hands clasped together on its dark glossy surface, nervously chewing the skin inside his lip as he observed what he would call a trial – with Gabriel being both judge and executioner. Viola and Louise stood before him, trembling in fear.

Inhaling a breath into the depth of his broad chest, Gabriel focused on Viola. "Louise, you may leave without fear of punishment, for I know that she put you up to this."

Flashing Viola a terrified glance, she said, "I am as guilty as she – "

"The only thing you are guilty of is your loyalty. I wish I could say the same for her. Go."

"No." Louise squared her shoulders and took a firm stance, though with tears shimmering in her green eyes. "I will not leave her."

"Young woman," Gabriel fastened a blackened gaze upon her, "you will go willingly or you will be removed by my sentry who stands outside the door. Either way, you will go."

"Please, do as he says," Viola whispered. "Bad enough I got you into this mess."

"But, *Mademoiselle* – "

"Go."

Gabriel swung the door open and waited for her to leave. After she did, he shut the door and stood before Viola. "You not only put your own life in danger, but you endangered the life of your best friend."

"Gabriel – "

"You have not been given permission to speak." He advised her, with eyes as hard and cold as flint. "If you two had been caught by anyone other than myself or my sentries, right now Louise would be behind bars awaiting the guillotine for impersonating a man."

"I had not considered – "

"Fortunately for her, I admire her loyalty to you. And as for you, let me advise you that you are in my realm, and within my realm I have authority to dole out punishment as I see fit, and that includes the taking of your head."

"Gabriel, that would be rash!" Valmont scrambled around the desk to speak up in her defense. "I'm sure she has a reason for what she did."

"It was your name that she forged, and me that she deceived."

"I am willing to forget that."

"I am not," Gabriel stated. "You will leave us now."

"I would rather stay," Valmont stated.

"That was an order." Gabriel once more opened the door. "Don't go far. I will summon you in a bit."

Grumbling under his breath, Valmont vacated the room, leaving them alone. Gabriel slid the forged letter from the pocket of his black surcoat and thrust it into her hands. "Why?"

"I didn't know what else to do. You forbade me to go anywhere without you, and I had to."

"So you defied me."

"Yes."

"Again. For a married man. Who does not want you."

"What?" She shook her head. *"No!"*

"A man will whisper all kinds of horse shit into a woman's ear but when push comes to shove if he – "

"No, you misunderstand. "

"If he won't make you part of his life in an open honest way, he's lying to you."

Don't you understand? I can say nothing to you! You have drawn this conclusion that there was a man involved. I cannot give you the truth, for if you knew about my past, you would despise me even more. If I told you, all doors might slam in my face, and I may never find my child!

Stepping forth, he raised a hand to run the back of his bruised knuckles along the curve of her cheek. "I loved you. I almost trusted you. Do you realise that?"

She shook her head, no. She knew he was fond of her, and jealous too, but she didn't know that it had so quickly grown into love, as her own feelings for him had.

"I thought that if I gave you your freedom, within reason for your own safety, we could build on this relationship. And you traded what I offered, for what? An absentee lover who could care less about you. So I took that freedom away to prevent you from making a fool of both of us, and you turn around and do it, anyway. Have you not one damn thing to say to me? Anything at all? Give me one reason why I should not take your head."

"I am guilty." She whispered, not at all believing that he would threaten her life in any way, because she had felt and seen the good in him – he, who would offer a wild cat shelter in his own chamber, he, who would not hesitate to come to her aid.

He held her face between thumb and fingers of one big hand and lifted her chin to peer into her eyes. "Have I not been good to you?"

A tear dropped off her lower lashes and spilled down her cheek. "You have been the very best."

"Did I not tell you straight away that if you told me how marrying me might help you fulfill your mission more expediently, I would help."

"Yes."

"And have I not asked you what it was that you needed from me, to make this work?"

"Yes."

"Then why, Viola? Why did you do this to me? Why did you trick me into believing that you were beginning to care for me, just to turn around and stab me in the back?"

"I was not thinking clearly."

"You were thinking, all right. You were thinking about how to secure your domicile in France so that you could sneak off to be with him while you were married to me. And what's worse, you used my boy and pretended to adore him to win me over. Perhaps blind me to your truth."

"No! My love for Xavier is true! You must know that!"

"What was today's plan, hm? Were you going off to meet him? Planning a little get-away together? What?"

"No."

Gabriel made a sound of disgust in his chest and strode past her to fling the door open. "Jean!"

"Yes, Your Lordship." The sentry appeared at attention.

"Take her down to the dungeon."

Valmont, who also stood in waiting outside the door, jumped in anxiously, "Gabriel, that is not necessary!"

"Yes, Your Lordship," the sentry replied, as he took Viola's elbow and led her away.

Gabriel added, "And bring my blade."

Viola's heart nearly stopped beating. She spun around and fired Gabriel a glance, the terror in her eyes flashing like black diamonds in the glow of the overhead torch. She performed the Sign of the Cross – and then dropped to the floor, unconscious.

"Have mercy!" Valmont exploded. "Do not do this! I will return her to her father a first light!"

"That option is no longer available." Gabriel squeezed through their midst, stepped over Viola, and marched toward the foyer, his heavy black boots hammering into the wood. "Carry that woman down to the dungeon."

There was too much fury, too much rage boiling inside of Gabriel's head to be able to think straight. He could not think. He could only feel. Only react to the fire blazing in his heart and in his embittered soul. That wildfire blew out of control in the root of his person – in that place within which love grew and, when betrayed, turned itself inside out like a wild beast thrashing about, trying to find some way to release itself from a trap, even if it meant chewing off its own leg. The first betrayer he had not beheaded, and had allowed her to continue hurting him over and over and damn well over again until the day she died, and the pain never stopped even when her breath did. This one would not.

He marched down the dark, narrow hall beneath the rear stairwell, and entered the *guarde robe*, where he filled a basin with cold water to splash his face. It was nearly pitch dark, but the sun would rise soon. Better to get this done with before first light. Better to take the pain and eat it before it ate him.

Without bothering to grope through the dark for a towel, he dragged his sleeve across his face and left. He found Valmont still lingering in the foyer, his visage drawn with angst. "Where is she?"

"Jean carried her down. Gabriel, do not do this, I beg you."

"Come with me. I require a witness to note the time of death, the reason, so on and so forth. Get your quill and parchment and bring it to the dungeon."

"Gabriel, do not shed her blood. You will regret it."

"I regret many things, but most especially, I regret having been used again. Get what you need. I will meet you down there."

"I do not want to partake in this."

Gabriel's nostrils flared, yet he didn't raise his voice—and it was always, always worse when he spoke in that quiet, controlled tone, for someone always died. "It is your responsibility to *partake*. You are my brother and nothing in this world will ever break that bond, but you are also my Vassal, responsible for carrying out orders as dictated by your Lord, who happens to be me. Get moving, before everyone awakens. I don't want an audience."

Swearing under his breath, Valmont hurried to his study. Gabriel left the building by the rear door and marched around the side of to the west end, where there was a heavy wooden door that had only been opened thrice since he had inherited the castle. Once, when he and Valmont had discovered this dungeon as mere boys and also discovered the mounds of old bones heaped up down there. The second time was when he had ordered Gaston to have someone come in to remove those bones so that his brother could play down there without falling over them. But even after the bones had been removed and they had opened that door the third time, they could still feel the pain and essence of those who had been tortured and died within, circulating in the cold, damp air, so they had not gone back in.

He depressed the latch and shoved the heavy door all the way, causing it to moan in its wide yawning. There was a lighted lantern sitting upon a massive wooden butcher's block upon which a body could be secured by leather straps, to be tortured in every way imaginable. It was stained with the blood of many, dating back four hundred years. Alongside the lantern, his freshly-sharpened sword glinted with its own cold anger.

It was a vast, morbid space. The damp stone walls were lined with weapons of torture hanging from roughly hewn racks, the rusted blades also stained with old, black blood. There were racks upon which to stretch a body until its limbs separated at the joints. There were instruments to cut off fingers, toes, hands, feet. Whips. Knives. It was all there.

He strode through the room until he came to a second door, and entered. In here, there were multiple restraints hooked up to the walls, where once so many captives had been held and starved while they awaited torture. The screeching of rats and the many webs of spiders told of its present occupants.

He found Viola sitting on the floor against the wall, with her knees drawn up to her chest. He could not see her face or her eyes, for it was too dark with only the meager glow of the lantern in the other room flowing within. Neither did he want to look into her eyes. "Get up. Come with me."

She rose and followed him her head down.

He gestured toward a stump on the stone floor, close to the butcher's table. "Kneel and bend over. Hang your head over the side."

She knelt and stared into the rusty pail below. It would catch her head when it fell.

"Stay as you are until my brother arrives."

He turned his back to her, unable to look.

Valmont finally entered with his quill, ink, and parchment. "I do not want to do this, Gabriel."

"Nobody's asking you to hold the sword. Do you have a timepiece with you?"

"Yes."

"Stand ready." He grabbed the blade by its handle and lifted it off the butcher's block, the tip of the cold, deadly metal singing as it scraped across the wood. Bracing his feet at shoulder's width apart, he raised the blade high.

Viola began to shake so violently that she grabbed the sides of the stump to prevent from collapsing. How difficult it was to lamely present one's neck for execution, how difficult not to fight and claw and scream, but to what avail? It would happen one way or the other. It was too late for regrets, too late for apologies, and too late for tears. All she could do now was pray, and so she did. Her voice quiet as a whisper, she prayed to God to forgive her for her many sins, and to take her soul, and to please, please look after her daughter and Louise, and to take away Gabriel's pain, for she had surely not meant to hurt him.

But she was weak. So weak and so afraid that if he did not get this done with very soon, her heart would stop and she would die before he had the satisfaction of killing her. She gasped involuntarily as Gabriel caught one side of the back of her gown and ripped it away from the other. *Our Father, Who art in Heaven, hallowed be Thy Name. Thy Kingdom come, Thy will be done, on earth as it is in Heaven...*

"Prepare yourself." He said, and replanted his feet.

Right away, Viola heard the whoosh of a blade slicing the cold air.

But the blade did not strike. Instead, she heard the sound of metal clashing to the stone floor, and an anguished, broken sob. "Damn my soul! I cannot do this!"

"Thank You! God Almighty, thank You!" Came Valmont's urgent whisper.

In her peripheral vision she saw Valmont's boots cross the room, and then she heard the scraping of the blade against stone as he picked up the sword and hastily left the dungeon with it. And then she felt a strong, trembling hand brushing over the back of her short hair. She slowly turned her head to find Gabriel kneeling beside the stump, looking at her. His dark eyes brimming with tears told her that she had broken something inside of him.

So close had she come to her own last mortal breath that the shock of still being alive rushed like needles of ice through her veins. Was it over? Was she going to be allowed to live, after all?

He whispered, "I loved you so damn much."

She could summon no strength to respond.

"Get up. Get out of here."

She tried. She wanted to get out of this horrible place more than anything on earth, but her body was paralysed, as if the blade had severed her head, but it still remained attached. *I cannot move!* She wanted to tell him. She opened her mouth, but no sound came out.

Viola turned her face toward the darkness of the pail for she could not bear to look at the misery she had caused him. For very long, heavy moments there was no sound at all. Then, as she began to accept that she would live, after all, she heard the soft "tap" of her own tears landing at the bottom of the metal pail.

She heard him rise to his feet. "Get up when you can. The door will be open." On that, he left.

Viola slid back to sit on her heels and had to use all of her strength to complete the simple act of pushing herself away from the stump. She stayed as she was until she felt as if she might be able to stand, and finally, after a couple of tries, was able to. It was with tears still streaming down her face that she left the dungeon and stepped out into the rising sun of a brand new day.

Louise came peeling around the corner of the castle, sobbing, with her arms held open wide. "Are you all right, *Mademoiselle?*"

"I don't know."

"Let's get you to your quarters. I will stay with you while you rest."

*   *   *

"I wanted to let you know that I am packing my things. I will leave on the morrow." She found Gabriel in the stable, brushing his horse, shortly before the noon's meal the next day. He was alone, his expression sombre. Dark circles around his eyes betrayed that he had not slept a wink the night before.

"Where will you go?" He asked.

"I don't know."

"Then you will stay."

"I cannot imagine why you would allow that."

"If you remained, would you still be a good mother to my son?"

"What I feel for your son is true. He's been a God-send, bringing more joy than I ever could have imagined."

He quietly conceded, "I know that."

"None of this was intended to hurt you, for you have been so good to me. Much better than I deserved."

He stopped brushing momentarily to glance at her. "Do you think that I don't understand what it feels like to be driven by a demon? To do things that you know will get you nothing but pain?"

"I don't know. You tell me nothing of your history."

" I *do* understand and if you had but trusted me, Viola, you may have...never mind, damn it. What's done is done. I have danced with that devil, and I lost. You too will lose, for those who love you will come to you freely, and they will stay. You do not have to chase after them."

"And if I stay, Gabriel...then what? What of us?"

"I will marry you as I have agreed to do, for my son does need a good mother. Despite your deception toward me, I concede that you have done more than enough to prove your devotion to him." He dropped the brush to the floor to approach her. "That was all I had in mind at the start, and that is what I will revert to."

"But in doing so, you tie yourself up to me for life, which would prevent you from finding someone you want to be with. Someone better than I."

"Do you seriously think that I will *ever* love again?"

She whispered, "I hope and pray that you will, for you deserve a good woman and a good home. I regret that it won't be me."

"It won't happen." He vowed. "There is one condition."

"And that is?"

"You are to forget Mark Simone and put your efforts into raising my son and managing our home."

"You would still take me?"

"Yes."

"If I requested to go away for a day or two with Louise, and if I swear to you by all that I hold sacred, that it will not be to do anything untoward, would you allow it?"

A bitter smile touched his mouth. "You want me to believe that by any oath that you make to me, even by all that you hold sacred, that you will begin to be honest with me *now*, after all these lies?"

"My word is all that I have."

"But your word is no damn good, Viola."

She dared to step closer to place a hand upon his chest. "I beg you to just try to trust me, for I promise you with all my heart that I will not betray you. Not ever."

His dark gaze dropping to her hand, he took it into his own and removed it. "Do not touch me."

The yearning in her steadfastly growing, she pressed on by reaching up to take his face between her hands. "I am so sorry that I hurt you."

"Don't!" He growled, and then on the next breath, slammed her against his chest and locked her into a steely embrace with his mouth hungrily devouring hers.

A fire burst within her, whose origins she could not guess for one moment it wasn't there and then it was consuming her in its infernal heat. She slid her arms upward and locked them around his neck, to greedily take whatever form of acceptance he was willing to give.

But he tore away from her in anguish and retreated as if she had burned him with her heat. "Don't ever touch me again!" He turned on his heel and marched out of the stables, into the high noon sun, his heels pounding his wrath into the earth below.

Viola left the stable and went to her room, where she decided she would remain for the rest of the day. She curled up in bed and slept through most of it, until Louise came up to deliver the evening meal, which she accepted but could not eat. It went cold on the vanity while she retreated to the balcony, where she sat at the small wrought-iron table and watched the lanterns begin to light the windows in the modest homes across the river.

Not being able to see clearly prompted her memory of the many months in that chateau, somewhere in France, while she had carried her daughter. How often had she sat at her window late at night, when her back ached from the weight of her child, staring out at nothing, imagining what the Aristocrat might look like. Assigning him a particular kind of nose, mouth, skin.

She had built him from imagination and had fallen in love with that fabrication. In her vision, the Aristocrat was the ideal man, against whom every other man in the world would have to be measured. They would have to be as tall as he was and feel the way he had felt. And of course, they would have to be gentle and soft-spoken and whisper all sorts of romantic things all of the time, no matter what life threw at them. Someday, she had so often told herself, she would meet a man just like him, and together they would have many beautiful, perfect children, and live in a peaceful place where nobody ever fought. And most of all, he would love her so much that he would never raise his voice to her in anger.

In her innocence and desperation, she had needed to be loved in a way that she had never been, and to be touched as if she were special. Yes, she had relived that passionate night with him over and over again, until the escape from her ugly reality had become so real that her heart believed it. And lastly, she had vowed that she would never marry until she found a man just exactly like him.

She had not known that to love someone, one must actually be able to put a face to them. A real face. Mustn't they need to know them in their moments of anger and sadness and joy and fear and all of those things that reality entailed? It would never be enough to just know how someone felt in bed, even if that touch was so memorable that it could still the heart time and time again. It all had to come together to form a complete picture, enhanced by the lover's beauty and bitterly challenged by the shortcomings that only love itself knew how to overcome before one could call it love and call it real.

The way she now felt for Gabriel, even after all that they had put each the through, *was* real. Even with their arguments and their unexpected moments of tenderness, and burning passions, and at last, when in his anguish he wanted to take her life but could not hurt her...that was as real as love could get.

She resolved to try her best to be a good wife and mother. Perhaps in time, he would forgive her. If she was fortunate he might learn to trust her, and if a true miracle were to happen, he would fall in love with her again.

As the cold evening breeze swept in from the Loire River, she entered her chamber and shut the door. Grabbing her black veil off of the vanity, she covered her hair, blew out the candle, and went downstairs to find Louise.

"She went out," Chantalle grumbled, as she picked up a stack of dishes and rammed them onto a shelf along the wall.

"Out?" Viola echoed, surprised. "Where?"

"For a ride with Monsieur Ste. Germaine."

"A ride?"

Chantalle whipped around to face her, hands on hips. "Are you losing your hearing, My Lady? That is what I said. She went for a ride with *Monsieur,* on horseback."

"Where is Xavier, then? Has he been put to bed yet?"

"His father is bathing him."

"Doesn't Denise do that?"

"She went out. Again."

"Oh." She turned and left the kitchen, in search for a place of warmth, for it was a chilly evening. She found it in the sitting room.

It was not a particularly large room, and it wasn't very furnished, but there were a lit hearth and a red chaise on the opposite side of the room. Red velvet drapery hung on the tall, narrow windows flanking the stone hearth, and a red and cream floral rug sat on the wood floor before it. Aside from that, there was nothing.

She sank onto the chaise and brought her knees up to hug them, and stared into the flames. Not five minutes later, Gabriel entered the room with his son in his arms. She dropped her feet to the floor and shifted to a more ladylike position, while Gabriel sank onto the mat before the crackling hearth. The child's hair was a mess of wet curls. He wore a blue nightshirt to his feet, and those adorable toes and hands poked out the hem and sleeves.

Gabriel himself wore a pair of black hose and nothing else. Splatters of water glistened across his broad shoulders, reflecting the orange light pouring out of the hearth.

He avoided acknowledging her presence, so she swallowed her disappointment and watched quietly while he played with the child on the floor for the next half hour or so. It was odd to hear Gabriel laugh so jovially, strange to see the glow in his eyes when he did. How different he was with his boy. Finally, as Xavier began to yawn, Gabriel drew him to his chest, whispering, "Have you finally exhausted yourself?"

"Kaput." The child grinned and sank into the warmth of that gentle hug. Placing the boy's cheek against his shoulder, Gabriel stroked his back while the child commenced sucking his thumb.

Viola's heart nearly burst as Gabriel closed his eyes and began to hum a lullaby, while rocking him to and fro before the crackling fire. Such a tiny little child, so secure in those large dark hands, upon a thick, powerful chest. Such a lovely illustration of strength protecting fragility. A thought came from nowhere that brought tears to her eyes.

Why can't you hold me thus? I never had that when I grew up, but I could use one of those big warm hugs right now.

And Heaven help her, but she was jealous. Jealous that he was able to hold his son in his arms and rock him to sleep, while she could only imagine and dream about doing this with her own child. She had almost found her daughter. She had got so close.

Gabriel finally stopped humming and turned his head toward her. "Are we talking or pretending the other does not exist?"

Chapter Eleven.

"That is your decision."

"I have lived that way before, Viola, and I cannot stomach the notion of doing it again."

She stood and crossed the room to drop to her knees beside them. "May I hold Xavier?"

Gabriel transferred his boy into her arms. In spite of his lingering pain of betrayal, Gabriel longed to put his arms around her. Now that his rage had exhausted itself and he was able to process things more clearly, he finally understood that she too suffered the most bitter agony she had ever known. He felt it. She loved a man who was not free and obviously would never make himself free to be with her.

Gabriel loved her. Still. He did not have whatever it took to make that go away. He had seen that wistful yearning in her whisky-brown eyes when she had set them upon Mark's little girl for the first time. He had seen it. *I wish you were mine.*

What was she doing now, as she so gently rocked Xavier? Did she imagine, in her sad, distant fantasies, what their lives together would be like if they had borne all of those children of his together? Her and Mark? In spite of his own hurt, he felt hers. Moving behind her, he closed a hand over each of her shoulders, whispering, "Viola, I am told that time heals all wounds."

"There are some beyond time's reach."

He remained as he was for a moment, then placed a gentle kiss upon her shoulder and stood. Without another word, he left the room. He was not sure that it was the right thing to do, but he didn't know what was. Of late, he had spent hours contemplating this morbid turn of events, and after the initial rage had subsided, a slew of questions had come at him from the dark, accusatory corners of his own mind.

Theirs had been a relationship built on secrets from the get-go, him keeping his from her and her holding hers from him. In truth, who was he to demand transparency from her when he did his almighty best to protect his own sordid past? Things had gone as wrong as they possibly could, and he was ashamed of himself, for nothing could be worse than a man threatening to take a woman's life in the heat of jealous rage. He hadn't been able to go through with it but all the same, he had done it. So, if she was reluctant to trust him now, who could blame her?

He went for a long stroll around the property, trying to second-guess what might be going through her mind in regards to how badly he had treated her, and he came up empty. Eventually, he returned to find her asleep on the floor with his son on top of her, also sleeping. The fire in the hearth had burnt away, leaving only smouldering embers, and a chill had crept back in. He quickly strode out to the foyer to ensure that the torches were lit along the stairs, and then returned to the sitting room to extract Xavier without waking either of them.

He carried his son upstairs, tucked him in, and then returned to the sitting room. Viola still lay sleeping on the floor. She hadn't moved a muscle, but the tracks of her dried tears extended from the corners of her eyes, back into her hairline. He collected her into his arms and carried her up the stairs, where he paused outside her door, but continued to his own quarters, instead.

It was very chilled, as his cat had come and gone again, and had left the doors open. But the servants had kept the fire in his hearth going strong. He lay her down carefully upon his bed and then strode to close the French doors. At the end of the bed, he paused to remove her shoes before stretching out alongside her.

His gaze lingering on her mouth, and then the small dark fans of her eyelashes, he thought, *I love you, my lady, and for so many reason, and I will eternally regret the abuse that I threatened against you.*

He loved that she could crack the hard shell of his sobriety and make him smile. He loved that she stood up to him when backed against a wall. He loved that she had a scared little girl inside of her that required him to step it up and become her hero. He even liked that she kept her own counsel because he was that way, too...but did she have to do that around *him?* He admired that she would rather die than let go of what she believed in. It took the bullocks of a stallion to do that.

When he had slashed open her gown to make her neck more readily accessible for her beheading, he had seen the grid-work of white scars etched across her back from floggings she had taken in her past. It was then that it struck him like a bolt of lightning – she and he were even more alike than he had realised. She too bore the physical scars of battle. That iron-clad will that made a person arrive at a place where they thought, *damn you, you can beat me, you can torture me, you can rip me to shreds, and you can even take my life, but you WILL! NOT! BREAK! ME!*

It was in that life-changing moment that the question roared inside his head—*what the hell has this woman endured? Who has done this to her?* He had realized in that instant that she was who she was because someone or something in her past had made her that way. That was when his hands began to shake around that sword's handle. That was when he broke.

He understood this woman, even though she didn't seem to realise it. He understood that if one wanted a thing, they had to chase after it...but he just hated that it wasn't him she wanted.

Still, hadn't he done the same damn thing in his first marriage? Hadn't he put up with her horse shit, time and time and time again, always rationalising on her behalf because he just hadn't wanted to see what was real. His love for her had blinded him to the truth.

And so it was for Viola. She, being ten years younger than him, still had to learn this. And if he were any kind of man he would have taken that knowledge and offered her compassion when he had caught her trying to sneak off, instead of losing his head and wanting to take hers, too. But his deeply-rooted fear of failing at this game again had sent him over the edge. The only question now was, what would he do about his feelings for her? What were the chances of her ever loving him when she loved another?

Gabriel slid his arm under her head, and the other around her waist, unintentionally crushing her in his embrace as a rush of emotion tore through him.

She stirred, her smoky eyes fluttering open to gaze into his, and sat up with a jolt. "I'm sorry. I fell asleep. I'll leave now."

"Stay. Be my wife tonight. Let the ceremony be the formality to satisfy the church and the law, but let us make this commitment to each other in the flesh tonight."

"What?" She blinked.

"Stay with me tonight."

She stared at him in disbelief. "What happened? What changed?"

"*I* have changed. Stay with me tonight." He repeated yet again.

"Um...I cannot do that, Gabriel. I have made enough mistakes in my life, enough immoral acts to earn me the beheading that I almost got from you. I don't want to add to them."

"Is it that you don't want me touching you in that way?"

"You are a beautiful man." She whispered. "I would be insane not to want that with you."

"Is that what you really feel?"

"Yes. It is."

"Then stay, and just let us allow ourselves this time to get close in other ways. We could simply talk."

"You want this, after all that I have done?"

"My behaviour was even worse. I was an abominable beast, and I am very sorry."

"As am I."

"I detest losing control over situations going on right under my nose." He said. "Can we try this again?"

She reclined on her side and slid her arm about his waist, whispering, "Yes, please."

"Will you stay?"

"I will."

Snuggled into his warm embrace, Viola realised that she felt truly safe for the first time in her entire life. As the hours of darkness passed and the fire in the hearth died out a distinct chill swept over her, but she did not move. She lay still, inhaling the masculine scent of him, and listening to his deep, steady breathing.

She brought her hand around to place it over his beating heart, knowing that he held a part of her within its chambers. She felt the hardness of his thighs sealed against hers and longed more than anything to wake him up and accept his offer, but she didn't do that, either. Time was needed to heal the wounds that they had inflicted upon each other.

So many volatile moments had exploded between them in so short a time. Was that what passion did to a person? Did it make them insane? Did it drive them to do things that they would not ordinarily do? Did it, in spite of one's most profound sorrow and most agonising fury, create a new place within that allowed forgiveness of the unforgivable?

Did it drop you to your knees?

With tears welling up in her eyes, she slid her arm around his waist and sealed her face into the warm crook of his neck. She vowed that somehow, some way, she would tell him soon about her past and all the terrible things that she had done, and try to put enough trust in him to give him the benefit of the doubt.

Trust had to begin somewhere, and in these moments, she decided that it would start with her. On the morrow, she decided, she would tell him all of her secrets and hope for the best. With that thought in her mind, she fell asleep.

In the hours of predawn the sound of a child crying awakened her with a jolt. She sat up and stared into the blue light of dawn creeping in through the French doors, listening to hear it again. Was it real? Or had she dreamed of birthing her daughter again?

The cry came once more.

Xavier! She carefully extracted herself from Gabriel's arms and left the room, to find the poor thing crawling around in the corridor. Scooping him into her arms, she whispered, "Shhh, little man. Let us not wake up your Papa, all right? He is tired. She noticed then that the child was soaked in urine. He locked his small arms around her neck and held on for dear life as she carried him into her own chamber.

She whispered, "Did you have a bad dream?"

"I dreamed I was fa-falling!" He sniffed, "I made a mess in my bed...I called Denise to he-help me...but she di-didn't come!"

"Do you know," she whispered, "when I was your age, I wet the bed so many times. I was terrified of spiders, and there were many of them in my room at the back of the palace."

He stared at her through shimmering brown eyes, his small body shivering, he said, "I'm cold. Denise forgot to fire my hearth."

"Well, look out the window over there." Mindless of his urine seeping into her own clothing, she carried him across the room. "See? Dawn is chasing away the night, and Mister Sun is on the rise. We will go to your chamber and get you some fresh clothing, and then we will take these wet ones off. We will go downstairs and clean you up and dress you. If there is any of Chantalle's delicious bread left, I will put some Punic Apple sauce on it for you to eat. How does that sound?"

"Good." With one long, shivering inhale, the last of his tremors passed, and he relaxed in her arms.

Kissing his cheek, she left her chamber and carried him down to his, where together they selected an outfit from his bureau. Viola sat him at the end of his bed and began removing his blue nightdress, which was a tricky task when the wet fabric wanted to cling to his skin. As she managed to pull it up over his head, her heart nearly stopped, for there in the pit of his tiny arm, was a birthmark somewhat like her own. There could not possibly be two birthmarks like this in this whole wide world, could there?

She nearly dropped to the floor like a stone, but very quickly recovered her senses for his sake. Her mind raced with thoughts that made sense but more that did not. She had given birth to a girl, hadn't she? They all said so – the housekeeper, the groundskeeper, the midwife, *Monsieur* Ste. Louis – they all said she had birthed a daughter! How was this possible? Had they deliberately lied to her to keep her in the dark? Why not? They would have done anything to guard that child's identity. Was Xavier her son? Was it possible that this birthmark was a coincidence? Was Gabriel the Aristocrat?

Could this be?

She did not have time to indulge herself at present because the child was freezing and afraid, and he needed her to be strong. Though her hands shook, she finished disrobing him and wrapped him in a small blanket, which she found in his bureau. She gathered up his clean clothing and carried all of this down the two sets of stairs.

She followed the lights of the wall torches in the narrow hall of the back end of the castle, finally finding Chantalle already hard at work in the kitchen. The head servant didn't look up from her task of pounding dough.

"What rouses you at this hour?" the Head Housekeeper mumbled.

"Xavier wet the bed. I must clean him up."

Chantalle hurried around the table with both beefy arms open. "Give him to me. I will take care of things from here."

"I can do it."

"You can go clean yourself up. You too, reek of urine. Give him to me. If you will, My Lady."

"Xavier, do you want to go with Chantalle?"

Xavier locked his arms around the woman's neck. "Yes."

Viola nodded and stepped back. "As long as he feels safe and warm, that is all that matters."

"Indeed." Grunted the servant. She stepped around Viola and headed down the hall. "That miserable woman did not return when she was supposed to."

Following her, Viola inquired, "About whom do you speak?"

"Denise! Who else? She was supposed to return yesternight. She did not. Again! I have been telling his Lordship for months that she was useless but does he listen? No. How did you know he was having a problem?"

"I found him crawling around in the corridor."

"Well, thank God somebody is looking out for him! He could have fallen down the stairs and killed himself! Grab me a torch from the hall, will you?" She commanded, as she straight-armed the door and entered the dark *guarde robe.*

Viola snagged a torch from the wall and carried it in. She used it to light several candles and then knelt before the small hearth in the bathing room to begin arranging kindling to start a fire.

Chantalle asked, "Do you know where Yolande sleeps?"

"I have never been into the servants' quarters."

"Continue down the corridor to the end. Rap on that first door and tell her to get up, that you want her to quickly boil some water for a small bath."

"I could boil the water."

"That is not your duty." Chantalle tightened the blanket around Xavier's body and sat him upon a stool near the tub. "You stay there, beloved. You are safe now."

"I wouldn't mind."

"I would." Chantalle turned to face her, and her big square face was red with fury. "Don't you see, this is our problem around here? Those who are supposed to do their jobs do not. Those who are not supposed to, cover the tracks of the lazy ones. We require at least four more indoor servants, but we have me, one lazy cow, one who is supposed to tend to that child's every need but her head shoved up the arse of whichever man she is obsessed with that week. Louise has been God-send, but the rest are useless! Everything runs amok! His Lordship thinks he has everything under control, but he is not a woman, he does not do these menial chores, ergo, he seems to think that they get done by themselves when it is I who breaks my back trying to keep up!"

Chantalle sucked in a deep breath before continuing on with her rant. "So, do I require you to boil water? *No!* I require you to own your position as the future Countess of this place, and help me to get this mess organised! I don't need another lazy Countess who cares more about shopping for jewellery than selecting the proper servants to get things done!"

Viola stood back in utter shock, her mind still reeling from the new-found hope that Xavier might possibly be her own child, and now, listening to all of this from a woman who seldom spoke and when she did, it was always just an irritated grunt or insult. But alas, she understood what the problem was.

"Nobody listens!" Chantalle finalised.

"I was not aware. But now that I know, you may count on me to do what must be done." Viola turned and left the room to hurry down the hall and rouse the sleeping Yolande. Afterwards, she took a pitcher of water from the vat in the kitchen and returned to her chamber to remove her wet clothing and get washed up.

It was only as she stood naked before the looking glass and raised her arm to inspect her birthmark, that she broke down and cried. How in the world was she going to ascertain if Gabriel had been the Aristocrat? A thing so small as a birthmark could be just a coincidence. Really, the child did not resemble her in the least. He was identical to his father. But supposedly, the Aristocrat had died of Lung Fever. Or perhaps that was also a lie. What a mess this was.

She could ask, she thought. But then quickly dismissed that notion. As she dried her eyes with her towel and marched into the adjoining dressing room to select a gown, she thought that while she was ready to begin trusting, Gabriel was not exactly willing to talk about anything in his past. It was entirely possible that if he was the Aristocrat, he had intimate relations with her behind his late wife's back in order to create an heir, which could have, in some way, led to her demise. That could be a very touchy subject, and she certainly didn't want to set him off again. Not this quickly after the last go-round. No, she had to find out another way.

"Mademoiselle?" Louise called from the corridor and knocked on her door. "May I enter?"

"Come in!" She called out, as she slipped on white underdress and did up the front lace.

Louise wandered in with a basin full of water. "I brought you...oh."

"Yes, I have already washed. How are you?"

"I am fine, *Mademoiselle.* How are you?"

"Everything is working out." Viola tied a bow at the front of her underdress and tucked it inside, then reached for the pale green gown that she had not yet worn.

Louise hurried over to help her slide the bulk of it over her head. "He is speaking to you again?"

"Yes. But Louise," Viola poked her head through the top of the green fabric, "I discovered something that has got me in knots."

"What is that?"

"Xavier has a birthmark under his arm, just like mine."

"Has he?"

"Yes."

"And?"

"He could be my son."

"You gave birth to a girl-child, *Mademoiselle.*" Adjusting the many folds of this extravagant gown, Louise glanced up at her with a gentle smile.

"You were in that room with me when I gave birth. Did you actually see her girl parts?"

"Well, no. The midwife wrapped her so quickly. I only believed what they said to you—that you had a girl."

"That's my point. And now, this birthmark."

"Many people have birthmarks in exactly the same places but are not in any way related."

"I know, Louise, but my babe did have one there. I saw one before they took the child away."

"*Mademoiselle,* the babe was covered in blood. Your water broke many hours before your very traumatic delivery. It was a dry birth, and you bled a great deal. The lighting was inferior. It could have been a spot of dark blood or tissue or something stuck to the flesh."

"Louise, please? Can I not grab onto something to believe in?"

Issuing a heavy sigh, Louise whispered, "Perhaps there may be more to it. How will you find out?"

"I don't know." Viola's shoulders sagged. "After my near-beheading, I'm reluctant to do anything so possibly volatile as ask him outright if he fathered a child with a stranger in the dark. No, it's too touchy. He hates talking about his past as much as I do."

"Well, if he had the chance to take your head and did not, he won't hurt you now."

"I'm not worried about him laying a hand on me in anger, Louise. I'm worried about our relationship. We require time to mend things before jumping on another ride that might pound the hell out of both of us."

"Turn around so I can lace you up."

Viola turned, her mind still processing.

"I have an idea."

"What is that?"

"Well, if you could recreate that night...no, never you mind   Hang that idea," Louise said.

Viola spun around. "Finish your thought. I am desperate here."

"No, it would require you to perform an indecent act."

"Tell me!" She nearly shouted, and then quickly added on a quieter note. "Please."

"I am sorry I mentioned it at all."

"Louise. What were you going to say? If I could recreate that night...?"

"Well, you have often told me that the touch of the Aristocrat was one you would never forget as long as you lived. Yes?"

"Yes, and....oh. Oh...I understand..."

"Yes. But you would have to get into His Lordship's bed and

do...*things*...with him, in a completely dark room, to see if you note anything familiar about the way it does...*it*. And if you are wrong about this, then you would be guilty of bedding a man before wedlock."

Viola slanted her a moot glance. "Don't you think it's too late for me to worry about my chastity at this stage of the game?"

Louise shrugged. "I was simply pointing that out."

"The idea has merit."

"But if you get caught...oh, dear."

"How does one get caught when one is doing something the other will surely enjoy, and when the process of ascertaining certain facts only transpires inside of one's head? If he turns out to be the Aristocrat, then I may rejoice for I have found my dau—I mean, son. Whatever. And if he turns out not to be, then I will have to continue my search, only be more careful about it in the future."

"I am sure you will find a way to botch it up." Louise frowned. "You always do. And I mean that in a nice way."

"Well..." She couldn't dispute that fact, so she had no comment. But she thought, *the only question now, is how do I go about climbing into his bed to do any of this, when just last night I declined in favour of behaving in a morally acceptable manner?*

"I can see your wheels spinning," Louise twirled her index finger through the air, "and that frightens me."

"Shhh. I'm thinking." She turned around. "Please finish lacing me up while I process this some more."

After Louise left with the basins and dirty towels, she returned to deliver a treat to Viola. Some of Chantalle's bread with reheated gravy from yesternight's meal, and a pot of mint tea. It wasn't quite breakfast in bed, but it was close enough, for this was another day she was still alive – she was counting them now that she had come so close to losing her head. The sun was shining, and she might be one step closer to finding her child and getting the man of her wildest dreams.

She smiled at her dearest friend. "Thank you."

"Where do you want it, *Mademoiselle?*"

"Out there." She gestured toward the balcony and quickly opened the door.

Louise set the tray down out on the table and then turned to leave.

"Aren't you going to eat with me? There's enough for two."

"I would love to, but I must go help in the kitchen."

"I understand Chantalle has a horrible time getting things done around here."

"Yes. I am glad to help." Louise said. "It makes me feel useful."

"She appreciates it."

"She doesn't show it." Louise showed her a twisted grin. "But that is all right."

"She said you were a God-send."

"Did she?"

"Yes."

Louise's green eyes twinkled. "I am glad."

"I am going to try to get more help in here."

"That would be nice. Thank you."

"May I ask you something?"

"You may ask me anything," Louise said. "You know that."

"You have gone riding with *Monsieur*, correct?"

A warm glow instantly infused her cheeks. "Yes."

"Is there something developing with him?"

"Something small," Louise admitted. "I am drawn to him."

"He's a wonderful man. I would find him appealing myself if he didn't have straw for hair."

"He has lovely hair. It's soft and nice to touch."

Viola's dark eyebrows lifted. "What were you doing with your hands in his hair?"

"I'm not telling."

In spite of herself, Viola had to grin. "All right then. I meant the colour. I don't like like that color of hair on men."

"I like it. It's almost like mine. May I go now?"

"Of course. Have fun pretending not to notice him moving about down there. It works like a charm, I hear."

Viola stepped out onto the balcony, and into the fresh spring air and warm, glowing sunshine.

"Good morrow." Gabriel's sleep-ridden voice came from the other side of the partition.

She hurried to peer around the stone wall. "Good morrow. Did you sleep well?"

"Like a log." He said. "Yourself?"

"Good." Her gaze skimming down his front, she admitted shyly, "You are very nicely put together."

"Not too shabby for a man who slept in his hose?"

"I would imagine you look even better without them."

"You've already seen me bare arsed in the tub."

"I didn't allow myself to look."

He reached for the drawstring on his hose. "I could sate your curiosity in a heartbeat."

"No, don't!" She laughed. "At least, not yet."

His smile draining, Gabriel leaned both elbows on the ledge and gazed out at the river. "I enjoy taunting you, as I'm sure you know. But you don't have to feign interest if it is not genuine, Viola."

"It is genuine, I assure you."

"Is it?" He glanced toward her, his eyes searching hers.

"You're utterly gorgeous, Count Gabriel. If I wasn't trying to turn over a new leaf so as to become a woman of honor, Lord knows what I would do to you right now. I doubt that you could summon up those images even with your overactive imagination."

"Good God. Is there a beast lurking within you, that is yet to be unleashed?"

"There might be."

He reached over to lightly grace the back of his knuckles down the side of her neck and across her collarbone. "You had me the minute I saw your face. Do you know that?"

"I didn't know that."

"You with that insanely adorable boy's hair cut. But what pretty well sealed the deal was when you told me to kiss your *bony arse*."

"I did say that, didn't I?"

"Yes. And the more I envisioned myself doing that, the more I wanted to. I still do." He leaned further to graze his lips over her neck, "I want to possess you and obsess you and set a fire in your belly that will never give you peace."

Her eyes fluttering shut, she nearly lost her balance but caught the stone ledge to stabilise herself. "Please do."

"I don't know what has changed within you to have you behaving this way toward me, but I'm going to make it my life's work to make you forget Mark Simone, beginning right here and right now."

"Mark who?" She teased.

"Are you seeing me as I touch you, Viola? Or him? I need to know that."

"There is only you. I was never interested in him in the way that you assumed, nor him in me."

"I know what I saw."

"You *think* you know." She said. "But you were wrong. You allowed your temper to rule your thinking, as I so often do myself."

"Prove it."

"How?"

He made direct eye contact with her. "Marry me today."

"Say again?" She blinked.

"Forget all of the pomposity that everyone else would want to drown us in, and marry me. Just you and I, and two witnesses. I cannot wait anymore to have you as my lover and my wife."

"Just like that?"

"I'm waiting for an answer, Viola."

"When and where?"

"At the Cathedral. I will meet you there at eight this evening. I will bring Valmont as a witness, and you may bring Louise." He withdrew out of her sight.

"Gabriel?"

He reappeared. "Yes?"

"We need more indoor servants."

"Do we?" His forehead creased. "I thought we had plenty. There are only three of us to tend to. Four with you, I suppose, but even so."

"We need more servants," she repeated, "because this is a massive castle. Haven't you noticed that most of it never gets cleaned properly?"

"I never bother to look. I trust that they will get the job done."

"It isn't getting done."

"Then get more from the outbuilding and bring them inside. Lord knows we have the space to keep them."

"How many more?"

"Whatever you think, my lady. You don't need to ask my approval for this sort of thing. Just do it."

"Seriously?"

"It's your home. Manage it. I will frankly be relieved not to have to think about it anymore."

"Thank you."

"No worries. Anything else?"

"No." She answered.

"I will see you at eight. You had better not run away again."

She feared that he was beginning to be able to read her mind, because all of a sudden that thought *did* cross her mind. As crazy as she was about this man, what was his reaction going to be when he learned about her sordid past, and that it was unfitting for her, as a commoner with no noble blood, to marry a Count without first telling him of her true lineage—or the lack thereof.

Oh, my God. What have I gone and done this *time?*

"Chantalle, I have rounded up a dozen women from the outbuildings to help inside. They are in the foyer, awaiting your instructions."

"A dozen?" The head servant tossed another block of wood into the outdoor spit, to get a good fire going before hooking a side of skewered beef over the rack.

"Yes." Viola nodded. "Select the best ones, as only you know what you need, and simply dismiss the ones you don't need. You may put them up wherever you deem fit."

"As you wish, My Lady. How did you get him to agree to this?"

"I asked."

"Well," she said, straightening up to jam her hands onto her wide square hips, "I asked before, but I couldn't even get an answer."

"I suppose it's imperative to get his full attention first."

"How does one accomplish that?"

"Um..."

"Never you mind." The Head Housekeeper relented a small grin. "Thank you."

"Is there anything else you needed, Chantalle?"

"It would be nice to have some furniture in the place, but perhaps not so much that Xavier will ram his chair into it."

"All right. Do you want to shop for these things?"

"No." Chantalle said. "I have already too much to do. You do it."

"I have terrible taste in furniture. And I've never done this before."

"Ask someone who knows. There are people to give advice about these things. *Monsieur* Ste. Germain can direct you."

"All right. Did Denise return?"

"Yes. Finally. She's in her quarters resting. She said the visit with her *kin* was a tiring one."

"Is there nothing else she can do that would be more suitable? Perhaps she doesn't enjoy children."

"Pah! All she wants is to marry and have someone else take care of her." Chantalle huffed, as she tossed another log into the spit. "She's but a peasant who wants the life of an Aristocrat's wife, that one."

"What should we do about her?" Viola inquired.

"Send her to the outbuilding where she belongs. She can do outdoor duties. Her life has been too soft."

"Well, I don't want to do that, but add her to the clean-up team who will work on the old section of the castle. Perhaps if she can head that group. A bit of empowerment may get her on the right track."

"What will we do with that space?"

"I don't know. We can figure that out later. Where is Xavier?"

"He is with *Monsieur* Ste. Germaine. Yolande! Yolande, where are you taking that beef?"

"To the kitchen."

"Then why am I firing up the outdoor spit? Do you think I have been stoking this fire for the good of my health?"

"Oh, *shit!*" Viola exploded, as she turned suddenly and ran around the end of the castle, nearly knocking over Yolande. She tumbled into the front door, bellowing, "Louise! Louise! I need your help!"

Chapter Twelve

At eight that evening, a carriage pulled up to the side street upon which sat the Ste. Michel Cathedral, just as Father Jacques left the building to stroll around the property. It was a lovely evening, and he appeared to be simply getting a breath of air as Valmont and Gabriel approached him.

Seeming to expect opposition from the priest, Gabriel squared his shoulders before informing the good Father that he wanted to marry Viola—immediately. Father Jacques was clearly displeased. "Marriage is sacred and ought not to be entered into in such an impulsive manner."

"Well," Gabriel said, as he ticked off the numbers on his long fingers, "there are three ways that we could do this. One – you could marry us to assure your own good conscience that our marriage is condoned by our church and our religion. I am Catholic, and so is my betrothed so we would prefer that. Two – I could get the King to declare us married, which would not be condoned by the church, but still be legal according to the laws of the Franks. Or three—I could exercise my own authority as Lord of my region and pronounce us married after two individuals witness the physical joining of our flesh as one. Which would you prefer?"

Father Jacques shuddered. "That is fairly close to bestiality, to perform such illicit acts before others."

"They would be outside the room, but they would be close enough to hear. Either way, it's going to get done today. What say you?"

On a heavy sigh, the priest turned and swung open the side door.

"Very well. Where is the bride, then?"

Gabriel glanced at Valmont. Valmont shrugged. "I gave orders to Jean, the sentry, to deliver her and Louise here for eight, by carriage. I apprised Louise of the situation much earlier today."

"Well, Hell's breath!" Gabriel swore, "I bet she ran again! I bet you she is halfway back to Italy by now. That woman is going to drive me insane!" He pivoted to leave but stopped abruptly to turn and point at the priest. "You. I want you to go to my home and wait there for me there. Bring your Bible!" On that, he stalked toward the carriage with Valmont trotting behind.

"Gabriel, what are you planning?"

"I'm going to find that woman, and she will marry me—*tonight*."

"If she has decided to run off again, how will you accomplish that?"

"We're going to see my father. He will dispatch soldiers to find her and bring her back. This wedding will get done, by God!"

*   *   *

Viola and Louise were, indeed, about to leave the city boundaries when they were stopped by two Knights, by order of King Charles VII. They had been able to persuade Jean, the sentry, to allow them to ride to the church on horseback so that Viola could go to the cathedral to marry Count Gabriel. The excuse that she gave this time was that they all wanted to return to the castle in one carriage. The sentry had seemed pleased that this marriage would finally be over with soon, and let them go.

At the last minute, Viola could not bring herself to marry Gabriel without him knowing that she was a commoner, which wasn't something she had concerned herself about while searching for her daughter had taken priority. Actually, it had been the least of her concerns. However, when push had come to shove, and she realised the severity of the crime she would be committing by marrying him under false pretences—she had panicked. The last go-round of nearly getting her head chopped off had sent her into a blind fury. He had to know who she really was before the marriage could happen...and she needed time to work up the courage to tell him these things. Just a few days, she had told herself. And then she would return to the castle and get this all straightened out. Alas, here she was, once again nabbed while trying to make a run for it.

"I told you this was a bad idea," Louise whispered, as the Knights walked them toward a carriage that they had brought with them, which driven by another Knight who sat up in the driver's box, and a fourth Knight who sat inside the carriage to ensure that they did not somehow slip away again while in their custody.

They climbed up into the carriage and remained silent after that. Viola's heart thundered during the long ride to the castle and raced even faster as they were led from the carriage, into the front entrance of the building.

Gabriel was pacing in the formal foyer when they arrived. He glanced at Viola with a deeply furrowed brow, but commanded the Knights to bring them into the Great Room, while leading the way.

There sat the King of France, the priest, and *Monsieur* Ste. Germaine, at one of the tables. The Knight escorting them addressed the King. "Your Majesty. We found them as they were about to leave the city."

King Charles VII stood. "Shut the door on your way out, Guillaume." He waited until the door clicked before turning his eyes on Viola. "Lady Viola, why did you run? Do you not want to marry Gabriel?"

I am in so much trouble. Viola offered a nervous bow and saw absolutely no way to wriggle her way out of this one. "Your Majesty, it behoves me to admit that if I married him, I would be doing so under false pretenses, for I am not of noble blood."

"Explain yourself," Gabriel demanded. "And for the love of all that is holy, don't lie again."

"I...I was adopted by the Medici's." Viola confessed.

"Which Medici is your father, again?" The King wanted to know.

"The Baron," Gabriel grumbled. "Mario."

"Ah, yes." Said the King. "So, *you're* the adopted one."

Viola's brown eyes snapped up to meet his. "You know about me?"

"I know more about Mario than he knows I know, my dear." The King began to pace, while he spoke. "The Medici family goes back to the closure of the 12th century. They were a Patrician class—not noble, so even your braggart of a father has no noble blood in his veins.

Through commerce, they acquired enormous wealth and the political influence which inadvertently accompanies this prosperity. Eventually, a member of this family held the post as a *Gonfaliere* of Florence. That family's wealth and political influence increased until *Gonfaliere Salvestro* de Medici led the commoners in the rebellion of the *Ciompi*. Salvestro's brutal regime ultimately led to his own downfall. He was expelled in 1382. The family's fortune then diminished. Giovanni de Medici, who became *Gonfaliere* in 1421, eventually restored their wealth, and in fact, added to it. Giovanni's son, Cosimo, came into power in Florence, in 1434. Mario was a common farmer before the very generous Cosimo provided him with a palace and a post in Florence. I believe he's in charge of tax collection, is he not?"

Viola nodded.

"His palace was a gift from Cosimo." Said the King. "Pardon my vulgarity but that narcissistic little prick, Mario, bestowed the Baroni title upon himself and nobody bothers to correct him, as he is a trifle daft and suffers from delusions of grandeur, to boot. Mario is what I would call an opportunist who rides on the coattails of his illustrious cousins. Ergo," King Charles VII flicked a wrist dismissively, "I knew all along that you had no true noble blood in your veins, so it appears to bother you more than me. Does it bother you that she has no noble blood, Gabriel?"

"Hell, no!" Gabriel spat. "Why should it?"

"Marry them. I will be a witness." His Majesty turned his eyes upon the priest. "Get it done fast. I want to go home and get some sleep."

Without much ado, the priest flipped his Book to the appropriate page, and within moments, Viola was a married woman. Whether she wanted to be or not.

Fortunately, she wanted to be. This time.

*   *   *

Viola stood before the vanity mirror with not a stitch on, deciding that looked like a picket. If one were to line up a few hundred like her, they could plant them into the ground to create an enclosure for pigs. She dropped into a chair before the vanity with her face in her hands.

What a day. I need a drink.

Her husband awaited her in the adjoining room, and she was afraid to go to him. Not because she wasn't looking forward to this intimacy. She craved it with all her being, but she was back to worrying about her most urgent situation again. She was afraid of what she might discover in the dark, in his arms. If he were the Aristocrat, she would have to reveal to him that she was the woman he had bedded in the dark to create his son – the same woman who had agreed never to return to France in her lifetime. The same one who had been willing to do something so horrible as to sell her own son. How would he take that?

If he were not the Aristocrat, she would still have to tell him about her past because she could no longer keep this secret from him. She had put this off as long as she could and her time had run out. How would he react?

Regardless of which way it went, she would look evil. Even so, she prayed with all her heart that he was the Aristocrat because then, she will have found her child, at long last. If he was not, then she already did find the most wonderful of loves. She hoped and prayed that he would still love her after he discovered her dark, sordid past.

I seriously do need a drink. Or ten.

A few more moments wouldn't hurt anything, she decided. She threw on her long grey nightdress in the event that she ran into anyone, and left the room. The corridor was barely lit, for there was only one torch burning and it was spasmodic. A tiny flicker here and there, too small to be useful. The others had burned completely dry.

She began tiptoeing down the corridor to prevent Gabriel from hearing anything, but then she spotted the barely distinguishable form of a female person exiting Murielle's room. Or it could be male if he was wearing a long tunic, she supposed. It was hard to tell. She quickly darted back to her room and shut the door, leaning back against it. Who was that? And what was she or he doing in there?

She opened the door a crack to peer out. There was no-one. People did not just disappear. Her heart hammering, she temporarily forgot about her mission to find a drink and decided to investigate.

Darting to the intersection of the corridors, she turned right and proceeded slowly down the hall until she came to the door that separated the front of the castle from the rear, and then followed the narrower corridor to the stairs. Which way to go? Down the stairs? Or down that narrow hall to those dark, tiny, dingy rooms? She peered down the totally dark hallway and decided against that. The person could be in any one of the rooms. On the other hand, if she encountered her or him in the stairwell, that could be just as dangerous.

She decided to turn back and did so swiftly. She entered her room and knocked on the adjoining door, whispering, "Gabriel?"

He answered, "Come in."

"We may have a problem."

The door swung open, and he stood in the glow of his blazing hearth, wearing only a towel and a smile. "You didn't have to knock."

"We may have a problem." She repeated.

"We have had problems from the get-go." He smiled. "What is it this time?"

"I was headed down to the kitchen for a bottle of wine when I saw someone coming out of that chamber at the end."

"Are you sure?" His smile drained.

"I'm positive. I could not tell if it was male or female as the torches in the corridor have burned dry. But I saw someone. I ran back here and ducked into my own chamber, then when I peered out, there was nobody. I went down the halls to investigate but saw no-one, and I didn't want to venture into the back end rooms because they give me chills and it is pitch black there."

"Coming to fetch me was the right decision. Come in, my lady." He tugged her into his room and, with his back to her, dropped the towel and reached into his armoire to yank out a fresh pair of hose. Hauling them on, he said, "Stay put. I will return as soon as I can."

"All right."

He headed for the door leading to the corridor. "There are a few bottles of excellent wine in the corner out on the balcony. And a corkscrew on the table out there, as well." He gestured toward the hearth, "Keep the fire going."

Gabriel inspected the entirety of the third level, including Murielle's old chamber and the small chambers at the back, and found absolutely no-one. Xavier was sound asleep. He descended the stairs and went to Valmont's chamber to rap on his door.

His brother answered the door naked and flushed, with heavy-lidded eyes. "This had better be important."

Beyond Valmont's shoulder, Gabriel spotted a flaxen-haired woman with pale flesh lying in the bed with her back to the door. He had an idea who that might be but pretended not to notice. Where Valmont dipped his wick was nobody's business but his own. "There may be an intruder on the property."

"What do you mean?"

"Viola spotted someone on the third level, but then he or she disappeared. I searched that level completely and saw nothing."

"Go back to bed and get laid," Valmont said. "You might be easier to live with. I'll go round up a few sentries to search this place from one end to the other."

"Do you think that's necessary? Presently, we need only be concerned with who is inside. Right?"

"Right. So what are you proposing?"

"Come with me. We will split up. I will take this level, you can have the main. Check every chamber. If all is well, then leave a note under my door, and I will do likewise for you. If there is a problem, send someone up here to get me. And bring a blade with you just in case."

"All right. I will get a few sentries to stand guard at the front and rear doors for the rest of the night."

"Perfect." Gabriel nodded. "Hopefully, we will both get back to bed before the hour."

"Let me get dressed and I'll be on my way."

One hour later, Gabriel returned to his quarters and quietly let himself in. Neither he nor Valmont had found anyone in the castle who shouldn't be there. The fire in the hearth was dead as a doornail. His bride was sound asleep across his bed with an empty wine bottle lying beside her, and the glow of a full moon slanting in across her face.

Disrobing, he thought that given the occasion, she might have stayed awake. But then he decided that she must feel safe in the knowledge that he would handle things for her to relax this much. That was, decidedly, very good. He bypassed the trouble of creating another fire and stretched out alongside her, placing his hand on her belly. "I am back."

She groggily peeled her eyes open. "I fell asleep. I'm sorry." A bit of a slur, there, too. "Did you find anyone?"

"Nobody at all."

"I know what I saw." She slurred.

"Yolande entered Murielle's room because somehow the door had come ajar. She went in to see if anyone was in there and promptly left. She returned to the main floor by way of the turret stairs."

"Oh," Viola muttered. "I wonder how that door came open by itself?"

"You didn't go in there, did you?"

"Me? *Noooo.*"

He studied her closer. "You're lying again."

"Um..." she twirled a finger in the air. "Maybe just for a few moments. To get cosmetics. To make Louise look like a man. That night. When we rode off. That night. Maybe I didn't close the door. Um...properly."

Observing her profile illuminated in this silvery moonlight, he whispered, "Forget it. You are exquisite."

"I am a bony wreck."

"Ah, but you are *my* bony wreck, and I adore you." Gliding his palm over her belly, Gabriel asked, "Were you so afraid that you had to get sloshed?"

"Still am."

"Of what?"

"I don't know what to expect." She shyly admitted.

He rolled onto his back and pulled her atop himself. She whispered. "You're naked."

"You're only noticing now?"

She laughed. "*Really* noticing now."

"Are you sorry that we had somewhat of a forced wedding?"

"No. I suppose I was worried about nothing...that noble blood thing, I mean."

"You need to get over your habit of running away." This was very nice, he thought. It was different than he expected. It was comfortable. Easy. It felt *right*. "Tell me something. From where did you get the scars upon your back?"

"You noticed that, did you?"

"Yes."

"Floggings. I was committed to a convent for five years. I tried to escape. I got caught."

"I am sorry to hear that. Do they bother you?"

"No." She studied his eyes and drew a fingertip down the length of his nose. "I earned every lash. I truly did."

"No woman deserves that, Viola."

"I did. I have not been a very good person. Do your scars bother you?"

He shook his head. "I'm used to them. I forget they're there. Do you find them unsightly?"

"I like them." She said. "They are part of you."

"I've managed to acquire most of them in the past three years." He admitted.

She began to laugh, a slightly drunken bubbling sound.

"What's funny?"

"We're comparing battle scars."

"I suppose we are." He slid both hands down to graze them over the mounds of her behind, with only a light film of fabric preventing full contact, which was actually more sensual than skin-to-skin right then. Lightly squeezing her globes, he murmured. "What a nice handful." Even in very subtle light, he could see that she was embarrassed. "Though you may not be entirely chaste, your experience is not as extensive as I may have thought."

"One time only. I told you that."

His eyebrows pinched together. "I don't want to hear about it. *Ever.*"

"Am I pressing too hard on your wound? Does it still hurt?"

"I am prepared to suffer through that so as to feel you pressing hard on something else."

Bringing her mouth close to his, she whispered, "I want you inside of me."

His gut knotted into a very tight, hard fist, a pang of yearning so volatile he wanted to haul up her wretched, ugly grey gown and impale her upon himself. But she crawled off him and staggered across the room to shut the drapery, enveloping them both in total darkness. While she was trying to slowly feel her way back to the bed, he quickly pulled the covers, crawled under, and made a space for her.

"Ow."

"That corner post is a bitch."

"Yes." The end of the bed dipped from her slight weight, and she crawled toward him. "Where are you?"

"Right here." He said. "You ought to have left the drapery open."

"I'm too shy." She settled in beside him, found his arm, and settled her cheek against it.

He thought that he would rather have seen her in all of her naked glory, but this was fine. Rising up on one elbow, he whispered, "You need not be afraid. I will not hurt you in any way."

"My insides wrench when I feel you this close. The complete maleness of you, the hairs on your legs brushing against me makes my skin come alive."

He made no verbal response but slid a hand down to explore the lean curves of her body from armpit to knee, marvelling at how very much that simple black frock had concealed on the first night they had met. But even if these slender contours didn't exist and she was straight as a board, it wouldn't matter. Nor would it matter if she was heavy. None of that mattered. It was her face that never failed to take his breath away time and time again, with as much impact as it had at first glance. And it was the lively, vivacious, saucy spirit of hers that had won his heart. Yes, even all the trouble and misery she had caused him had contributed to making him love her all the more. She was what she was. And she was finally his.

Closing his eyes, he raised his hand to explore her intricacies lightly with his fingertips, her eyelashes, the bridge of her nose, the curve of her cheek, her incredibly luscious lips that trembled and parted and issued a breathless sigh.

What glorious torture this was! What a blessed dream, to know that the lonely, aching flesh would at last merge with its soul. He wasn't entirely sure what he had finally done right to have this battling she-warrior drop her armour long enough to come into his arms, but he wasn't going to look a gift horse in the mouth.

So he took his time, drawing out the moments as if each one was attached to the moon on one end and the sun on the other, and the endless space between them was filled with the bliss of exploration. This sort of agony was sublime. The waiting. The anticipation. The expectation. The catching of the breath. The denial of self. The glorious pleasance of her arms and legs and hands and slender arching back, desperately trying to coerce him into the quenching of her fire.

All of the I love you's, and I want you's in the world would not have roused his flesh so robustly as the complete surrender in each one of these whimpering sighs. He caressed her through the thin fabric until she began to scratch at him, and then peeled her nightgown off and began the whole exploration from start. Callused hands roaming over soft skin and gentle curves defined her femininity contrasting his maleness – an extra charge to feed his fire.

Finally, with mouth and tongue, he focused his attention on the heat and moisture between her legs, her nearly instantaneous climax rewarding him for having taken his time. She wept her way through the convulsions – and through another two for good measure.

At last, in the sinking of his root deeply into her warmth, time ceased to exist anymore. All thoughts disappeared. There was just the awareness every nerve and muscle coiling up tighter with every thrust, and then at last...the sensation of control dissolving into complete madness.

In the quiet of the aftermath, he lowered his head to nestle his nose into the warmth of her sweat-slickened neck, whispering, "In you, I have found the better part of myself."

"I have never experienced anything so intense in my entire life." She said. "I thought the top of my head was going to blow off."

"Well, if you check the ceiling in the morning, I'm sure you'll find mine up there." He laughed, as he slid off of her, and then pulled her into the crook of his arm. "You are insanely passionate."

She tried to roll over onto her side, but he held her where she was, with a hand on her breast. He reached up to remove the pillow from under his head and slide it under her bottom. "Stay there for a bit."

"Why?"

"I don't want you spilling my seed before it takes root."

"What?"

"I want you to have my child."

She made no reply, but he felt the shuddering of her shoulders and chest as she began to weep.

"Would that not be a good thing?"

"It w-would." She said, in broken whispers. "You are...the one."

These words turned everything that had ever been wrong in his life, right-side up. He drew her closer and held her until he drifted off, very contentedly, to sleep.

Viola lay awake staring, staring, staring through the dark, until a cool blue twilight filtered through the cream-coloured drapery.

"I don't want you spilling my seed before it takes root."

Those were nearly the same words that the Aristocrat had spoken that night. The voice was different, but the Aristocrat had been very ill with Lung Fever. The Aristocrat had been much leaner, but then again, he had been dying of Lung Fever. His manner and his technique had been different. While the Aristocrat's touch had been soft as silk at the start, he had got a burst of much-needed energy and was driven at the last. This time, he was gentle all the way through. The only explanation had to be that he had somehow recovered from Lung Fever.

She reasoned that men did not always make love the same way, every time. Did they? His final request before he dozed off would have landed her on her backside had she not already been there, for up until that moment she had not been certain, but those words confirmed her suspicions. Gabriel was the Aristocrat. And Xavier was her son.

And she didn't know what to do now.

After the fact, she was wholly terrified because part of the accord that she had signed – that he had insisted upon having in writing – stated that she would never in her life return to France. Never, ever try to take back her child. These conditions, she had been completely fine with before she had felt her child growing and moving within her own body.

How in the world was she going to tell Gabriel that she was that faceless woman that he had lain with in total darkness to create an heir? What would he think of one so purely selfish and without morals, that she would agree to sell her own child? How could she stand to lose this man, now that she had fallen in love with him? Would he send her away? How could she go, now that she was finally reunited with her beloved child?

Her heart torn asunder, she very carefully extracted herself from his limbs and left his chamber to find sanctuary in her own, for she knew that she would not be able to look him straight in the eye again until she purged her soul. This could wait no longer. She did not have one single moment left to hide in.

*   *   *

Gabriel slowly emerged from a deep, restful sleep, reached out to hold his beloved, and instead found empty space. He was disappointed but not surprised. It seemed she couldn't sit still, or lie still, for that matter. A sleepy smile warming his heart, he swung his legs over the side of the bed and got up.

He was anxious to see her, so he threw some clothing on and rapped on the adjoining door. She answered it immediately and the instant he lay eyes upon her, he knew something was very wrong. "What is the matter?"

"We must talk."

"About?"

"Follow me." She stepped away from the door, strode across the room and out onto the balcony.

After they were both seated on either side of a small wrought-iron table, solemn silence descended. He gazed at her studiously, but she seemed afraid to look directly at him. She shifted her eyes toward the glowing east beyond his left shoulder. In this soft morning light, they were as potent as the strongest whisky.

A glimmer of moisture forming along her lower lids, she whispered, "There is something that I must confess, but I don't know how."

"Heed, you know that regardless of how I approach matters I manage to say the wrong thing, so I would be the first to accept an awkward confession from anyone."

"Thank you." She clutched something between her slender hands, as though she needed to do so for courage.

"Gabriel, last night may not have been the first time you and I were intimate."

"Impossible." He laughed softly. "I would surely know if I had bedded you before."

"There is no way to do this but to be blunt." Viola opened her hand

212

and showed him a small ring box. She opened it to show him a ring, which was a small, square ruby set in gold. "Do you recognise this?"

Gabriel shook his head. "No. Viola, what is going on?"

Dragging a hand across her eyes, she said, "You must recognise this. Gabriel, you sent it to me through *Monsieur* Gaston Ste. Louis when my child was born. He – he told me that you had died."

"No, there must be a mistake. What child? I didn't know you had one."

She went on, "I signed an accord, the conditions of which were that I would come to you in the dark, never know who you were, nor would you know me. I only knew you as 'the Aristocrat.' The purpose of this...venture...was so that you would sire a child before you died. You had Lung Fever, and you wanted an heir. Another part of the accord was that I would carry your child in an undisclosed location and that the child would be removed from me immediately at birth. And finally, that I would leave France, never to return...and there was a substantial remuneration involved...this makes me ill."

"Go on." He gazed at her curiously, while a very sick feeling began to settle in his gut.

"I was blindfolded and brought to you, and it was completely dark. Afterwards, I was blindfolded again, and we rode in a closed carriage for many hours until I was brought to a chateau in the middle of the wood. There I remained until my babe was born. I'm getting the details all turned around, but you know what happened as well as I." She inhaled a deep, sobering breath, "Let me remind you of something that no other would know. After it was over, you placed a pillow beneath my hips so that I would not spill your seed – using almost the same words that you told to me last night."

"God Almighty." He fell back against the chair and studied the ceiling of the balcony, his head spinning. And then it dawned on him. It more than dawned on him. Dawn was generally soft. This was liken to a kick in the gut. He lowered his head to look at her. "Now I understand. You think I have your son and you're here to get him back. You would do anything to have him. Even—even fall into my bed and pretend to enjoy it. Even marry me. I understand it all very well now." He shoved out of the chair and stalked into her chamber.

Viola followed him, "Please, can we not talk about this?"

"You have had plenty of opportunities to tell me anything you wanted to, yet even if you talked without a pause for a solid hour, I wouldn't know what part of it to believe and what part to reject, because you've been lying to me from the start."

"I have not lied. I have withheld information."

"It's the same damn thing! We have discussed this before, and I told you the same thing then, too. I have asked you so many times to just trust me and tell me what was going on. Look, I have finally figured you out. You coerced your father into arranging this – this marriage – to reclaim the child that you thought we created together. That is the only thing that makes any sense."

"No, I didn't know where Xavier was! He was the one that I was risking life and limb to find. There never was another man in the picture at all! It was him! Your son! *Our* son!"

"You did not hear me, Viola. We never shared a bed before last night, and Xavier is not of your flesh."

"Gabriel," she rushed over to grab his arm, "I don't think you heard me. He was the one I was searching for when you caught me running off with Louise."

He tore his arm out of her grasp. "It seemed odd to me that the Medici's would want to form an alliance with my father when Cosimo was already an alliance of his. Now, it all makes sense. Damn, you are good, I will give you that. You had me believing that you cared for me and that in some small way you needed me, that – that I was your hero." He spat the word as if it made him sick. "Poor little homeless, loveless, abused Viola! Poor little thing, who so desperately needed saving that I jumped in to rescue you. You knew the way to this warrior's heart. You played me like a fine-tuned violin!"

"No! It was not like that! I didn't know Xavier was mine until I saw his birthmark."

"What birthmark?"

"I didn't suspect that he was my son until I saw one under his arm that resembles my own. It was only then that I thought you might be the man I came to that night."

"How many times must I tell you that he is not your son? But just as importantly, was that why you wanted no light yesternight? To see if I would feel the same, and act the same, and touch you the same as your child's father did?" He shook his head, and exploded, "You could have asked me! You could have asked me that *before* we married! You didn't have to pretend to want me! For the love of God, Viola, you didn't have to marry me under the pretext of wanting to be with me for this! I would have answered your questions! Damn it, Viola!"

"Please, can we be reasonable?"

"Reasonable?" He fumed. "All this time you have been lying, sneaking off, dragging my damned heart through hell, even allowing me to harbour mistrust and resentment toward a man who has been a trusted friend all of my life – all to hide your secrets. And now you want *me* to be reasonable?"

"I never meant to hurt you!" She wept.

"Well guess what—you did."

"There must be a way to work this out, Gabriel. We have a child together!"

"For the love of God! Listen to me! Xavier is not your son! I know! I was *there* when Murielle gave birth to him!"

"His birthmark – "

"That is not a birthmark! It is the result of a broken blood vessel that never healed properly! Stop this!"

"No." She whispered. "Don't do this..."

"He is not your son!" He shouted.

"Gabriel, no..." she whispered, as the truth finally penetrated her heart like a serrated blade, and all hope within it drained. "He has to be...he has to be."

"Don't look to me for pity! While I vowed my life to you before the King, the priest, and witnesses, and while I made love to you with my whole heart, you were only experimenting to see if I was the man who took your child away! I am done!" He turned and left, slamming the door.

*　　*　　*

Gabriel marched down the stairs to find his brother. No time to mourn the loss of something that he had come to believe in, he had to sit down with Valmont and work out the details of this accursed tax raise to support a battle that he was damned sick and tired of fighting. Life had to go on, even when all the joys of living it were gone.

He no sooner entered and shoved up his sleeves than he and Valmont heard the heavy clomping of boots beating across the foyer. One of the sentries appeared in the doorway, panting.

"Your Lordship, a messenger arrived with most important news – about the war."

"Go ahead."

"Kyriell's forces have defeated us in Valognes." The sentry paused to suck in a deep breath, "He has rounded up another eighteen hundred men, and as we speak they move toward Bayeux."

Gabriel grumbled under his breath, "Shit."

"Two French armies are positioned south of the Cherbourg Peninsula. They are preparing to engage the English. Three thousand men under Count Clermont are now at Carentan, and a second force of two thousand under Richemont departed from Coutances to join Clermont's army."

"Continue." Valmont prompted.

"They intend to intercept Kryiell and his English soldiers before they reach Bayeux, but our side is still outnumbered. His Majesty calls for all available men to join up with Clermont's army so that we will not be defeated as we were in Valognes. You would be under Clermont's direction, Your Lordship, so sayeth the King."

Automatically sliding into his well-worn warlord's mindset, Gabriel commanded, "Go round up all the serfs that we have. Fit them with armour and tell them to prepare for immediate departure. The same applies to the sentries. Leave only one sentry posted at the front and rear gates. Those who man the watchtowers are to come with us. Go!"

The sentry turned and ran. Valmont said, "I'll go suit up."

"The hell you will. You remain here to look after my wife and son."

"But you require soldiers."

"I require my brother alive. If anything happens to me, my son will require a man to help raise him."

"But, Gabriel – "

"Would you feel better if I allowed you to come along, and then we returned to find all of the women and my son dead?"

"What are you talking about?"

"Don't you recall that messenger we sent to Italy to appraise Cosimo of what the Baron was up to? Do you think for one moment that this fat bastard won't retaliate? He will. You will need to be here to defend these women and my son if that happens while I'm gone."

"Shit." Valmont frowned. "As you wish."

"What you can do for me is fetch my armour. Not the chains mail, the metal plate. We'll be departing as soon as our men are ready. I must go up to my quarters and change."

"Can you not sit this one out? You are not yet healed from the last battle and you are damned terrified of going back, Gabriel. Your fear alone could get you killed."

"That's a chance I'll have to take. If anything happens to me you'll see to it that you, Viola, and Xavier equally share the inheritance. You'll manage her finances because the French law somehow always orchestrates a way to deprive women of financial independence, so she will have her own, but it will appear that her share belongs to you. Understand?"

"Yes."

Good, he thought, because he sure as hell did *not* understand why he would take care of her this way when she had done nothing but lie to him. But after last night she may well be carrying his child, and he had to be a man about that. "I'm going to change. I will return shortly."

Viola strode along the row of hedges in the front yard, now just beginning to flower, the green more than green in morn's bright sun. The edges of the leaves were dipped in silver. A new spring was dawning. New life, and yet she felt dead inside.

How could she have been so wrong? She had been so sure that she had finally found her child. So sure! In her desperation, she had placed Gabriel into a role that he didn't fit, and from there revealed to him, absolutely everything that had gone on the night that her child was conceived. How could things have gone so wrong? Now, she wasn't sure if she still had a husband, either. Decidedly, it was her own fault.

She ought to have trusted him but how to do that? How? When she never learned to open up to anyone? She never learned how to be vulnerable. Always, every damn day, every step of the way, life had been one struggle after the other with her adoptive family – every one of them – out to stab her in the back. Could all of that change in a heartbeat just because she wanted it to? Could she relearn how to relate to people in a non-defensive way, or to be open and forthcoming when never a crumb of bread had ended up in her stomach that she hadn't had to fight for? Never a day of freedom from slavery had she got unless she had lied and said she was going to Mass. All of her life, lying, stealing, and cheating had been the only way to keep her blood from spilling in a sea of sharks.

But there were moments when she grew so tired of the struggle. Today, she was that tired. A man she loved with all her heart had rejected her because she could not for the life of her, trust.

She heard a scuffle at the other end of the property and glanced toward the sound. More than a dozen men, serfs and sentries included, rushed into the outbuilding beside the carriage house. She snapped her head toward another sound and spotted Gabriel exiting the front door, approaching her in his long strides, his armour clanging noisily. Under his arm, he carried a helmet. He paused before her and met her gaze, but there was no warmth. Only the hard, flinty eyes of her accuser.

She said, "What's going on?"

"The English forces advance toward Bayeux. We were called to duty."

"You're going to war?" Her blood drained from her head.

"Yes."

"Should I pack my things and leave while you're gone?"

Chapter Thirteen.

Gabriel behaved as if he hadn't heard her question. "If anything happens to me, you will be well cared for. Valmont has instructions – "

"You will not perish. You have a son who needs you."

"Will you take good care of him in my absence?"

That meant he wanted her to stay, she concluded. ""I will protect him with my life."

"Should I not return," he repeated, his voice still matter-of-fact, as if he were giving orders on the battlefield, "be sure that he never forgets me. Children need to know their parents. Never forget to tell him that you are proud of him. I grew up wondering if..." he paused, and his eyes and voice softened somewhat, "if my mother would be proud of the man I had become. There is something powerful between a father and son, this I learned from my boy. But there is also something nearly divine about the love that a boy feels for his mother. It's ethereal. I loved her." He paused, squaring his shoulders resolutely. "I know that your love for Xavier is great, and in truth, you are more of a caring mother to him than his own mother was when she was alive...but I digress. The point is – "

"Tell me what happened to your mother, Gabriel? I want to know something about you. Anything."

He withheld a sigh. "I will share this with you for Xavier's sake. This would not make a terrific bed-time story so save it till he grows up. Five years after my birth she married a cursed sot who would give her another child, Valmont, and more abuse than she could abide. Her husband caused her more damage, internally, with his beatings than we realised at the time. We could not afford a leech to find out, but she used to shove us aside and take beatings for us. At least she did when she knew it was happening. He beat her too much one night, and she died in our arms. I was ten. Valmont was seven. Thereafter, that useless bastard fled and neither of us has seen him since. Were it not for my father stepping in to take care of us, we probably would have died of starvation."

"I am so very sorry."

"Not a pretty tale, but that is why I do not condone the abuse of women in any way, shape, or form, and you are to raise him the same way. Raise him to respect women and to always be a man about that. Someday, if he wants to know about my past and his grandmother, that is the story. I must leave soon."

I cannot let you go! She thought, suddenly panicking. *Not with this wall between us. Not like this.* She placed a hand over his cold metal breastplate. "Don't go? What difference would one less warrior make?"

"I am a Warlord and I have an army to lead. I must do this for my son, that he may grow up in times of peace."

Viola hurled herself at him, locking her arms around the massive bulk of his heavily armoured waist. But he was cold and hard as stone, not budging one inch, not giving at all. Not even one touch for her to remember. Nothing. She pulled away, whispering, "I know you don't want to believe me, but I do love you."

"I would give everything I own to be able to believe you, but I don't."

"I suppose I don't blame you." She whispered, lowering her head. "I have lied from the start. It is as you said."

"Know that when – *if* – I return, I will help you find your child."

Up snapped her head. "You would do that?"

"And if I do not return, Valmont will help you. One way or another we will sort this out. Let us just get through this cursed battle first."

"Why would you do this for me, after all of my deceptions?"

"You really don't know the meaning of integrity, do you?" He turned and marched off without a backward glance.

She stared at his back. Whom did he suppose she could have learned integrity *from*? The Baron? He was without scruples. Her adoptive mother? Hardly. She had always been too busy fancifying her home to please her haughty friends. Her sisters? They all hated her and had no time for her. From whom could she have learned these things?

What little morality she did possess, she had learned at church when she had been able to sneak off to Mass, and later at the convent. But even those teachings had failed to explain to her how to survive in a den of wolves.

Nothing in her past had prepared her for life with a man of honour.

*   *   *

On the fifteenth day of the fifth month, at the noon hour, Clermont's forces advanced east, quietly approaching Krystal's English camp. Gabriel, moving among Clermont's group, volunteered to move on ahead in hopes of obtaining information.

Those among Clermont's group who rode horseback alit, and they awaited Gabriel's return. After an hour of moving through the bushes, attempting to do so quietly in his noisy armour, Gabriel finally managed to get close enough to view the goings on in a valley below.

Kyriell was in the process of organising his soldiers in the formation used at the battle of Crécy. Gabriel estimated that roughly seven to nine hundred armed soldiers dismounted and formed three wedges of longbowmen.

Scanning the assembly, he noted that roughly three thousand archers were positioned behind planted stakes and low moats. They stood with had their backs to a waterway that ran south to the Aure River. A bridge constructed of stone passed over the waterway, in the midst.

Hearing a sound behind him, he quickly crept back from the edge of the hill and disappeared within the tree. Making quiet haste, he returned to where he had left Clermont's army and relayed the news of their strategy.

Clermont stood upon a large boulder, addressing his army. Gabriel forced himself to pay heed. Clermont, a stout man with piercing blue eyes, announced, "We will do this in three stages. First, the foot soldiers will attack, followed by the mounted. Your Lordship, Count Gabriel—you know how to operate the two-wheeled culverins, don't you?"

"I do. If we breech-load them, they'll deliver at a more rapid speed."

"Then you'll be in charge of that task. Gather a few foot soldiers to move both culverins at once, coming in right after the mounted force. The bastards won't know what hit them. All right men. Assume your formations and let's go. May God go with us all."

Gabriel knew what he was getting himself into. He had been in this situation many times before. But this time the fearless Warlord began to sweat like a pig inside his armour, and to shake like a child. He was terrified. And the pain lingering in his side, aggravated by the hard, metal armour, was a brutal reminder of how close he had come to losing his life. He wished he could have stayed at home.

*   *   *

Just after the noon's meal two Italian soldiers quietly scaled the curtain wall and slew the sentry guarding the entrance. They lowered the drawbridge, allowing a group of soldiers to stampede into the castle grounds. They mounted their waiting horses and joined them.

Xavier, who wheeled his chair outside in the backyard with a new minder assigned by Chantalle, snapped a gaze toward them and burst into terrified sobs. The new minder, Sylvie, froze. It was all around her. The pounding of horse hooves, the snorting of horses, clumps of damp earth spewing in all directions. The cold hands of dread held her paralysed. One of the soldiers thundered toward her while another rode toward Xavier. She saw the soldier leaping from his horse, swooping down to take the child, and remounting. She wanted to run to his rescue, but her legs wouldn't move.

Another soldier carried a dead man slung over the front of his saddle. He rode up to the castle and hurled the body over. It dropped and rolled at the door of the portico. Sylvie recognized him as the messenger, Benoit. The handle of a dagger stuck out of his forehead.

A soldier stopped his horse to glare down at her with cold black eyes. He gestured toward Xavier and spoke French with a thick Italian accent, "Is this the son of Count Xavier Gabriel Valois?"

"Wh-what do you want with that boy?"

"Tell the Count that Baron Mario de Medici sayeth: An eye for an eye! Let's go!"

Sylvie glanced toward the door in time to see Valmont racing out, armed with a crossbow. Leaping over Benoit's corpse, he shouted, "You swarthy bastards!" He stole but half an instant to assess the situation, noting that they wore everything but helmets. One of them held a shrieking, terrified Xavier in the crook of an arm. In no way could he chance firing in that direction.

Sylvie yelped, "They are Mario de Medici's soldiers! He told me, an eye for an eye!"

Valmont aimed and fired at another soldier. His arrow did not miss its target but went into straight into the back of his neck. The soldier fell forward upon his horse while the animal continued galloping toward the gate. Chasing after the others, Valmont reloaded his bow.

One of the soldiers paused and returned fire, his arrow piercing Valmont's thigh. Operating on pure rage, he ignored the hot searing pain and attempted to take his best shot, but his severely punctured thigh muscle gave out, and he collapsed, knees first. His arrow whizzed straight upward.

Seemingly from out of nowhere, Gabriel's big mountain cat lunged onto a horse with a ferocious growl and then locked both paws around a soldier's throat. Sinking her long fangs into his jugular, she hauled him off his horse. The horse ran wily-nily around the property, while the lion feasted on the dead soldier's throat.

The other three soldiers rode through the gate with a shrieking and terrified Xavier, which prompted the big cat to race after them.

"Shit!" Valmont swore. *"Shit!"*

All of the female servants appeared, also armed with bows, but it was too late. The abductors were long gone. Tossing aside their weapons, the women crowded around him, dropping to their knees. The last to charge through the door were Louise and Viola.

Viola raced toward them, shouting, "What in God's name has happened? We heard the racket all the way to the – Valmont, your leg!" She dropped beside him, her face nearly white as snow.

Clutching his thigh, Valmont issued through ground teeth. "Haul that bastard thing out of me! I must go after them! They have taken

Xavier!"

"Who has?" Viola pressed, anxiously.

"Your father's soldiers. Gabriel's lion chased after them. Ah, shit—this has to come out!" He grabbed the arrow and broke off the tip, then growled viciously as he shoved it around the bone, and through the other side of the long frontal muscle. He passed out cold from sheer pain before he could yank it out the other side. His eyes rolling backwards, the full weight of his broad torso whacked against the badly torn up grass.

"Get the leech!" One of the servants cried.

"The leech is gone off to war, just like every other man!" Chantalle hissed, while completing the task that Valmont had begun. She locked her big square hand around the arrow's head and tore it out. Then she sealed both hands over the wound to slow the bleeding. "Quick, someone tear a strip off your frock and tie it above the wound before he bleeds to death. Stop your useless screeching and move!"

Nobody moved. And Viola couldn't think clearly. Grabbing her head, she screeched above them, "Shut the hell up, all of you!"

Silence fell fast. She reached down and tore a strip off the hem of her cream-coloured gown, handing it to Chantalle. She lifted Valmont's thick, muscular leg while Chantalle wrapped and tied it above the wound.

Viola's mind continued to race. *What do I do? I cannot allow my father to steal Xavier.* Her heart hammering, she said, "Chantalle, Louise and I will go after Xavier. We will need men's clothing. We cannot move in these cursed gowns and corsets."

Chantalle growled, "You heard her. Go get what she needs! What else do you require, My Lady?"

"Two muskets."

"There are two on the rack in Monsieur's study."

Scrambling to her feet, Viola vowed, "Louise and I will bring Xavier home."

Two streams of dust they left in their wake, as they thundered out of the stables and charged toward the drawbridge.

*   *   *

224

"Load!" Gabriel shouted over the war whoops, the shrieks of the dying, the clashing of armour, and rumbling of horses. Overhead, lightning flashed across the undersky, the long, claw-like tentacles needling the earth on the horizon. He and his group were a fair distance from the nucleus of the battle, on the periphery to the north.

The battle was going full boar, the archers and longbowmen on both sides launching their weapons en masse. It looked like the sky was raining arrows. Others engaged in hand-to-hand combat in the core of the melee. As they slew one another, the soldiers behind them stepped over the dead and continued fighting.

The ground was littered with blood and corpses of men and horses and dismembered parts, and shields, and swords and bows. Both sides suffered terrible casualties, ergo, it was impossible to say who was winning.

This one is for Xavier. Gabriel's wet, cold arm plates scraped his forehead as he dragged his arm across his face to clear the rainwater impeding his vision. He lifted the heavy steel hammer, swung with all his might, and blasted the tip of the cartridge protruding from the breach of the culverin cannon.

Boom!

The explosion resounded over all other noise as the gunpowder ignited within the tube, and the cannonball launched through the air in a long, wide arc. It struck with massive force, taking out an enormous "V" of English soldiers advancing at the rear.

"Load!" He shouted again.

One soldier opened the breech door, and two more hoisted up the large tubular cartridge containing both gunpowder and a cannonball. He stole a glance about to assure himself that no English soldiers encroached their circle, but as he did, he spotted another group of soldiers appearing on the horizon to the south.

"Shit!" He shouted and pointed. "Behold!"

"What is it?"

"Richemont's army approaches on the south! We've got the short-arse bastards beat now, by God!" He raised the hammer and lambasted the pin with all his might.

The cannonball soared, taking out another large cluster of English soldiers. A skirmish ensued as Kryiell, the English leader, hastened to redirect his soldiers. Those who were not in the nucleus made an about-face, forming an outer half circle to defend themselves against Richemont's thundering army of mounted soldiers, numbering approximately one thousand, not counting another eight hundred or so archers coming in behind them.

In the ensuing hour, the two French armies defeated the English. Kyriell was apprehended and taken prisoner. The entire English army was captured or slain.

Tho' bone tired, wet, and sore all over, the French erupted into whoops of victory, while hugging one another. It was late at night and still storming viciously when they regrouped to assess their losses. Then, while Clermont and Richemont's soldiers herded up the surviving English and led them off, Gabriel sank to the ground for a moment's rest before heading home. The men he had brought with him folded to the muddy ground along with him, savouring the rain pelting down upon their heads. With the sounds of war still rebellowing in his mind, Gabriel enjoyed the subtle "pinging" of rain against his steel armour.

I have survived another one. Thanks be to God. And now, to deal with the battle at home.

*   *   *

Viola and Louise didn't have to ride too far before they found a dead, bloody soldier on the road between the cow pasture and farming land. His throat had obviously been ripped out by a wild beast. A bit further they found a second one who had met the same fate. Out near the field where Gabriel had taught her to ride, there was a third soldier, backing away from the mountain cat. Beside his horse, on the ground, Xavier sat weeping and screaming. Viola alit to pick him up just as the big cat lunged upon the soldier, dealing unto him the same fate as had met the others. The victims' screams were blood-curdling. She pressed Xavier's face into her neck to prevent him from witnessing the slaughter, and knew she had to get him out of there but fast, before the cat turned on them, too.

She handed Xavier up to Louise quickly and climbed up onto her horse as the blood-soaked beast abandoned its kill to race toward her. Viola's heart leapt up into her throat. It paused abruptly to stare up at Xavier, growled, and then turned to gallop down the road from whence they had come.

"Mel!" Xavier cried. "Mel!"

"Let's get him home," Viola said. She had no idea what *"Mel"* meant, but she was ever so grateful that the beast had not attacked them, and that Xavier was alive and unharmed.

* * *

Having heard the racket of so many soldiers riding onto the property, all of the servants rushed to the door, armed with bows, and dreading another onslaught of Italians.

Instead, they saw their own men riding toward the stables, and Gabriel tiredly approaching the portico in his long strides. They dropped their weapons, issuing audible sighs of relief.

Valmont appeared at the door with a makeshift crutch braced under his arm. He limped through their midst toward his brother, so damn glad to see him alive. Gabriel tossed his helmet through the air, and it landed upon the torn-up dirt. His face smeared with mud and his jaw covered in dark whiskers, he said, "We won. But what the hell happened to you? Did Louise bite back?"

Stopping awkwardly before his older brother, Valmont said, " Mario's soldiers attacked us."

"I knew it would happen. Is your leg going to be all right?"

"In time."

"Was anyone else hurt?"

"They made off with Xavier. At least three of them did. They took me out with an arrow to the leg. By the time I regained consciousness they were all long gone."

"What?"

"They rode onto the property and absconded him while he was out with the minder. They dumped Benoit's body on our doorstep. He had a dagger thrust into his forehead."

Gabriel spun around and marched off. "That whoreson will die!"

"Wait! I'm not done. There's more."

"*What!*" He pivoted.

"Viola and Louise went after them. So did your cat."

"*What?*" Gabriel repeated yet again.

"I went unconscious. I would have tried to go after them but—"

"I am going after them."

"I'm not done! Will you cool your hot head for a moment!" Valmont growled.

"Will you just spit it out, then! Get to the point!"

"The soldiers didn't get very far. The cat killed them. Viola and Louise brought him home, safely."

"You could have just said that in the first place! I'm going to clean up."

"There's something else," Valmont said.

"Whatever it is, it can wait. I have to go see my father before I do anything else. It's urgent."

Gabriel removed his armour in the stable and strode to the front gate in front of the Loire river, where the sentries let him out. He began peeling off his dirty chemise as he descended the stone stairs leading down to the water. There, he stripped down to his skin and stepped down into the river to wash off the dirt and grime he had accumulated on the battlefield. His cat was already there, having a drink. He asked, "You didn't get hurt, did you, Melanie?"

She lifted her head to glance at him with those golden feline eyes, while water dripped off her tongue and chin. *I'm fine, human. Don't get your hose into a knot.*

He sank down over his head, and then emerged, shouting up to the sentries, "Go fetch me some clothes, will you? And a towel! And get them to saddle me up a fresh horse!"

*   *   *

Arriving at his father's castle, he found him in the back courtyard, soaking up some sun with a strong snifter of some sort of amber liquid in his thin, aging hand. Except for the entourage of armed sentries surrounding the garden of flowers, trees, and chirping birds, His

Majesty was alone. Gabriel took a seat on the other side of the black, wrought-iron table. Keeping his voice low, he said, "Good day, Father."

"Good day, my son." He smiled. "I heard that we won this battle."

"We most certainly did."

"I am proud of you."

"Thank you."

"Have a drink." The older man refilled his own silver snifter and passed it over.

Gabriel downed the liquid, enjoying the heat infusing his throat and chest, and then he said, "I need help with something."

"I'm listening."

In the quiet of the garden, and in whispers, he relayed the story that Viola had told to him about the Aristocrat and her missing child, wrapping it up with, "Gaston never mentioned such an arrangement to me, however close we were."

"Gaston was iron-willed when it came to honouring confidentiality," His Majesty said. "That's why he was so valuable to me—and to you."

"Yes, I know. And business is business – an affair apart from the very close bond that I had with him."

"Indeed. But how may I help?" The King asked.

"I'm trying to help her find her child. Do you know anything about that?"

"I don't generally concern myself with family matters, except for that wedding of yours. That was quite enjoyable, actually. I deal mostly with war and trying to get back my damned country." He said, slicing the air with a sharp gesture. "However, he did come to me in confidence to give me a certain document pertaining to the birth of a child. I wondered why he was giving it to me. I meant to ask him about it, but then he turned around and hung himself at his other home in *Tours*. I understood then that he wanted someone to have it in case it was ever needed."

Sliding to the edge of his chair, Gabriel said, "What was in this document?"

"I never read it." His Majesty waved a hand, and a servant in a brown frock came running out the door.

"Yes, Your Majesty?"

"Go into my chamber and get me that silver box hidden in the safe behind the portrait of my father."

"Yes, Your Majesty." The servant bowed, turned, and ran.

His Majesty said, "So then, you think that Viola might have been that young woman?"

"It's a very unusual circumstance. I can't imagine her *not* being the child's mother. My question is, who was the child's father? And where is her child now?" He nervously bounced his leg until the servant returned with the box.

Leaning forward, His Majesty motioned for the servant to leave them and then opened the silver box, which was about the length of a letter but half as wide, and not very deep. He carefully pulled out several folded sheets of parchment, until he lifted the final one at the bottom. Opening it, he scanned the contents and then passed it over to Gabriel. "Perhaps I ought to read these things now and then. Her signature is on it. It appears that after she signed it, he filled in more detail at the bottom before giving it to me. He names this 'Aristocrat.'"

Gabriel read it. "I'd known this man for years, yet he never once told me that he paid a woman to have his child."

"Who knows why people do the things they do?" His Majesty shrugged. "I stopped wondering a long time ago. You should, too."

"Thank you, Father. I am indebted to you."

"Go do what you must, Gabriel. Your leg is shaking my table."

*   *   *

"The Countess has departed," Chantalle informed Gabriel, as he entered the kitchen late that night with five-year-old Lise Simone in tow. "I see we have a visitor."

"Yes. Would you bring her up to Xavier's room? They can share a room for tonight."

"For tonight? What does that mean?"

"It's a long story, Chantalle, and I am too exhausted to indulge you."

Chantalle slanted him a frown. "I do not know why there always has to be so much secrecy in this place, but fine! I will take care of this child. Come, little one." The Housekeeper took the little girl's hand and began marching toward the door.

"Wait. Where did Viola go?" Gabriel asked.

"She didn't say. And why would she tell me? I am not her grouchy husband, you are."

The blood drained from his head. "Do you mean, she has left for good?"

"I'm sure I don't know that, either. Perhaps you've finally driven her away. She was the best thing that ever happened to you. Are you happy now?"

"No, I am not happy. When did she leave?"

"They left on horseback. She and Louise. Your brother tried to tell you that, but you waved him off. You said you had to go see His Majesty before anything else. You said it was urgent business."

Wracking his brain, Gabriel tried to remember the details on the document that his father had shown him, at last recalling part of the added notation at the bottom, which stated that Gaston had initially found Viola in *Tours*. He recalled her so desperately asking him if she could go away for three days, and some quick calculations brought him to realise that it would take one day to get there, one day to do some searching around for information, and one day to get back. Gaston had once lived there, and perhaps she had gone there hoping to find him. Maybe she thought he would tell her who the Aristocrat was, not knowing that Gaston was dead.

Damn it, woman! Why could you not have waited for me to help you?

It was early eve when Gabriel arrived in *Tours* the following day, and those who lived in the streets were plenty. He strode about in the rain, offering payment to anyone who could provide him with information on a young woman named Viola de Medici, who used to live in the vicinity roughly five years ago. Was there a particular place she would gravitate toward? People were creatures of habit, this he knew.

His stomach growling, he finally stopped to purchase a handful of nuts from a vendor who had set up her cart under a selar. Being as he asked everyone else in the area already, he said to the old woman, "There used to be a young lady who lived in this area five years ago. An Italian lady. Her name was—"

"I know her." The old rag grumbled. "She spoke French with an Italian accent. She used to come here and crush my Punic Apples to smithereens with her fondling. They are strong fruit but not safe in her hands!"

Gabriel's pulse leapt. "That would be her. She loves the things. Do you know where she would go if she were to return here today?"

"She used to visit a gentleman by the name of *Monsieur* Dupuis. He lives two blocks over, above the leather merchant's shop. He owns the shop, but—*Monsieur*, your change!"

The old vendor's face puckered in confusion as the well-heeled gentleman tore down the street, leaving his nuts and his money behind. She worked her gums a few times and decided she had called him once. If he was feeling particularly generous, she would not spoil his day by chasing after him.

Gabriel was about to give up when at last the door opened after the third rap, and then he understood why it had taken so long. *Monsieur* Dupuis was small and crippled, his left shoulder substantially higher than the left. His skin was pasty white and very wrinkled, the thin flesh of his eyelids drooping like onionskin over a pair of bright grey eyes. Draped loosely about his shoulders was a grey wool blanket.

He stood at the door leaning on his cane with both hands, while his gaze travelled down along Gabriel's attire. "Yes, how may I assist you?"

"Good day," Gabriel said, his insides fluttering with hope. "I am Count Xavier Gabriel, and – "

"Ah, yes." The old man smiled and made an effort to bow. "His Majesty's bastard. I am honoured to have you grace my doorstep, Your Lordship."

Thrown off balance, Gabriel queried, "How do you know me?"

"Oh, my distraction is endeavouring to ascertain the true genealogy of the noble. For future generations, you understand. I have no other legacy to offer as I squandered most of my personal fortune long ago.

Please, come in."

The ceiling was unusually low. Gabriel had to duck to follow the old man into a small room containing only two chairs, a writing table, and several shelves chock-a-block with scrolls. The mixed scents of burning wood, India ink, and burning whale oil hung in the air. The walls were dark wood, unfinished. Along one wall was a stone-block hearth that cast a warm amber glow and a most welcome warmth throughout the room. At the corner of the table was an oil lamp throwing a glow across a sheet of parchment upon which sat a quill. A jar of ink sat at the front of the table. At the end was and a rather ornate blue glass decanter partly filled with dark, rich liquid.

The irregular edges of the grey blanket swung side to side while the old man shuffled toward the roughly-hewn writing table and sat. He gestured toward the chair at the opposite side and went on, "Those who keep records seem to conveniently omit individuals such as yourself. What can I say? The whole thing amuses me. I've little else to pass my time in the winter of my life. I hope I did not offend you when I called you His Majesty's bastard."

"Not at all." Gabriel folded his tall frame into a chair designed for one much shorter. His knees were well above hip level. "It's the truth."

"Would you care for a spot of whiskey?"

"Thank you, I would."

The old man scooped two glasses out of a drawer, grasped the blue decanter in his gnarly fist and commenced to pour. "I had this brew imported all the way from Scotland. It is quite superb."

"I would imagine."

"Now then," he said, as he slid one of the small glasses toward Gabriel, "how may I assist you, Your Lordship?"

"I'm looking for my...for a friend who has gone missing. Viola de Medici. I was told that you knew her."

"I do, but she hasn't shown up at my door. You say she is missing?"

"Yes."

"Well," the old man smiled, "she may have decided that it was time to move on again."

"What do you mean, *again*?"

"Let me tell you something about this young woman. If she has decided to make herself scarce, I doubt you will locate her. She's very bright, she knows how to survive in the streets, and she has the tenacity of a Bull Mastiff. She will be most difficult to find."

"How can she know how to survive in the streets? She is the daughter of Baron Mario de Medici, of Florence."

Monsieur Dupuis raised his glass, uttering, "to good health," and downed its contents. "I suppose she didn't tell you."

"Tell me what?"

"She fled from Italy at oh...sixteen or so, because her father was trying to force her to marry a man old enough to be her grandfather. A disgusting old pig, according to her description. She was living in the streets and thin as a stick when I found her. She had been for months."

His interest peaking, Gabriel leaned in closer. "I had no idea."

"You say she's a friend. How long have you known her, if I may be so bold?"

"Actually, she is my wife."

"I suspect there's much you don't know. It took me eight months to get her to trust me." *Monsieur* Dupuis shifted positions, so obviously to relieve an ache in his aging soul case, and went on, "She told me that poverty was not such a difficult thing to abide. She said that when it strikes, your mind quickly learns to stop expecting food at certain times, and your stomach grows accustomed to not having. You learn to survive on less than you're used to, and apart from knowing that you must put something into your body every few days in order to survive, you stop anticipating food for its taste at all. You just eat to live when you can get it."

"I know that feeling. I was born into poverty."

The old man slanted him a grin. "I know."

"Please, tell me more about Viola. Anything you know might give me clues as to where she may have gone."

"I can say that I'm honoured to have known her. She regularly visited me. She was able to speak, read and write in three languages. French, English, and Italian."

"She's able to write in all three languages?"

"Oh, yes, indeed. You can imagine what a great gift that was to a man such as myself, who needed her skills to translate documents and write letters. With her help, I obtained a great deal of information that I needed to forward my research. Apart from that, she cooked for me and cleaned up after me once a week. I missed her terribly after she moved on. I still do."

"I am dumbfounded."

"Drink, Your Lordship. It is freezing out there this eve."

He drank the whiskey, and it burnt beautifully all the way down. "Thank you."

Grasping the bottle in a gnarly fist, the old man refilled both glasses. "Her childhood was not a pleasant one. Mario's eldest daughter, Maria, found Viola as a newborn shortly after she was born, in a back alley. Her mother lay dead beside her. She is a beautiful woman, and so I would imagine she was a beautiful babe as well."

"Absolutely." Gabriel pulled his chair close to lean both elbows on *Monsieur* Dupuis' writing table.

"Maria brought her home and promised her father that she would take care of the babe herself, and she did—until she died of intestinal poisoning at sixteen. Viola was two by then. Now, while endeavouring to raise his own power to match that of his cousins, Mario produced no sons but many daughters, whom he would later marry directly back into the most revered among the Medici's, which raised his own rank by association, you see. So Viola, who was adopted by him, grew into a beautiful young woman who became a bartering tool, and possibly his most valuable one because of her extraordinary beauty. His own daughters are, I hear, rather unpleasant to behold. Viola would be sought after by many, and he could use her to wheedle his way deeper into the glory of the noble, which he somehow thinks he deserves. But pamper her, or treat her equal to his own blood, that he did not do."

"Did she tell you this?"

"Yes. After quite some time, mind you. We became companions, me in my old age and her in her loneliness. One would think she wouldn't know how to cook, clean, launder, make soap, these sorts of tasks, but I didn't have to teach her any of those things. She already knew. She was little more than a servant to Mario and his brood when he wasn't trying to trade her off. But when he knew that wealthy old widowers would be coming to the palace, he would stuff her into a very elaborate gown and parade her as though she were his pride and joy, the scheming bastard. He began doing this to her when she was twelve. She was terribly abused since she was two."

Gabriel gazed studiously into those sharp grey eyes. Suddenly, Viola's tendency to treat her handmaiden as a best friend, her lack of finesse among royals, the way she flinched when he touched her without warning, and her overly modest self-image made sense. "Thank you for educating me."

He nodded.

"So she hasn't come back here, then?"

"If she had I would be celebrating her return. But if she thinks that you will come here looking for her, assuming she wanted to disappear, then I'm doubtful that she would return to me. She would be too cunning for that."

"Have you any ideas where else she might go, then?"

"Does the wind tell you where it goes when it passes through?"

"No."

"That's right. If you are quick enough to chase it, you might discover its destination, but most of us are not. What I would suggest to you, if I may be so bold, Your Lordship, is to go home. Or go to wherever it was that you saw her last, and wait there. When and if she wants to see you, she will return."

"That's not what I wanted to hear."

After he left, he rode across town to the home where Gaston Ste. Louis had once lived and found it boarded up, which would be precise what Viola would see as well if she happened to come this way. Where else would she have gone? What in hell was she up to?

Gabriel searched every town between *Tours* and *Orléans* but returned to the castle nine days later, empty handed and empty hearted. She had not told Chantalle that she was leaving forever, but she hadn't specifically said that she would return, either. After their last fight, she may have assumed that he would hate her forever. He decided that he was going to ride all the way to bloody Italy if he had to, but he was bringing his wife home.

He passed Valmont in the narrow service hall at the back of the castle, and inquired, "You haven't heard anything yet?"

"No." Valmont replied. "When did you get back?"

"A few minutes ago. I'm going to clean up, eat, and leave again.

How are the children?"

"Good. Don't worry about them. Bring our women home."

"I'm going to take a bloody army of soldiers with me this time," Gabriel grumbled, as he entered the *guarde robe* and slammed the door.

Valmont continued on, stepping out the back door to examine the sky for the placement of the sun. It was getting late, and he was tired in his soul, for he missed Louise something terrible. On impulse, he strode to the stable, saddled up his horse, and went into the city to visit the tavern. He figured it would do him good to be in the company of *normal* men.

As he dismounted in front of the tavern, he spotted Louise darting between two buildings across the street and bolted in that direction. He caught up with them as they were hurrying toward a bench near a flower bed on the next road. What they were doing there, only God knew.

"Louise!"

♥ *Chapter Fourteen.*

Louise and Viola stopped suddenly and turned.

Valmont ran – or rather, limped on one foot and ran on the other – to catch up. Impulsively, he grabbed Louise's face between both hands. "I have been worried sick about you! Er..." Catching himself, he released her to step back a respectable distance. "What have you two been up to? And why did you think you had to run away again?"

Viola rolled her eyes. "We were not running away. We were simply investigating. Go ahead and kiss her. I'll wait."

"It's—it's fine. You could *investigate* while still living at the castle, could you not?" Valmont argued.

"We just returned," Louise supplied. "We have been all over the place. We were going to go to the castle soon."

"I see." Valmont nodded.

Crossing her arms, Viola said, "*She* was going to go to the castle to see you. *I* was going to wait here in the city for her. Your brother seems to want me to remain at the castle to be Xavier's mother, and I'm honest when I tell you that there is nothing I would love more. But Gabriel— he will want me to tell him where I'm going and when I'm coming home, and he will want to know every little thing about me, but I have been chewing on this thought for a spell, and the more I chew, the worse it tastes."

"And what is that?"

"I just told you, *Monsieur!*" Viola said.

Valmont was totally confused. "What did you just tell me?"

"He wants to know everything about me, but he tells me nothing about himself. That has to stop."

"Have you told him that?"

"Do you think it would matter if I did? He hates me now!"

He thought about that. "He keeps his own counsel. I understand your conundrum."

She sighed. "Then, *do* something about it. Louise may return to the castle, but my feet are not stepping onto that property until I know who the hell Count Gabriel really is, what the hell he is always so secretive about! I am his wife, and if I am to live in that place, I demand to know! But he never talks! Do you understand? I'm tired, my arse is sore from riding, and I'm frustrated! But if I go back to that castle, he will keep me a damned prisoner after this round, so I can't go back until I find what I'm searching for! I have lost his love and his confidence. All that I have left is my child, and I intend to find her, come hell or high water!"

Valmont placed a fingertip over her very active mouth. "Countess, please take a breath. Calm yourself for a moment. Louise, would you excuse us, please? Just...just go have a seat on the bench while we go for a little stroll about the garden." Valmont took Viola's arm and led her slowly along. "I will tell you what you want to know since he most likely never will, as this has to get resolved before he drives me completely mad, as well. However, you must not tell him that I told you, or he will have a fit. Agreed?"

"Fair enough." She nodded. "Tell me about who he is, inside. And about what went wrong with his marriage, and all of that."

Valmont chose his words carefully. "Gabriel is certainly not a refined sort of gent, as we both well know. He was never a child, as Xavier is or even as I was, for that matter. He took up arms and began fighting for his country when he was thirteen and has spent most of his life doing just that ever since. He is good at that...a damn good Warlord."

He paused to shake the stiffness out of his leg, and then continued. "I'm getting ahead of myself. Chantalle raised us as if she was our mother. The King appointed her as our guardian when His Majesty learned of our mother's untimely death. Gabriel was ten at that time, and I was seven. It was then that he received his title as Count, the region of Bellefleur, and the castle—along with a great many serfs to care for a property that size. Up until then Gabriel had no idea that his real father was the King. Our mother had never spoken of the involvement that she had with His Majesty before Gabriel's birth. There was a period of adjustment for us, as you can well imagine, for we went from abject poverty and near-starvation, to wealth and power. A gentleman by the name of Gaston Ste. Louis managed the finances until I was old enough to be trained and take over that aspect. While we were growing up, there was another group of people assigned to educate us properly, and teach us the ways of the noble. With Gabriel, they had to wait until he was available, between battles."

"I knew *Monsieur* Ste. Louis, only briefly." She said. "Please go on. He was always going to war? Even that young?"

"Yes. I suppose he carried a great deal of anger because of the manner in which our mother was killed, and fighting on the battlefield must have helped him to deal with that. I'm not sure, Countess. I didn't want to pry into the inner workings of his heart. I only know what he deems acceptable to entrust to me. You know how private he is. But you need to understand that how a man relates to other men on the battlefield and how he relates to women are two very different things. Warriors don't spend much time sharing their *feelings*. I don't know much of anything having to do with women. I, quite frankly, don't understand them. But I do know that he loves you and that love is true."

She said. "I know in my heart that he didn't kill Murielle. But who did?"

"Melanie."

"Who?"

"His mountain cat."

"He went to jail over a mountain cat?" She gawked.

"You heard about his jail time?"

"Yes."

"She's not just any mountain cat. Listen to this. Gabriel kept Xavier in his own chamber, in a bassinet, for the first few months after his birth, since Murielle didn't want anything to do with her son. His cat gave birth to cubs in your chamber at one time."

"I am not connecting the two. I am confused." She admitted.

"I'm getting there. Right after Xavier was born, he went down to the kitchen to grab a bite early one morning, and when he went back to his quarters, Xavier was missing. He heard the sound of a babe gurgling in the adjoining room so he raced in, and there was his son, curled up with Melanie's two cubs, suckling on one of her teats. She had taken him – by his clothing I would imagine – and brought him with her."

"That is *remarkable*."

"Yes. She is a remarkable cat. Henceforth, she treated Xavier as one of her cubs, always looking out for him. So, now we get to why he went to jail for her. When Xavier was six months old and teething, Gabriel couldn't seem to find a way to deal with this, so he asked Denise, whom he had brought in by then to help care for him, to bring the babe to the leech. This was in the dead of winter. Gabriel bundled him up nice and warm, and Denise left by the front door with the child. An instant later, his late wife also left. She was in the habit of always running around by herself and Gabriel had by then stopped inquiring about it. He gave up."

Viola inserted, "That's why he was so adamant about my not leaving the grounds without him."

"Perhaps. I don't know. Let me finish. He heard the babe wailing outside, and it was killing him, so he stuck his head out to suggest that Denise find an icicle for him to suck on until they arrived at the leech's home. I suppose he thought it would numb the pain. But as he opened the door, he heard Murielle ordering Denise to shut the babe to hell up, and then he saw her grabbing Xavier and tossing him across the yard. He hit the wrought-iron fence out there, and his back was broken."

"Dear God," Viola whispered, "I cannot believe that."

"When that happened, he raced out to Xavier but didn't know what to do. The boy wasn't moving, wasn't crying. But at that moment, Melanie came out of nowhere and launched toward Murielle, with intent to kill her, I'm sure. But being as she listens to Gabriel, she halted when he ordered her to stop. In my opinion, Countess, he should have let the beast eat her alive, but I suppose he was acting on instinct, not logic. Murielle left the property to do whatsoever was on her mind that day. Gabriel pressed his ear to Xavier's chest to see if he was breathing, and he was, so he told Denise to go fetch the leech and bring him back."

Inhaling a deep breath, Valmont went on, "Gabriel stayed home all the time to tend to his ailing son's needs, and Denise was afraid to go near him. Afraid to hurt him in his very delicate condition. Xavier slept in Gabriel's room, in a special bed that he created for him, with instructions that the leech had given him. He was giving him goat's milk, for Murielle even refused to feed him. Gabriel went downstairs one morning to warm some for him, and when he returned Murielle was in his chamber, leaning over the babe. He had no idea what she intended to do, but before he could intercept his cat came charging through the adjoining door – after Murielle. It all happened very quickly, he said. He ran to check on the babe, foremost, but as he was doing that, Murielle tried to escape the cat by running out onto his balcony—and Gabriel did nothing to stop the cat from attacking her this time. She climbed up on the ledge to try to get away, the cat lunged toward her, and she fell backwards. When he saw that Xavier was all right, he stepped out to look over the balcony ledge. Just then, the leech came around the front of the property. He had come by to see how Xavier was doing. The leech saw Murielle on the ground, dead, and Gabriel up on the balcony and drew his own conclusions. It was the leech who alerted the authorities, who then took Gabriel into custody. "

"But *Monsieur,*" she said, "why didn't he tell them what had really happened?"

"They would have killed Melanie. That creature took Xavier as her own. Dear God, that animal treated my nephew better than his own mother did. How then, could he let anyone kill her when she guarded that child with her life? We all knew that when we left Xavier in that mountain cat's care to go do something, she would watch over him. Heed, she even knew not to move him after his back was broken. She knew, Countess, and rather than try to carry him off as she did before, she simply sat beside his bed and watched him."

"Who cared for Xavier while he was in jail?"

"Myself, Chantalle, and the cat." He said. "As Xavier's pain became less and less, she would bring her cubs in and deposit them into the boy's bed to keep her babes all together. She thought he was one of her own. After her own cubs grew up and wandered off, she began to stay out of the castle for longer periods, but even today, she comes onto the property every night and stands guard to ensure that no-one threatens us. He claims that Melanie was well worth the eight months that he lost behind bars and I would have to agree."

"Thank you for telling me all of this, *Monsieur.*"

"I think it's about time you addressed me by name."

"And you as well, Valmont. Listen, I have another question. Do you know what went wrong in his marriage?"

"Yes. He did tell me about that. Within a year they fell apart when his father told him that Murielle had only married Gabriel to get to him —the King, I mean. He informed Gabriel that she had offered him a proposal, which was that she would leave him to become the King's primary mistress."

Viola's jaw dropped. "Why in the world would she do that?"

"She believed it would raise her to a more elevated social standing. Bear in mind that Gabriel was still madly in love with her that early on in their marriage, so Gabriel and his father fought very bitterly over that. Gabriel didn't want to believe him. All the same, he confided in me that she didn't want him touching her. She detested physical intimacy."

"That does not add up," Viola spoke quietly. "She would have had to be intimate with the King if he had accepted her offer."

"True." Valmont nodded. "Gabriel was quick to realise that she didn't want intimacy with *him*. So, he confronted her with the accusations that his father had made. This I overheard myself, as they were having a very loud fight in the sitting room. Murielle confessed that she had made that proposition to the King and then threw into his face that she would rather be intimate with a pig than the offspring of a Moor. She had a serious hatred against people of darker flesh."

"Oh, my God!"

"Which brings me to this: She was in her mid-thirties then and time was running out for her to bear a child. Gabriel wanted to continue his familial line because he was the only surviving male descended directly from Ma'n Taymullah, his maternal grandfather, from Africa North. So to avoid intimacy, she moved out of the adjoining room, down to the end of the corridor. He became very depressed over this. He thought that he constantly felt depleted because of his emotional state, and he frankly stopped caring about himself at all. Consequently, he ended up getting almost killed too many times on the battlefield. One day he went to see the leech, who diagnosed him with Lung Fever. There was an outbreak of it around here, so the leech assumed that he had it, as well. But one day Chantalle spotted Murielle slipping something into

Gabriel's soup. She brought a sample to the Alchemist, and he found a small dose of arsenic in it."

"What an evil bitch." Viola spat.

"Oh, yes. So, she forbade Murielle to go into the kitchen anymore, and then *they* started fighting between themselves. It got ugly, but Gabriel supported Chantalle because that horrible woman was poisoning him. She had been slipping these small doses of arsenic into his food over a long period of time. He loved her, Viola. You understand? He knew that she had been prepared to leave him for the King, but he didn't want to believe she would actually try to kill him, even though he was dying proof that she was. He kept on trying to make her love him. He bent over backwards—that is, until she tried to kill Xavier, and ended up getting killed herself."

She whispered, "If she didn't want him touching her, how did she wind up having his child?"

"In his misery, he got drunk one night while he and Murielle were at the King's palace. It was his birthday feast. Murielle also drank too much. So, they ended up in bed despite their growing resentment toward each other, and Xavier was conceived. She despised Gabriel even more for that, and once she gave birth to Xavier, she turned her back completely on the both of them. Ultimately, she also tried to kill her own child rather than raise what she called a *'Moorish spawn.'* And that is the whole story. Is there anything else you would like to know?"

"Yes, can you buy us a meal at the Bras d'Or? We're both famished. I may have more questions while we eat."

He smiled. "I would be delighted. On one condition."

"What is that?" She frowned.

"Come home, Countess. We miss you terribly."

"I suppose I can comply. For awhile. Maybe. I am exhausted, and I need to take a break from searching for a bit, anyway. Let's go eat."

*   *   *

It was late when Valmont returned to the castle. He led Viola and Louise into the sitting room and requested that they sit and wait. They complied without argument. Chantalle passed the door and looked in. "You're back."

Viola nodded. "It would appear so."

"Good, but you're even bonier than the last time I saw you."

"Where is Gabriel?" Valmont interjected.

"In your study—and he's not in a good mood, but that is nothing new," Chantalle grumbled, as she continued down the hall.

"Wait here." Valmont left the women in the sitting room and headed toward his study, feeling quite smug that he knew something that his older brother did not.

Gabriel sat at the writing desk, studying a map. His head popped up when he heard his brother's uneven footfalls. "I suppose you want your chair?"

"No. I have spoken to your wife."

"Where is she?"

"Not far from here."

"I refuse to play this game. Where in the hell is she?"

"She's in the sitting room with Louise."

The back of the chair hit the floor as Gabriel raced from the room.

As per his usual fiery nature, the first thing Gabriel did was scream, "Where the *hell* have you been!"

"Searching."

"I have dispatched an entire fleet of soldiers to search for *you!*"

"Clearly," Viola said, "they lack investigative skills. They didn't find me."

"What the hell am I going to do with you!" On his next breath, he crossed the room to haul her into his arms, and was relieved that she didn't push him away. He heard movement behind him and glanced back to see Louise creeping out. "Viola, you need to talk to me. Tell me what happened back then."

"I already told you."

"Not all of it. There was money involved. A great deal of money. Correct?"

Extracting herself from his embrace, Viola sighed and shifted her gaze toward the ceiling, as though she would see the answer scrolled across it. "When I went into that accord I had no idea what a profound experience it would be to feel a life growing inside of me. At the moment of my child's birth, I changed my mind, but they took the babe away before I could stop them."

"Yes, but how did you end up back in Italy? Was not the deal to provide the Aristocrat with a child in return for large sums of money? And also, never to return to France after the fact? And then, five years later, you end up back here with nothing. To be used as a damned bartering tool by that bastard, Mario." He said, his hand cutting the air in a gesture of disdain. "You could have used that money to build a better life for yourself. No?"

"I didn't take any money for my child. I couldn't sell my own flesh. Do you understand? I couldn't. But I have mourned that loss every day since my babe's birth."

Expelling a heavy, tired sigh, Gabriel said, "I wish you had told me what you wanted so desperately when we met. You needn't have gone through all of this alone."

"I couldn't have."

"I would have heard you out."

"No." She argued. "You would not have. You didn't trust me even to tend to your wound, for goodness' sake. You were hard, you were cold, you were stubborn, and you were dead set on doing everything just the way you saw fit. I understand that your trust was destroyed by your late wife but you made *me* pay for it, Gabriel. I couldn't talk to you."

He studied her thoughtfully. "You're right. I would not have listened. At least, not in the beginning. I was a miserable bastard and I know it. I take full responsibility for botching this up, all right? But I felt so betrayed by all of your games and your secrecy. Look, come with me to my chamber. I have something for you."

Without objection, she followed. He led her up the two flights of stairs, down the long corridor, and into his chamber. There, he said, "Get into that bed and just wait. There's no need to disrobe."

Her eyes steadily upon him, she followed him inside and crawled onto the bed, fully dressed.

"I shall return, briefly."

Viola curiously observed him as he left the room, leaving the door open. What was he doing? Long moments later he strode through the door, carrying Lise Simone, who was sound asleep. Coming round the bed, he tucked the child in beside her and then whispered, "Here is your beloved daughter."

Her lips turning white, she whispered, *"What?"*

Gabriel whispered. "She is your child."

"But the birthmark..."

"Forget the damn birthmark," Gabriel whispered, "you either imagined it or it was something stuck to her skin. Lise is your daughter."

"No..." she mouthed the word, but no sound came out. Her face twisting, the tears began to flow like a fountain.

"Yes. Your search is over, my lady."

"My God....oh, my God...are you *sure?"*

"I have found proof. We can discuss that later."

Viola couldn't hold the child. Carefully, so as not to wake her, she crawled off the bed and fled into the adjoining room. Gabriel followed and eased the door shut. Therein, she crumbled to the floor before she could make it to the bed, and sobbed.

Crouching beside her, Gabriel rubbed her back. "Do you not want her?"

"I was afraid to wake her!" She sobbed, "Afraid to frighten her! I couldn't hold it in!"

"Come here." He closed her into a tight embrace. She shook violently in his arms as her sobs tore through her chest and through her soul. When at last she was able to breathe, she whispered, "I am scared to death to hope again. What is this proof? You must not hold me in suspense."

"I have obtained the document signed by both you and Gaston. After you signed it, he added more information, which states that Arthur Stephan Simone was the Aristocrat. He gave it to my father for safekeeping and then hung himself."

"How can I ever thank you, Gabriel?"

Stroking her wet cheek with the backs of his fingers, he answered, "You can start by being more open with me. Can we try that?"

She nodded. "I am sorry for all the pain that I have caused you."

"Viola, it was my own fault that you kept me at arms' length because I wouldn't let you in, either. And later, the source of my rage was that I knew you would never love me in return. It was a bitter repeat of the way it had been with Murielle."

"Is that what you thought?"

"It is."

"Do you still think I don't love you?"

"I suppose I do, but I understand that you would go to any lengths to find your child. I would, too. Even right down to marrying a miserable bastard like me if it meant getting one step closer. I understand that."

"I cannot believe that you have no clue."

"Clue of what?"

"That I *do* love you, Gabriel."

Gabriel took her hand and kissed it tenderly. "You don't have to say that. All I ask is that we begin anew by trusting each other more. I shall never expect more than what you can give."

"My God. Were I able, I would tear open my chest, rip out this heart of mine, and place it in your hands for it is yours. I swear to you upon the head of my beloved daughter that I do love you...oh, God...so much." She took his face between her hands, whispering, "Though I came here to find my child, I also fell in love with the man who gave me a home while I was on that search. A damn good man who – in spite of all that I had done – found it in his heart to bring my little girl home to me."

Gabriel crushed her in a shuddering embrace. Standing, he collected her into his arms and transferred her onto her bed, where he stretched out alongside her and held her in poignant silence.

He eventually spoke. "You once said something that was so profoundly true. It continues to echo in my head."

"What was that?"

"You said we were both wounded. I don't know if I will ever be the sort of man who can think reasonably when things go wrong."

"I understand. But can you at least hear me out rather than to fly off the handle?"

"No." He laughed. "That would take a miracle. But what I'll do is fly off the handle first and then listen to your side later."

Viola lifted her head to stare at him. "That's what I just asked you not to do."

"I won't make promises that I know I can't keep."

"Well, I suppose there is merit in that, too." She conceded.

"Understand that I've spent a great deal of life on the battlefield, where the mentality is always first and foremost, survival. If I do not act immediately and with confidence, I will end up dead and cause the deaths of those who rely on me. There is no time to second-guess my actions. I've been living this way since I was not much more than a child, so it takes me a few weeks after I come home to adjust my brain to this other life that I lead. It is as I said when we first met. I am a Warlord, and I am no gem. But I do love you, and I hope that counts for something."

"It means the world. Gabriel, does Lise know that I am her mother?"

"Yes." He nodded. "Mark explained it to her. I'm sure he left out some details not appropriate for a child to hear, but she knows that you are her mother. And now, the two children – *our* two children – have been referring to you as their *Maman* in your absence."

"Have they?" She beamed.

"Indeed. Are you at last fulfilled, Viola? Has your wounded heart found a place to call home?"

"Completely. Thank you so much."

"Stop thanking me. It works in my favour, too." A few moments later, he said, "I am hungry. Are you?"

"No. My stomach is in knots. I want to go hold my daughter now. I've waited five long years for this."

He kissed her nose before leaving the bed. "Take your time. Come find me when you're through. I'll be outside."

After he left, Viola quietly crept back into Gabriel's chamber and lay down next to the child with the striking silver-grey eyes and dark soft hair. As she gently held Lise, new tears fell from her eyes while in her memory, she recalled the joy of carrying this babe in her womb, the pain of delivering her, and the sorrow of losing her.

She thought, all the while that she had believed her prayers were not being answered, all events were being aligned just properly by the merciful God before Whom she knelt each night. In the end, she had her child, and also the love of a man who, despite his own hurtful past, had found it in his heart to carry her sorrow, too. To make it his own. To love her enough to swallow his own pain and find a way to make all of this madness make sense. What a good, good man.

She finally carried Lise down the corridor to place her into bed beside Xavier. The new minder, Sylvie, quietly added a log to the hearth to keep the room warm. Viola whispered, "Thank you for doing that. You can get plenty of rest on the morrow."

"Thank you, My Lady."

"I will mind them during the days, and you, over the nights."

"Thank you, My Lady," Sylvie repeated.

Lise's eyes fluttered open as Viola kissed her cheek. "*Maman,* you're home."

"Yes. You must know that I love you." Viola whispered, as her heart nearly exploded with joy. *Maman.* What a beautiful word. *I will spend the rest of my life making it up to you. I promise.*

"Uncle Mark told me." The child whispered. "Are you truly my mother who gave birth to me?"

"Yes." Viola whispered, "You just don't remember me."

"May I continue sharing this room with Xavier?"

"Until it is no longer appropriate, you may."

Lise whispered, "He is afraid of falling. He likes it when I sleep on the outside so he can't fall to the floor."

Viola's heart twisted. Somehow, Xavier must have retained some portion of the memory of having been thrown. "You're a good girl."

"I will look after him," Lise promised. "He's my brother now. Uncle Gabriel said so."

"Uncle Gabriel is now your Papa. On the morrow, we will all do something together as a family. Go back to sleep now, little darling." Viola kissed both their cheeks and quietly slipped out before her heart broke right in front of them.

She found Gabriel outside on a blanket, on the grass, staring up at the stars. He cast her a smile and stretched out an arm for her to curl into. He said, "What a beautiful night."

"The most beautiful night that God ever made." Viola lay down beside him, head on his shoulder, and said, "Tell me again that you still love me."

"I still love you. I will always love you, Viola."

"And I will always love you."

"I will give you such a beautiful life that you will forget all the misery in your past." He promised. "One day you will wake up and think that you were spun from the dust of angels, for those ugly memories will be so far gone, you will have no recollection of your tortured youth."

"I believe you can make that happen."

"You watch and see." He said. "The whole world I will hand to you on a silver platter. You will know more love than you can imagine."

She smiled. "Gabriel, did you know Lise's father?"

"Very well. I met the Simone twins when I was ten."

"Was he a good man?"

"He was a very good man who loved his wife deeply. All that he did to acquire a child was for both of them, out of love."

"Good."

Stroking her arm, he said, "I'm sure you made him happy, Viola."

"And that was difficult for you to say." She said.

"It was hell." He grumbled. "So let's not talk about that night ever-more."

"I have one question, and then I won't bring it up again."

"Go ahead."

"Why did *Monsieur* Ste. Louis hang himself? Do you know?"

"I'm guessing, but if you changed your mind about giving up your child and he felt bound to honour his loyalty to Arthur as well, he might have been suffering terrible guilt for having allowed anyone to take your child from you. He was a very conscionable, tender-hearted man who understood the inability to sire children. He never had any, so your situation would have cut straight through his heart. But that is only my speculation."

"I would feel horrible if I thought he did that on account of me."

"My lady," he sighed, "we all have things that we feel horrible about. I am not insensitive to that. But sometimes we have to make choices that are very difficult, in situations where somebody wins and somebody, naturally, has to lose. That is the warrior's life, and you are a warrior."

"I guess I am. Are you ever going to trust me with the secrets of your heart, Gabriel?"

After a pensive silence, he explained, "It's difficult for me to do that, as much as I love you. The burdens I carry are heavy, and so I don't want to dump them on anyone else."

"Share them with me? Let me in?"

"Well, first there is the memory of my mother's death, and that I was unable to defend her. I tried but he was stronger than I. I failed. I've spent my life defending my country, but that doesn't make up for my weakness back then. And it doesn't change the fact that Valmont grew up without a mother. And then there is my—*our*—son, who may never be able to walk. He wets the bed at times because he cannot feel it happening until the wetness touches his skin. If a miracle does not happen, he will never know the love of a woman, or the joy of being a father. It is so hard to watch him live this way. I keep thinking that if I had got rid of Murielle as soon as Xavier was born, he would still be able to walk. I take responsibility for that. These realities send me into very dark places, Viola, and while I am in there, I cannot see the light. I cannot even see you, though you may be standing right in front of me."

"Besides working with Xavier on the swing you made, is there anything I can do to help?" She whispered.

Gabriel turned his face toward her. "Just wait for me, my lady. Just wait, and I will always, always come back to you. I promise."

"I will always be here when you do."

Silence descended gently, interrupted only by the sound of the Loire River bubbling beyond the gate.

In this peaceful quiet a mountain cat padded along the shore of the water, pausing to lap a few drinks before climbing the embankment. She came to the gate and was admitted by a sentry who knew her well. A deep purr rumbled within her chest as she crossed the grass in her predatory feline stride. Near the wrought-iron fence, she settled in for the night, intending to protect her family until morn's first light.

♥ *The End.* ♥

More Books By Ziana de Bethune.

Author-ize Me!
The Self-publisher's Desktop Mentor.

Non-fiction/Educational.

Everything you'll need to write YOUR book.

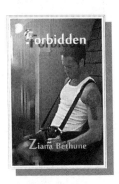

Forbidden.

Fiction/Bi-racial Romance.

A period piece – The Great Depression and WW11.

Valantinus.

Fiction/Vampire.

Vampires as you've never seen them before.

Other involvements.

Coming Soon...

Cover Art, Copy-editing, and Line-editing.

"The Fight For My Soul."

By James Larry Holmes.

A documentary-style book.

Cover Design, Copy-editing, and Line-editing.

"A New Destiny."

By Solomon Raju Vulamparti, in collaboration with Fr. Julian Policetti, Founder of the Mother Teresa Rural Development Society.

Ziana de Bethune

Author/Scriptwriter/Public Speaker/Mentor.

Ziana de Bethune's writing career launched with "Persistence Pays," in 1992, a category romance novel that was released by Kensington Publishers. Since then, she has published numerous books in the genres of Fiction, Non-fiction, Self-help, and Educational, under different pen names. As well, she has written numerous articles for writers' magazines, online publications, and blogs. Her work has been translated into several languages and published worldwide.

She has taught the craft of writing at workshops and seminars, and has mentored a number of now-published authors.

www.ziana-bethune.com

First Book "of the Press."

JdB

april 10 - 2019

Made in the USA
Lexington, KY
05 April 2019